AF147777

The Love That Prevailed

by

Frank Frankfort Moore

Double 9
BOOKS

The Love That Prevailed
by Frank Frankfort Moore

Copyright © 2024

All Rights reserved.

No part of this publication may be reproduced,
stored in a retrieval system, or transmitted in any
form or by any means, electronic, mechanical,
photocopying or Otherwise, without the written
permission of the publisher.
The author/editor asserts the moral right to
be identified as the author/editor of this work.

ISBN: 978-93-63056-85-5

Published by

DOUBLE 9 BOOKS

2/13-B, Ansari Road
Daryaganj, New Delhi – 110002
info@double9books.com
www.double9books.com
Tel. 011-40042856

This book is under public domain

ABOUT THE AUTHOR

Frank Frankfort Moore was an Irish writer, journalist, and playwright who lived from 1855 to 1931. He was a Protestant from Belfast and a unionist. But during the years of Home Rule protests, his historical fiction did not shy away from themes of Irish Catholics being pushed out of their homes. Moore was born in Limerick but grew up in Belfast. He remembers seeing religious rioters being chased by dragoons with sabers drawn in the street below his nursery window as his oldest memory. It was a pretty well-off family; Moore's father was a successful clockmaker and jeweler, and French and German were spoken. But because the older Moore was a member of the very strict Open Brethren sect, he wanted his kids to only read religious and educational books. The preacher Michael Paget Baxter often went there. He said that Emperor Napoleon III was the Beast from the Book of Revelation. Moore went to school at the Royal Belfast Academical Institution and quickly learned to take a step back from his father's views. He remembered that some slanderous lines called "Mr. Baxter and the Beast" were going around, "proving" that Baxter was the Antichrist.

CONTENTS

CHAPTER I

The old church ways be good enough for me," said Miller Pendelly as he placed on the table a capacious jug of cider, laying a friendly left hand on the shoulder of Jake Pullsford, the carrier, as he bent across the side of the settee with the high back.

"I ne'er could see aught that was helpful to the trade of a smith in such biases as the Quakers, to name only one of the new-fangled sects," said Hal Holmes, the blacksmith, shaking his head seriously. "So I holds with Miller."

"Ay, that's the way too many of ye esteems a religion—' Will it put another crown in my pocket?' says you. If't puts a crown in your pocket, 'tis a good enough religion; if't puts half-a-crown in your pocket, 'tis less good; if't puts naught in your pocket, that religion is good for naught."

The speaker was a middle-aged man with a pair of large eyes which seemed to vary curiously in colour, sometimes appearing to be as grey as steel, and again of a curious green that did not suit everybody's taste in eyes. But for that matter, Jake Pullsford, the carrier, found it impossible to meet everybody's taste in several other ways. He had a habit of craning forward his head close to the face of anyone to whom he was speaking, and this movement had something of an accusing air, about it—occasionally a menacing air—which was distinctly distasteful to most people, particularly those who knew that they had good reason to be accused or to be menaced.

"Jake Pullsford goes about the world calling his best friends liars without the intent to hurt their feelings," was the criticism passed upon him by Miller Pendelly. Other critics were not so sure on the subject of his intent. He had never shown himself to be very careful of the feelings of his friends.

"The religion that puts naught in thy pocket is good for naught—that's what you be thinking of, Hal Holmes," he said, thrusting his head close to the face of the smith. But the smith did not mind. The man that spends most of his days hammering out and bending iron to his will, usually thinks good-naturedly of one who uses words and phrases as arguments.

"I don't gainsay thee, Jake," he replied. "If you know what's in my thought better than I do myself, you be welcome to the knowledge."

"I meant not thee in special, friend," said Jake. "What I say is that there are too many in these days that think of religion only for what it may bring to them in daily life—folk that make a gain of godliness."

"And a right good thing to make a gain of, says I," remarked the miller with a confidential wink into the empty mug which he held—it had been full a moment before.

"Ay, you be honest, miller: you allow that I am right and you have courage enough to praise what the Book condemns," said Jake.

"Look'ee here, friend," said the miller, in his usual loud voice—the years that he had spent in his mill had caused him to acquire a voice whose tone could successfully compete with the creaking and clattering of the machinery. "Look'ee here, friend Jake, 'twould be easy enough for you or me that has done moderate well for ourselves in life, to turn up our eyes in holy horror at the bare thought of others being godly for what they may gain in daily life, but for myself, I would not think that I was broaching a false doctrine if I was to say to my son, 'Young man, be godly and thou 'll find it to bring gain to thee.' What, Jake, would 'ee have a man make gain out of ungodliness?"

"Ay, that's a poser for him, miller: I've been thinking for that powerful proposal ever since the converse began," said a small man who had sat silently smoking in a high-backed chair. He was one who had the aspect of unobtrusiveness, and a figure that somehow suggested to strangers an apologetic intention without the courage ever to put it in force. His name was Richard Pritchard, and he was by profession a water-finder—a practitioner with the divining rod, but one whose successes were never startling.

When he had spoken, all the room, to the number of three, turned anxious eyes upon him, as if they were surprised at his having gone so far and feared a painful sequel. He seemed to feel that he had justified their worst forebodings, and hastenēd to relieve their minds.

"I'm all friendly, friends, and Jake in especial," he said. "Don't forget that though a man on the spur of the moment, and in the fierce stress of argyment, may say a bitter hard word or two, there may still be naught in his bosom's heart but neighbourly friendship, meaning no offence to you, Jake, that be a travelled man, viewing strange cities quite carelessly, where plain and simple men would gape and stare."

Jake, the carrier, gave no sign of having heard the other speak.

"There's a many o' us in these parts as strong as in other parts, that be ready and willing to take things as they come," said he; "to take the parson's preaching as they take the doctor's pills."

"Ay, wi' a wry face," acquiesced the blacksmith with a readiness that one could see the carrier thought meant no good.

He leant across the table once more until his face was close to the smith's, and said:

"That's where you be wrong, Hal Holmes. You know as well as the most knowledgable——"

"Meaning yourself, Jake?" said the smith drily.

"You know well that though you may make a wry face when gulching down the doctor's pill, ye dursn't so much as show a wrinkle or a crinkle on your face when Parson Rodney is in his pulpit," replied the carrier with emphasis.

"'Cause why?" said the miller. "I'll tell ye truly—'tis because the parson gives us no bitter pills, only——"

"That's what I've been leading up to," cried the carrier triumphantly. "The parson, like thousands of the rest of his cloth throughout the length and breadth o' the land, is content to preach pleasant things only, even as the false prophets of Israel prophesied fair things."

"And why shouldn't he be content to preach pleasant things, friend Jake, if so be that we be content to hear them? and for myself I would muchly listen to an hour of pleasant things—ay, rather than half an hour of unhappy ones."

"Ah, miller, what would you say if the doctor, who, when he saw your body suffering from a canker, gave you a sugar-plum and withheld his knife from cutting out the plague spot because you were apt to be squeamish at the sight of bloodletting!"

There was an uneasy pause when the carrier had asked this rehearsed question. He asked it with a triumphant air, and, as if he felt it to be too large a question to be answered by the miller singlehanded, he, as it were, swept the whole company by a glance into his interrogation.

The water-finder made a motion with his hands as if trying to smooth away an imaginary roughness in the air. There was a general feeling that the carrier had triumphed in his argument. He was one of those people who, by speaking in an air of triumph, succeed in making some people believe that they have triumphed. The farmer shook his head with the disinterestedness of an arbitrator. The smith continued looking into the empty mug from which he had just drunk. The silence lasted several seconds, and every second of course added to the triumph of the carrier. The man was not, however, adroit enough to perceive this. He was indiscreet enough to break the silence. When his eyes had gone round the company they returned to the miller.

"Answer me that question, man!" he cried, and then everyone knew that he had not triumphed: the last word had not been said.

"I'll answer you when you tell me if you wouldn't bear friendly feelings for a doctor who gives you a sugar plum instead of blooding you when he finds you reasonable well," said the miller.

"'Tis when a man feels healthiest that he stands most in need of blooding," said Jake, not very readily and not very eagerly. "And so it is in the health of the soul. 'Let him that thinketh he stand take heed lest he fall.' Friends, is there one among us that can lay his hand on his heart and say that he believes that our parsons do their duty honestly and scripturally."

"It took you a deal o' time to lead us up to that point: you'd best ha' blurted it out at once," remarked Hal Holmes.

"Nay, we all knew that it was a-coming," said the farmer. "Since Jake found himself as far away from home as Bristol city, he has never lost a chance of a dig at the parsons."

"I don't deny that my eyes were opened for the first time at Bristol," said Jake. "Bristol was my Damascus, farmer."

The farmer gave a jerk to his head, for the carrier had laid undue emphasis upon the first syllable of the name.

"So bad as that?" he whispered.

The blacksmith laughed.

"Not so bad, farmer," he said. "'Tis only our neighbour Jake that compares himself with St. Paul, the Apostle."

"I heard the profanity. He would ha' done better to abide at home," said the farmer severely.

The blacksmith laughed again.

"There fell, as it were, scales from my eyes when I heard preaching for the first time—when I heard a parson for the first time," resumed the carrier, looking out of a window, and apparently unconscious of any of the remarks of his friends. "Ay, 'twas for the first time, albeit I had scarce missed church for a whole Sunday since I were a lad. That was what struck me most, neighbours—that I could go Sunday after Sunday, in good black cloth, too, and hear the holy service read, in a sort of way, and the sacred psalms sung, while the fiddle and the double bass and the viol made sweet music, and yet have no real and true yearning after the truth, seems little short of a miracle, doesn't it?"

"Not when one knows that your heart was hard, Jake—ay, sir, it must ha' been harder than steel," said the blacksmith, shaking his head in mock gravity.

"You scoff, smith, you scoff, I know; but you speak the truth unwittingly," said the carrier with some sadness. "My heart was like the nether millstone—your pardon, miller, I meant not to say a word that would cast a slight upon your calling: 'tis right for your nether millstone to be hard."

"The harder the better, and no offence, neighbour," said the miller generously.

"None was meant, sir," said the carrier. "We were discoursing of my heart—hard—hard. And I was a reader o' the Book all my life. That's the strange thing; but I sought not to understand what I read and I got no help from parson—-no, nor yet from Archdeacon Eaton, that I listened to twice—no, nor the Dean himself in his own Cathedral at Exeter. With the new light that came to me, I was able to perceive that their discourse was a vain thing—not helpful to a simple man who thought something of himself, albeit jangling with the other tinkling cymbals every Sunday, kneeling (on the knees of my body) when we called ourselves miserable sinners. Miserable sinners! I tell ye, friends, I gave no thought to the words. I slurred through the General Confession at a hand gallop—just the pace that parson gets into when he warms to his work."

"There's few left of the cloth and none of the laity can pass parson when he gets warmed to it. To hear him in the Litany is like watching him go 'cross country when he be mounted on *King George*, his big roan," said the blacksmith reflectively.

"There's none rides straightlier," said the farmer. "And there's no better or steadier flyer than *King George*, first foal to my mare *Majesty*. When I heard that parson had need of a flyer that was a flyer, after poor *Gossip* broke her neck at the Lyn and her master's left arm, I held back, not being wishful to put myself for'ard, though I knew what I knew, and knew that parson knew all I knew and maybe more; but he got wind o' the foal, and then——"

"One at a time, farmer—one at a time is fair play between friends," said the miller, nodding in the direction of Jake, who had suffered the interruption very meekly.

"Your pardon, friend," said the farmer. "Only 'twas yourself brought in the parson's pace. For myself, I think all the better of the cloth that rides straight to hounds."

"'Miserable sinners,'" said the carrier, picking up the thread which he had perforce dropped. "I tell ye, neighbours, that there's no need for any parson, be he a plain Vicar or of high rank such as a Dean—nay, a consecrated Bishop—no, I'm not going too far, miller—I say in cool blood and in no ways excited, a consecrated Lord Bishop—I say that not one of them need travel in discourse all his pulpit life, beyond that text 'Miserable sinners.' That was his text—the one I heard at Bristol. 'Miserable sinners.' For the first time in my life I knew what the words meant. I felt them—I felt them—words of fire—I tell ye that I felt them burn into me. That was at first—when he began to preach; a red-hot iron brand stinging me all over, and before he had done I felt as if all my poor body had been seared over and over again with red-hot letters that go to the spelling of '*miserable sinners*' You mind Joe Warden's trial when we were lads, and how he was branded in the forehead and right hand before he was sent to the pillory. He uttered neither cry nor moan when the hot iron burst his skin——"

"I smell the smell o' 't in my nose this moment," said the water-finder gently. The farmer nodded.

"But the look that was on his face when he stood up there a marked man forever!" cried the original speaker. "It told everyone that had eyes what the man felt, and that was how I felt, multiplied an hundred fold, when my preacher had done with me. I felt from the first that he had singled out me—only me out of all that assembly, and when he had done with me, I say that I could feel myself feeling as Joe Warden felt, the rebel who suffered for slandering the King's Majesty."

"'Tis no marvel that the man has had most of the church doors banged in's face, if so be that he makes genteel churchgoers with ordinary failings to feel so unwholesome," remarked the smith.

"And so you comed away," said the farmer. "Well, I wouldn't look back on it as if I was satisfied. If I want that sort o' preaching I'll e'en throw myself prone on my nine-acre field when the seed's in, and command my man Job to pass the harrow o'er the pelt o' my poor carcase."

"I've only told you of that part of his sermon that made one feel sore and raw with hot wounds all over," said Jake. "That was one part. I told you not of the hand that poured soothing oil and precious ointment into the wounds—that came after. And the oil was as holy soothing as what ran down over Aaron's beard even unto the skirts of his garment, and the ointment was as precious as Mary Magdalen's of spikenard—in the alabaster box, whose odour filled the whole house. The whole life of me became sweetened with the blessed words that fell from his lips. I felt no longer the sting of the brand of the truth that had made me to tingle all over. Oh, the dew of Hermon's holy hill was not more soothing than the words of gracious comfort that came from him. I had a sense of being healed and made whole. The joy of it! A cup of cold spring water when one has toiled through a long hot harvest day. Oh, more than that. The falling of a burden from off my shoulders like the great burden of Christian, the Pilgrim; and then the joy—the confidence—the surety—I cannot tell you how I felt—'tis over much for me, neighbours—over much for me to attempt."

"Say no more, Jake; you have made a good enough trial for such as us," said the miller, laying his hand on the carrier's shoulder, and speaking only after a long pause. The others of the party began to breathe again, some of them very audibly.

The carrier's eyes were shining with an expression his friends had never before seen them wear. He had been swept away by the force and fervour of his words, and like one who has been breathing of a rarer atmosphere than that of the plain, he gasped for several moments, and then there was a sob in his throat. He went quickly to the door and, letting into the room the sudden glow of a beautiful Spring sunset, he passed into the open air, without speaking another word.

CHAPTER II

No one in the room had watched the man except in a furtive way, after he had spoken, although while he was speaking every eye had been fixed upon him. The sight of the effect of a great emotion makes some people feel strangely abashed, and the miller and his friends were among such persons. When the carrier had gone they remained silent for some time. Each of them seemed to be thinking his thoughts.

"Poor Jake!" said the miller at last. "He was ever the sort of man that would be like to have a twist, and he hath got one now. He's made us forget the cider, lads. Blest if the jug has been touched since Jake began his story! Hal, man, pass the jug to your neighbour.'Tis Jake that should have swallowed a mouthful before he left: talking is drouthier work than listening."

The smith passed on the jug of cider without replenishing his own mug; and then knocked the ashes out of the bowl of his pipe.

"I don't know that there's a deal in all this," he remarked. "What do you say, miller?"

"I don't say nought: I only looks on," replied the miller cautiously.

"Ay, that may be," said the smith. "We all know Jake. He never wronged his fellow—nay, there's some of us knows that if the worst came to the worst with us, Jake 'ud be the first to hold out a helping hand, with a guinea or two in it, as the case may be. Still there may be something in what he said about being brought to feel himself a miserable sinner."

"He allowed that the preacher on'y kept him in that suspensory way o' thought for a brief space," said the miller.

"Ay, there's men that be mortal sinners, and for all that their luck is tremendous and saves 'em from the eye of their fellow-men," said the smith.

"I feel bound to say this to the credit o' parson," remarked the water-finder with deprecatory suavity: "he never makes a simple countryman feel himself to be a miserable sinner. He is of such a good nature that he slurs over the General Confession so genteelly that I defy the wickedest of his churchful to feel in any ways as if parson was dictating the words to him."

"That shows that parson's heart be in the right place," nodded the farmer. "He gives us all to understand at a glance that he reads the words 'cause they are set down for him in the solemn prayer book, and hopes that there's none among his hearers who will hold him responsible as a man for their ungentility."

"True, sir, true; parson's an am'able gentleman, always 'cepting when the cock he has hatched from the noblest game strain fails him in the first main," said the blacksmith.

"And who is he that would be different, tell me that?" cried the miller, who had fought a few cocks in the course of his life. "Ay, we be well content wi' parson, we be so; but I don't say that if Jake's Bristol preacher came within earshot I would refuse to listen to him—only out o' curiosity—only out o' curiosity. But I do wonder much that a man o' the steadiness o' Jake Pullsford owning himself overcome by a parson that has no church of his own."

"'Tis as humble as allowing a toothache to be cured by a quack at a fair, when a wholesome Doctor of Physic, like Mr. Corballis, has wrestled, with it for a whole week," said the water-finder.

"I hope I haven't offended any friend by my homeliness when the talk was serious," he added, glancing around, not without apprehension.

No one took the trouble to say a word that might place him at his ease. The farmer took a hasty drink out of his mug, and sighed after. The blacksmith cut up some tobacco and rolled it between his palms. There was a long silence in the room. It seemed as if the weakness which Jake, the carrier, had displayed had saddened the little company. It was pretty clear that they were all thinking of it.

"Hey, neighbours," cried the miller at last, with a loud attempt to pull his friends together. "Hey lads, what's amiss? These be doleful dumps that have fallen on us. A plague on Jake and his quack preacher! Now, if I'm not better satisfied than ever with parson may I fail to know firsts from seconds by a sniff of the dust. Come, farmer, tell Hal what answer you gave to Squire's young lady when she asked you if you made the cows drink wine wouldn't they milk syllabub? He told me before you looked in, Hal! Droll, it was surely. You'd never think that the farmer had it in him."

"Nay, nay," said the farmer with a smile that broke up his face into the semblance of a coloured diagram of the canals in Mars. "Nay, miller, 'twas on the spur o' the moment. I had no time to think o' some ready reply that a young miss might think suitable to her station in life coming from a humble yeoman that has no learning but of tillage."

"I'll swear you'll esteem it neat as a sheep's tongue," said the miller. "Come, farmer, out with it, and don't force me to spoil it i' the telling."

"Oh, well——" began the farmer, pursing out his lips and assuming the expression of one who is forced into a position of enviable prominence.

"Oh, well, 'twas o' Tuesday last—or was it Monday, miller?"

"You told me Monday," replied the miller.

"Did I? Well, if I said Monday I sticks to it whatever may hap; for as ye know me, friends, I don't go back on my word, even though I be wrong, that being my way, so to speak, that came natural to me ever since poor father said to me——"

But the revelation as to the terms of his father's discourse which had produced so lasting an impression upon him, was not to be made at that time; for before the slow farmer had spoken, the porch door was opened, and there appeared against the background of the spring green side of the little valley slope, the figure of a young girl, rather tall, wearing a cloak by the lined hood of which her pretty face was framed.

"Hey," cried the miller, "this be an improvement. After all we won't need your story, farmer."

"Your servant, Master Miller—gentlemen, I am your most obedient to command now as ever," said the girl, dropping a curtsey first to the miller, then to his guests. "Oh, Master Hal, black but comely as usual, and rather more idle than usual. And Farmer Pendelly, too—fresh as a new-washed cherub on a tombstone. Master Pritchard, with his magic wand up his sleeve, I doubt not. I didn't know that you was entertaining a party, miller, or I—I——"

"Don't tell us that you would ha' tarried, Nelly; that would be to pay a bad compliment to my company as well as to me," said the miller.

"I was about to say that I would have hurried, not tarried. Maybe I'll not tarry even now, in spite of the attractions you hold out, sir."

While she spoke the girl conveyed the impression of making another general curtsey to the company, though she had merely glanced around at them with an inclusive smile. She made a pretty pretence of drawing her cloak around her—she had thrown back the hood immediately after entering the room—and made a movement towards the door.

"Don't you dare to think of fleeing, hussy," said the miller. "If you was to flee just now, there's not one of us here that wouldn't hale thee back by the hair o' the head—and a nobler tow line couldn't be found."

He had put his arms about her and patted her hair, which was the lightest chestnut in colour, and shining like very fine unspun silk.

"Hey, Nelly, where did ye pick up that head of hair, anyway? All your household be black as night," he continued.

"Where's the puzzle, sir?" said she, without a suggestion of sauciness. "I favour the night, too, only a moonlight night. My hair is the flash o' moonlight."

"The lass never was slack in speaking up for herself," said the blacksmith.

"True, friend Hal; but haven't I ever been moderate? Have I ever gone even half-way to describe my own charms?" said the girl with a mock seriousness that set everyone laughing—they roared when she looked at them more seriously still, as if reproving their levity.

"I'll not stay here to be flouted," she cried with a pout, giving the miller a pat on the cheek. "Ah, here comes Sue to protect me. Dear Sue, you come in good time. Tell these gentlemen that I haven't a red hair in my head, and as for its being good only to make towing lines of——"

Here she broke down and fell sobbing into the arms of Susan Pendelly, a girl of about her own age, who had entered the room by the door that led to the parlour. For a few moments Susan was puzzled, for Nelly went through her piece of acting extremely well, but the laughter of the miller and the smith—the farmer and the water-finder were not quite sure, so they remained solemn—quickly let her know that Nelly was up to a prank, so she put her arms about her and pretended to soothe her, calling the men ill-mannered wretches, and shaking her fist at them. Susan was a little heavy and homely in her comedy.

"Towing line indeed!" she said, looking indignantly over Nelly's bowed head at the men. "Towing line indeed! Why 'tis the loveliest hair in Cornwall."

"A towing line," said her father, laughing. "A towing line that has drawn more craft in its wake than any twenty-oared galley of a man-o'-war. Oh, the poor fools that try to get a grip o' that towing line! Let me count them. First there was Spanish Roderick——"

The girl lifted up her head from her friend's shoulder.

"Spanish Roderigo the first!" she cried. "Oh, miller, I did think that my reputation was safe in your keeping! Why, sir, there were three after me long before Roderigo showed his face at the Cove."

"I ask your pardon, madam; I did you an injustice; you began the towing business when you were twelve——"

"Ten, miller—ten, if you love me. You would not accuse a simple girl of wasting her time."

"Once again, your pardon, miss. I'll make it nine, if so be that you wish."

"I have no wish in the matter, sir. I'm nought but a simple country wench with no wish but to be let live in peace."

"Tell us how many lads are dangling after you at the present moment, Nell—dangling like mackerel on the streamers?"

"How could I possibly tell, sir? Do you suppose that my father knows to a fish how many mackerel are on his cast of streamers at any time? You should have more sense, miller. The most that I can speak for is the five that I angled for."

"The impudence of the girl! She allows that she angled for five!"

"Miller, you would not have me treat them like trout and whip for them with a rod and a single hook. Oh, no, sir, that would not be worth the while. You see, miller, there are so many of them swimming about—and—and—well, life is brief."

"'Tis my belief, Nelly, that there's a hook on every hair of your head and a foolish lad wriggling on it."

"You compliment my fishing too highly, sir. If I thought that——"

"Well, what would happen if you thought that, madam?"

"Oh, well, I believe that I would e'en weave my hair into a reasonable fishing-net to save time and a diffusion of wriggling. There now, miller, we have had said the last word between us of this nonsense. I know what I am, and you know what I am—a healthy, wholesome country wench, that two or three lads think well of, and as many more think ill of—they don't get distraught about me on the one hand, and they don't have any particular enmity of me on the other hand. That's the way with all girls, even such as are black-browed, and hard-voiced, which no one has yet accused me of being, and I've walked seven miles from Porthawn within the two hours to give you my father's message about Rowan's corner, and when I've given it to you, I have to trudge back with a six-pound bag of your best seconds to keep us from starvation for a day or two."

"You'll not trudge back before the morning if I have any say in the matter," cried the miller's daughter, catching up the other's cloak and throwing it over one arm. "Come hither, Nelly, and we'll have a chat in the parlour, like the well-to-do folk that we be; these men can have this place to themselves till the time comes to lay out supper."

"Supper! what good pixie made you say that word?" cried the other girl. "If you hadn't said it it would have clean gone from my mind that I brought with me a stale fish or two that was left over from our dinner on Sunday week. What a memory I lack, to be sure!"

She picked up a rush basket which she had placed on the floor when she was taking off her cloak, and handed it to Susan.

"You young rapparee!" said the miller. "Did it not cross your foolish pate that a basket of fish a week old and more is fully capable of betraying its presence without the need for a laboured memory?"

"I know that that basket betrayed its presence to me more than once as it hung on my arm after the first three mile hither," said the girl.

"As I live'tis a seven-pound pink salmon, and 'twas swimming in the sea at noon this day," said Susan when she had opened the basket.

"She must ha' heard that we were supping at the mill this eve'n, and that I was of the company," said the blacksmith. "Mistress Polwhele, my respects to you!"

"Nay, Master Hal, had I known that you were to be of the company, the salmon would ha' been a fifteen-pounder at least—that is if I wanted any of the others to have a mouthful," laughed the girl.

She was out of the room before the blacksmith had ceased rattling his chair in his pretence of rising to carry out the menace he made with his fist when she was speaking.

The miller and his guests watched in silence the door through which she had gone.

"A bit of a change from Jake Pullsford, eh, friends!" remarked Hal.

"That's what we needed sorely," said the miller.

CHAPTER III

Life did not seem to be strenuous in the valley of the Lana, seven miles from the fishing village of Porthawn, and thirty from Falmouth, when the eighteenth century still wanted more than ten years of completing its first half. To be sure, the high road to Plymouth was not so very far away, and coaches with passengers and luggage flew daily across the little bridge of the Lana at the rate sometimes of as much as nine miles an hour; and the consciousness of this made the people of the village of Ruthallion think rather well of themselves—so at least the dwellers in the more remote parts of the region were accustomed to affirm. The generous were ready to allow that the most humble-minded of people would think well of themselves if they were so favourably situated in regard to the great world as to be able to get news from London only a few days old, simply by waiting at the turn of the Plymouth road until a coach came up.

But of this privilege the people of that most scattered of all Cornish villages, Ruthallion, did not avail themselves to any marked extent, except upon occasions of great national importance; such as the achievement of a victory by King George's army in the Low Countries, or by the King's ships in the West Indies. In the latter case the news usually came from the Plymouth side of the high road. For the sober discussion of such news in all its bearings, it was understood that the Lana Mill, situated as it was in the valley within a few hundred yards of the village, and having a little causeway off the Porthawn road all to itself, occupied a most favourable position. There was no inn with a well-lighted bar-parlour within four miles of the place, and the miller was hospitable. He was said to be the inheritor of an important secret in regard to the making of cider, and it was no secret that his autumnal brew had a flavour that was unsurpassed by any cider produced in Cornwall, or (as some people said) in the very apple-core of Devonshire itself.

Miller Pendelly was known to be a warm man in more senses than one. He had not only a considerable amount of property apart from the mill, which the unfailing waters of the Lana fed; he was a warm-hearted man, though one of the most discreet that could be imagined. When it was a charity to give, he gave freely, but he showed himself to be well aware of the fact that sometimes charity consists in withholding one's hand. He was not a man that could be easily imposed upon; though, like all shrewd people, he allowed three or four ne'er-do-wells to borrow from him—*once*. He talked of every such case with great bitterness on his tongue, but with a twinkle in his eye that assured his confidants that he knew what he was about. To rid the neighbourhood of an idle youth who was robbing an easy-going father, was surely worth the disbursement of five guineas; and the expatriation of a hard-drinking husband was not dear at six.

He, himself, was a good husband to a good wife, and the father of a girl, who, though well favoured, was discreet—a girl who loved her home and all it contained better than she did any possible lover.

The miller's friends were just equal in number to the inhabitants of the valley and of the villages of Porthawn and Ruthallion. Even the mother of the worthless youth who had disappeared with the five guineas, and the wife of the bibulous husband who had not returned after contracting his loan of six, became, in the course of time, his friends, and almost forgave him for his exercise of generosity. But among his neighbours there were none whom he met on such friendly terms as those to whom he turned with a side-nod of his head when the girls had gone.

"They may spare their breath who would tell me that the ill-favoured ones are the best daughters," said he.

"I'll not be the first to advance that doctrine to the father of Susan Pendelly," said the blacksmith.

The miller laughed.

"Sue was not in my thought," he cried—"at least not when I spoke, though thinking of her now only makes me stronger in my opinion.'Twas the sight of t'other lass. Merry she be and with a sharp enough tongue, but was there ever a better daughter than Nelly Polwhele, tell me that, Hal?"

"A fine salmon fish it be surely," said the blacksmith. "Seven pounds, I'll wager, if 'tis an ounce."

"Out upon thee for a curmudgeon," shouted the miller, giving the blacksmith a push of a vehemence so friendly that he with difficulty retained his place on the settee.

"'Tis a mortal pity that so spirited a mare foal will be tamed sooner or later—that's the way with all female flesh whether well-favoured or black-a-vised," remarked the farmer..

Richard Pritchard, who was the only single man present, shook his head with as great a show of gravity as if he had spent his life taming spirited things.

His arrogance aroused his host.

"And what are you that gives yourself airs, my man?" he cried. "What call has a worm of a bachelor to let his tongue wag on a matter that might well make owdacious fathers o' families keep dead silence? Richard Pritchard, my good man, this talk is not for such as thee. Thou beest a middling silent man by nature, Dick, and for that thou shouldst be thankful when wild words be flying abroad on household matters."

"I allow that I went too far, neighbour, though I call all to witness that I did not open my mouth to speak," said the water-finder, with great humility.

"You are aye over daring, though never all through immoral, Dick," said the blacksmith gravely.

"I allow that I earned reproof, friend," said Richard.' "We all be human, and many have frail thought of high language, and a proud heart at the hope of wisdom and ancient learning. But I take reproof with no ill-feeling."

The miller roared at the success of his jest.

"Richard Pritchard, if I didn't know you for a brave Welshman, I would take you for a Dorset dairyman that's so used to the touch o' butter they say it wouldn't melt in their mouths," he cried when he found breath.

At this point Mistress Pendelly bustled into the room, which was not the kitchen, but only a sort of business-room of the mill, with the message that supper would not be ready so soon as she could wish; the salmon steaks took their own time to cook, she affirmed, and expressed the hope that her friends would be able to hold out for another half hour.

"Make no excuses, mother," said her husband. "Why, good wife, the very sound of the frizzling will keep us alive in hope, and the smell that creeps through the crevices of the kitchen door is nigh as satisfying as a full meal in itself."

"Speak for yourself if you are so minded, miller," cried Hal Holmes. "Sup off the sound of a frizzle mixed with the sniff of a well-greased pan, if you so please, but give me a flake or two o' salmon flesh, good mother, the pink o' the body just showing through the silver o' the scales. Oh, a lady born is your sea salmon with her pink complexion shining among the folds o' her silver lace!"

"Ay, sir, better than that your praise should be, for the fish's beauty is more than skin deep," said the housewife, as she stood with the kitchen door half open.

The miller winked at his friends when she had disappeared.

"Canst better that, Hal?" he enquired.

"Vanity to try," replied the blacksmith. "A man's good enough maybe for the catching o' a salmon, but it needs a woman's deft fingers to cook it. You see through my proverb, miller?"

"It needs no spying glass, Hal," said the miller. "The interpretation thereof is in purpose that it needs a woman's nimble wit to put a finishing touch to a simple man's discourse, howsoever well meant it may be. Eh, farmer?"

"'Tis different wi' pilchards, as is only natural, seeing what sort of eating they be," said the farmer shrewdly; he found that he had been wittier than he had any notion of being, and he added his loudest chuckles (when he had recovered from his surprise) to the roaring of the miller's laughter.

It was Nelly Polwhele who demanded to be let into the secret of the merriment so soon as she had returned to the room with Susan, and when the miller told her, with an illuminating wink and a shrewd nod, she laughed in so musical a note with her hands uplifted that the farmer pursed out his lips in pride at his own wit. He was not without a hope that he might find out, in the course of the evening, wherein the point of it lay.

Meantime Nelly was looking anxiously around the room.

"What's gone wrong wi' the girl?" said the miller. "Oh, I see how things be: 'tis so long since she was here the place seems strange to her. Is't not so, Nelly?"

"Partly, sir," replied the girl. "But mainly I was looking to see where Mr. Pullsford was hiding. You can't be supping in good style and he absent."

"Give no heed to Mr. Pullsford, whether he be here or not; spend your time in telling us where you yourself have been hiding for the past month," cried the miller.

"She has not been hiding, she has been doing just the opposite—displaying herself to the fashionable world," said Susan.

"Hey, what's all this?" said the miller. "You don't mean to tell us that you've been as far as Plymouth?"

"Plymouth, indeed! Prithee, where's the rank and fashion at Plymouth, sir?" cried Nelly. "Nay, sir, 'tis to the Bath I have been, as befits one in my station in life."

"The Bath?—never," exclaimed the miller, while the girl, lifting up her dress with a dainty finger and thumb to the extent of an inch or two, went mincing past him down the room, followed by the eyes of the blacksmith and the others of the party. "'Tis in jest you speak, you young baggage— how would such as you ever get as far as the Bath?"

"It sounds like a fancy freak, doth it not truly; and yet 'tis the sober truth," said Nelly. "At the Bath I was, and there I kept for a full month, in the very centre core of all the grandest that the world has in store. I didn't find myself a bit out of place, I protest."

"Hear the girl!" exclaimed the miller. "She talks with the cold assurance of a lady of quality—not that I ever did meet with one to know; but—and the fun of it is that she wouldn't be out of place in the most extravagant company. Come, then, tell us how it came about. Who was it kidnapped thee?"

And then the girl told how it was that Squire Trelawny's young ladies at Court Royal, having lost their maid, owing to her marrying in haste, asked her to take the young woman's place for a month or two until they should get suited. As she had always been a favourite with them, she had consented, and they had forthwith set out for the Bath with the Squire's retinue of chariots and horsemen, and there they had sojourned for a month.

"'Tis, indeed, like a story o' pixies and their magic and the like," said the miller. "I knew that the young ladies and you was ever on the best o' terms, but who could tell that it would come to such as this? And I'll wager my life that within a day and a night you could tire their hair and dust it wi' powder with the best of their ladyships' ladies. And, prithee, what saw you at the Bath besides the flunkies o' the quality?"

"Oh, sir, ask me not to relate to you all that I saw and noted," said the girl. "Every day of my life I said, 'What a place the world is to be sure!'"

"And so it be," said the farmer approvingly.

"Oh, the rank and fashion, farmer, such as would astonish even you, and you are a travelled man," said she.

"Ay, I have been as wide afield as Falmouth on the west and Weymouth on the east," said the farmer. "Ay, I know the world."

"Your travels have ever been the talk of the six parishes, sir," said the girl. "But among all the strange people that have come-under your eyes, I'll warrant you there was none stranger than you might find at the Bath. Have you ever in your travels crossed ladies sitting upright in stumpy sentry boxes with a stout fellow bearing it along the streets, winging 'twixt the pair o' poles?"

"Naught so curious truly; but I've seen honest and honourable men that had heard of such like," said the farmer.

"And to think that I saw them with these eyes, and link boys, when there was no moon, and concerts of music in the Cave of Harmony, night by night, and two gentlemen fighting in a field—this was by chance, and my lady passing in a chariot sent forth a shriek, so that one pistol exploded before its time, and the bullet graded a peaceful gentleman, who they said was a doctor of physic coming quick across the meadow, scenting a fee!"

"Pity is 'twasn't a lawyer. I hoard the thought that in case o' a fight 'twixt friends, the lawyers hurry up as well as the doctors in hope of a job," said the miller. "Well, you've seen the world a deal for one so young, Nelly," he added.

"And the concerts of singing and the assemblies and the beautiful polite dance which they call the minuet were as nought when placed alongside the plays in the playhouse," cried Nelly.

The miller became grave.

"There be some who see a wicked evil in going to the playhouse," he remarked, with a more casual air than was easy to him.

"That I have heard," said the girl.

"They say that a part o' the playhouse is called the pit," suggested the farmer. "Ay, I saw the name over the door at Plymouth, as it maybe did you, miller."

"And some jumped at the notion that that pit led to another of a bottomless sort?" said the girl. "Well, I don't say that'twas the remembrance of that only that drew me to the playhouse. I did get something of a shock, I allow, when my young ladies bade me attend them to the playhouse one night, but while I sought a fair excuse for 'biding at our lodging on the Mall, I found myself inventing excuses for obeying my orders, and I must say that I found it a good deal easier doing this than t'other."

"Ay, ay, I doubt not that—oh, no, we doubt it not," cried the miller, shaking his head.

Richard Pritchard shook his head also.

"I found myself saying, 'How can the playhouse be a place of evil when my good young ladies, who are all that is virtuous, find it a pleasure to go?'"

The miller shook his head more doubtfully than before.

"I think that you left the service of your young ladies in good time," muttered the miller.

"Do not dare to say a word against them—against even Mistress Alice, who, I allow, hath a tantrum now and again, when the seamstress fails her in time or mode," said the girl. "Of course when I reflected that I was but a servant, so to speak, and that my duty was to obey my mistresses, I would hesitate no longer. Duty is a virtue, sir, so I submitted without a complaint."

"Ay, you would do that," murmured the blacksmith.

"I said to myself——"

"Oh," groaned the miller.

Nelly ignored the groan. She went on demurely from where she was interrupted.

"I said to myself, 'Should there be evil in it none can hold me blameworthy, since I was only obeying the order of them that were set over me.' I went and I was glad that I went, for I saw no evil in word or act."

"I'm grieved to hear it, Nelly," said the miller.

"What, you are grieved to hear that I saw nothing of evil? Oh, sir!"

"I mean that I don't like to think of a girl like thee in such a place, Nelly. But let's make the best of a bad matter and recount to us what you saw. It may be that by good fortune we may be able to find out the evil of it, so that you may shun it in future."

"Alack, I fear the chance will not come to me in the future," said Nelly mournfully.

"I trust not. Who was the actor that night, do you mind?" asked the miller.

"Her name was Mistress Woffington, and now I mind that one of my ladies said that Mr. Long had told her that Mistress Woffington had been to dinner with the learned provost of Dublin College in Ireland—a parson and a scholar."

"Oh, an Irishman!" was the comment of the miller.

"Let the girl be, miller," said Hal Holmes. "She's making a brave fight in the way of excusing herself. Go thy gait, Nell; give us a taste of the quality of this Mistress Woffington."

"Oh, Hal, she is a beauty—I never thought that the world held such. The finest ladies of quality at the Bath, though they all copy her in her mode, are not fit to hold a candle to her. And her clothing and her modesty withal. They say she does the modest parts best of all."

"Ay, I've heard that the likes of her are best in parts that have the least in common with themselves," murmured the miller.

"Oh, to see her when she vowed that she would be true to her lover albeit that her ancient father, stamping about with a cudgel and a mighty wig, had promised her to a foolish fellow in yellow silk and an eyeglass with a long handle, and a foppish way of snuff-taking and a cambric handkerchief! La! how the lady made a fool of him under his very nose. This is Mistress Woffington: 'I protest, Sir, that I am but a simple girl, country bred, that is ready to sink into the earth at the approach of so dangerous a gentleman as your lordship.' And she make a little face at her true lover, who is getting very impatient, in blue and silver, at the other side of the room. 'Stap my vitals, madam,' lisps the jessamy, dangling his cane in this fashion—you should see them do it on the Mall—" She picked up a light broom that lay at the side of the hearth and made a very pretty swagger across the room with her body bent and her elbow raised in imitation of the exquisite of the period, quite unknown to Cornwall. "'Egad, my dear, for a country wench you are not without favour. To be sure, you lack the mode of the *haut ton*, but that will come to you in time if you only watch me—that is, to a certain extent. My lady, the Duchess says, "Charles is inimitable." Ah, her Grace is a sad flatterer, 'fore Gad, but she sometimes speaks the truth.' 'What, Sir,' says the lady, 'do you think that in time I should catch some of your grand air? I beseech you, Sir, have pity on a poor simple maiden; do not raise false hopes in her breast.' 'Nay, pretty charmer, I do not dare to affirm that you will ever quite catch the full style—the air of breeding, so to speak; but you may still catch——' 'the smallpox, and faith, I think I would prefer it to him,' says Mrs. Woffington in a whisper, that all in the playhouse can hear. 'Eh, what's that?' lisps Mr. Floppington. 'Oh, sir, I was just saying that I fear I am sickening for the smallpox, which runs in our family as does the gout, only a deal faster.' 'Eh, what, what! keep away from me, girl, keep away, I tell you.' He retreats with uplifted hands; she follows him, with her own clasped, imploring him not to reject her. He waves his cane in front of her as if she was a bull ready to toss him. They both speak together, they run round the table, he springs upon the table, she tilts it over—down he goes crying, 'Murder—murder—stop her—hold her back!' He is on his feet again, his fine coat torn in half at the back. She catches at it and one whole side rips off in her hand. He makes for the window—finds it too high to jump from—rushes to the door and down goes the lady's father, who is in the act of entering, with a bump, and down goes the fop with the half coat in the other direction. The lady sits drumming with her heels on the floor between them in a shrieking faint—thus!"

She flung herself into a chair and her shrieks sounded shrill above the laughter of the others.

Suddenly the laughter came to an abrupt end, as though it were cut in twain with a sharp knife. The girl continued for a few seconds shrieking and rapping her heels on the floor, her head thrown back; then she clearly became aware of the fact that something unusual had occurred. She looked up in surprise at the men on the settee, followed the direction of their eyes, and saw standing at the porch door a man of medium stature, wearing a long riding cloak and carrying a book in one hand. The doorway framed him. The dimness of the shadowy eventide made a background for his head, the candle which Susan had lighted in the room shone upon his face, revealing the thin, refined features of a man who was no longer young. His face was sweetness made visible—eyes that looked in brotherly trustfulness into the eyes of others, and that, consequently, drew trust from others—illimitable trust.

The girl stared at the stranger who had appeared in the doorway with such suddenness; and she saw what manner of man he was. There was an expression of mild surprise on his face while he looked at her, the central figure in the room; but she saw that there was a gentle smile about his eyes.

"I hope that I am not an intruder upon your gaiety," said the stranger. "I knocked twice at the door, and then, hearing the shrieks of distress, I ventured to enter. I hoped to be of some assistance—shrieks mixed with laughter—well, I have stopped both."

The miller was on his feet in a moment.

"Foolery, sir, girl's foolery all!" he said, going towards the stranger. "Pray, enter, if you can be persuaded that you are not entering a Bedlam mad-house."

"Nay, sir," said the newcomer. "'Twould be foolish to condemn simply because I do not understand. I am a stranger to this county of England; I have had no chance of becoming familiar with your pastimes. Dear child, forgive me if I broke in upon your merriment," he added, turning to Nelly; "Good sir,"—he was now facing the miller—"I have ridden close upon thirty miles to-day—the last four in the want of a shoe; my horse must have cast it in the quagmire between the low hills. Yours was the first light that I saw—I was in hopes that it came from a blacksmith's forge."

The miller laughed.

"'Tis better than that, good sir," said he. "The truth is that the smith of these parts is a fellow not to be trusted by travellers: his forge is black tonight, unless his apprentices are better men than he. He is a huge eater of salmon and divers dainties, and he will drink as much as a mugful of cider before the night is past."

"But he is a fellow that is ready to sacrifice a cut of salmon and a gallon of cider to earn a sixpence for a shoe, sir," said Hal Holmes, rising from the settee and giving himself a shake. "In short, sir, I be Holmes, the smith, whose lewd character has been notified to your honour, and if you trust me with your nag, I'll promise you to fit a shoe on him within the half-hour."

The stranger looked from the smith to the miller, and back again to the smith, and his smile broadened.

"Good neighbours both, I can see," he said. "I thank you, smith. How far is it to Porthawn, pray, and what may this placed be called?"

Before he could be answered the door opened and Jake Pullsford entered the room. The sound of his entrance caused the stranger to turn his head. Jake gave an exclamation of surprise.

"Mr. Wesley!" he said in a whisper that had something of awe in its tone. "Mr. Wesley! How is this possible? I have spent the afternoon talking of you, sir."

At the sound of the name the miller glanced meaningly at the smith. They were plainly surprised.

"Well, my brother," said Mr. Wesley, "I ask nothing better than to give you the chance of talking to me for the next hour. I remember you well. You are Jake Pullsford, who came to see me a month ago at Bristol. You have been much in my thoughts—in my prayers."

CHAPTER IV

Jake was so excited at finding himself by a curious accident once more face to face with the man who, as he had happily confessed to his friends, had produced so great an impression upon him as to change the whole course of his life, that he began to talk to him in his usual rapid way, as though Mr. Wesley and himself were the only persons in the room.

The miller remained on his feet. The blacksmith was also on his feet. He had assumed a professional air. After all, he was likely to be the most important person present. The girl in the chair remained with her hands folded on her lap. She had the aspect of a schoolgirl who has broken out of bounds and awaits an interview with the schoolmistress. She had heard during her visit to Bath of this Mr. Wesley and his views—at least such views as were attributed to him by the fashionable folk who assembled to have their gossip and intrigue flavoured by the sulphur of the waters. He was not so easy-going as the clergymen at Bath. She could not doubt that he would esteem it his duty to lecture her on her levity. It was known that he abhorred playgoing. He was naturally abhorred by the players. They had the best of reasons: when he was preaching in any town that had a theatre, the players remained with empty pockets.

The appearance of Mrs. Pendelly announcing that supper was ready was a great relief to her.

She jumped up with alacrity. Jake Pullsford came back to earth. He was breathing hard. The visitor had signified his intention of resuming his journey, if his horse could be shod. Jake was entreating him to pass the night at his house, only a mile up the valley.

The miller was beginning to feel awkward. He was hospitably inclined, but he was not presumptuous. The blacksmith was fast losing his professional bearing; a sniff of the salmon steaks had come through the open door.

It was the visitor whose tact made the situation easy for everyone.

"Sir," he said to the miller, "I have arrived here so opportunely for myself that I will not even go through the pretence of offering to go to the wayside inn, which our good friend Jake Pullsford tells me is some miles away. I know that I can throw myself on your hospitality and that you would feel affronted if I hurried on. I have no mind to do so—to be more exact, I should say no stomach."

"Sir, if your reverence will honour my house I can promise you a wholesome victual," said the miller. "Even if you was not a friend o' my friend Jake here, who might, I think, have named my name in your ear, you would still be welcome.".

"I know it, sir," said Wesley, offering the miller his hand. "I thank you on behalf of myself and my good partner whose bridle I hung over your ring-post. A feed of oats will put new spirit in him in spite of the loss of his shoe."

"The horse shall be seen to, Mr. Wesley. Susan, the stable bell," said the miller, and his daughter set a bell jangling on the gable wall.

"Again my thanks, good friend," said Wesley.

"May I beg your leave to be presented to my fellow-guests at your table, sir?"

He shook hands with the farmer, the water-finder and the smith, saying a word to each. Then he turned to where the two young women had been.

They had fled through the open door, Nelly having been the one to judge of the exact moment for flight.

They appeared at the supper table, however, but not taking their seats until they had waited upon all the others of the party. That was the patriarchal custom of the time. Nelly Polwhele only wished that the severe discipline of a side table for the serving girls had been in force at the Mill. Remote from the long oak table on which generations of her family had dined, she might have had a pleasant chat with her friend Susan, and then steal off, evading the lecture which she felt was impending from the strict Mr. Wesley. As it was, the most she could do for herself was to choose an unobtrusive place at the further end from the clergyman.

She hoped that the excellence of the salmon which she had carried through the valley of the Lana would induce him to refrain from asking any questions in regard to the game that was being played at the moment of his entrance.

But Mr. Wesley was vigilant. He espied her before he had finished his salmon, and had expressed his thanks to her for having burdened herself with it. It was his thirst for information of all sorts that had caused him to enquire how it was possible to have for supper a fish that must have been swimming in the sea, or at least in a salmon river, which the Lana was not, a few hours before. Was not Porthawn the nearest fishing village, and it was six miles away? Then it was that Mrs. Pendelly had told him of Nelly's journey on foot bearing her father's gift to his friend the miller.

"I should like to have a word or two with you, my dear," said Mr. Wesley when he had thanked her. "I wish to learn something of the people of Porthawn. I am on my way thither to preach, and I like to learn as much as is possible of the people who, I hope, will hear what I have to say to them."

Nelly blushed and tried to say that she was afraid she could tell him nothing that he could not learn from any other source—that was what was on her mind—but somehow her voice failed her. She murmured something; became incoherent, and then ate her salmon at a furious rate.

The miller, although he had felt bound to offer hospitality to the stranger who had appeared at his door, knew that his other guests—with the exception, it might be, of Jake Pullsford—would feel, as he himself did, that the presence of this austere clergyman would interfere with their good fellowship at supper and afterwards. He and his associates knew one another with an intimacy that had been maturing for thirty years, and the sudden coming of a stranger among them could not but cause a certain reserve in the natural freedom of their intercourse.

The miller had a constant fear that this Mr. Wesley would in the course of the evening say something bitter about the parsons who hunted and bred game-cocks and fought them, laying money on their heads—on parsons who lived away from their parishes, allowing indifferent curates to conduct the services of the church—of parsons who boasted of being able to drink the Squires under the table. The miller had no confidence in his power of keeping silent when he felt that the parson with whom he was on the easiest of terms and for whose gamecocks he prepared a special mixture of stiffening grain food was being attacked by a stranger, so he rather regretted that his duty compelled him to invite Mr. Wesley, of whom he, in common with thousands of the people of the West country, had heard a great deal, to supper on this particular evening.

But in the course of the meal he began to think that he would have no reason to put any restraint upon himself. He soon became aware of the fact that this Reverend John Wesley was not altogether the austere controversialist which rumour, becoming more and more exaggerated as it travelled West, made him out to be. Before supper was over he had come to the conclusion that Parson Rodney as a companion could not hold a candle to this Mr. Wesley.

The compliment in respect of the salmon had pleased both the miller and his wife, even though it had made Nell blush; and then a bantering word or two was said to Hal Holmes and his fine taste for salmon, and forthwith Mr. Wesley was giving an animated account of how he had seen the Indians in Georgia spearing for salmon on one of the rivers. This power of bringing a wide scene before one's eyes in a moment by the use of an illuminating word or two was something quite new to the miller and his friends; but it was the special gift of his latest guest. With thin uplifted forefinger—it had the aspect as well as the power of a wizard's wand—he seemed to draw the whole picture in the air before the eyes of all at the table—the roar of the rapids whose name with its Indian inflections was in itself a romance—the steathily moving red men with their tomahawks and arrows and long spears—the enormous backwoods—one of them alone half the size of England and Wales—the strange notes of the bird—whip-poor-will, the settlers called it—moonlight over all—moonlight that was like a thin white sheet let down from heaven to cover the earth; and where this silver wonder showed the white billows of foam churned up by the swirl of the mad river, there was the gleam of torches—from a distance they looked like the fierce red eyes of the wild beasts of the backwood; but coming close one could see deep down at the foot of the rapids the flash of a blood-red scimitar—the quick reflection in the passionate surface of the water of the red flare that waved among the rocks. Then there was a sudden splash and a flash—another scimitar—this time of silver scattering diamonds through the moonlight—another flash like a thin beam of light—the fish was transfixed in mid-air by the Indian spear!

They saw it all. The scene was brought before their eyes. They sat breathless around the supper table. And yet the man who had this magic of voice and eye had never once raised that voice of his—had never once made a gesture except by the uplifting of his finger.

"Fishing—that is fishing!" said Hal Holmes. "I should like——"

The finger was upraised in front of him.

"You must not so much as think of it, my friend! It would be called poaching on our rivers here," said Mr. Wesley with a smile.

"Then I should like to live in the land where the fish of the rivers, the deer of the forests, the birds of the air are free, as it was intended they should be—free to all men who had skill and craft—I have heard of the trappers," said Hal. "It seems no sort of life for a wholesome man to live—pulling the string of a bellows, hammering iron into shoes, for plough-horses!—no life whatsoever." Wesley smiled.

"Ah, if you but knew aught of the terror of the backwoods," said he. "If you but knew of it—one vast terror—monstrous—incredible. A terror by day and by night. I was used to stand on one of the hills hard by our little settlement, and look out upon the woods whose skirts I could see in the far distance, and think of their immensity and their mystery. Hundreds of miles you might travel through those trackless forests until the hundreds grew into thousands—at last you would come upon-the prairie—hundred and hundreds of miles of savage country—a mighty ocean rolling on to the foot of the Rocky Mountains! Between the backwoods-and the mountains roll the Mississippi River—the Ohio, the Potomac. Would you know what the Mississippi is like? Take the Thames and the Severn and the Wye and the Tyne and the Humber—let them roll their combined volume down the one river bed; the result would be no more than an insignificant tributary of the Mother of Waters—the meaning of the name Mississippi."

There was more breathlessness. When Hal Holmes broke the silence everyone was startled—everyone stared at him.

"Grand! grand!" he said in a whisper. "And your eyes beheld that wonder of waters, sir?"

Mr. Wesley held up both his hands.

"I—I—behold it?" he cried. "Why, there is no one in England whose eyes have looked upon that great river. Had I set out to find it I should have had to travel for a whole year before reaching it—a year, even if the forests had opened their arms to receive me, and the prairie had offered me a path I spoke with an Indian who had seen it, and I spoke with the widows of two men who had gone in search for it. Four years had passed without tidings of those men, and then one of the Iroquois tribe found a tattered hat that had belonged to one of them, on the borders of the backwoods, not a hundred miles from his starting place. Of the other nothing has yet been forthcoming. I tell you, friends, that I was used to let my eyes wander across the plain until they saw that forest, and they never saw it without forcing me to look upon it as a vast, monstrous thing—but a living creature—one of those fabled dragons that were said to lie in wait to devour poor wretches that drew nigh to it. Nay, when I looked upon it I recalled the very striking lines in John Milton's fine epic of 'Paradise Lost':

'With head uplift above the wave, and eyes
That sparkling blazed; his other parts besides
Prone on the flood, extended long and large,
Lay floating many a rood,—"

"One must needs be a dweller among the adventurers in America in order to understand in its fulness how terrible a monster those backwoods are thought to be. There it stretched, that awful mass—that monstrous mother of that venomous brood—the huge snakes that lurk in the undergrowth, the fierce lynx, the terrible panther, the wolf and the wildcat. I have heard, too, of a certain dragon and the vampire—a huge bat that fans a poor wretch asleep by the gentle winnowing of its leather wings only to drain his life's blood. These are but a few of the brood of the backwoods. Who can name them all? The poisonous plants that shoot out seeds with the noise of the discharge of a musket, the swamps made up of the decay of a thousand years—breathing fevers and agues—the spectre of starvation lurks there unless you have weapons and the skill to use them—fire—they told me of the prairie fires—a blast of flame five miles broad—sometimes twenty miles broad—rushing along driving before it beasts and birds until they drop in sheer exhaustion and become cinders in a minute—these are some of the terrors that dwell in the backwoods, but worst of all—most fierce—inexorable, is the Red Indian. Tongue of man cannot tell the story of their treachery—their torturings. Our settlers do not fear to face the beasts of the backwoods—the rattlesnakes—the pestilence of the swamps—the most cruel of these is more merciful than the Indian."

They listened as children listen to a fairy tale, and they knew that they were hearing the truth. There was not one of them that had not heard something of the story of the founding of the settlement along the coast of the new Continent, from the Bay Colonies and Plymouth Rock in the North to Carolina in the South. The spirit of adventure which had given Drake and Raleigh their crews from the men of the West country gave no signs of dying out among their descendants. They listened and were held in thrall while this man, who had come among them with something of the reputation of a pioneer—a man boldly striking out a new track for himself, told them of the perils faced by their countrymen on the other side of that sea which almost rolled to their very doors. He carried them away with him. They breathed with him the perfume of the backwoods and became imbued with the spirit of mystery pervading them. He carried them away simply because he himself was carried away. He felt all that he spoke about; this was the secret of his power. He could not have made them feel strongly unless by feeling strongly himself.

But his aim was not limited to his desire to arouse their interest in the romance of the backwoods. He spoke of the troubles of the young settlement to which he had gone out, of the bravery of the settlers, men and women—

of the steadfast hope which animated them in facing their anxieties—their dangers. What was the power that sustained them? In one word, it was faith.

Without the least suggestion of preaching, he talked to them of Faith. He talked as if it was not merely a sentiment—a cold doctrine to be discussed by the aid of logic—nay, but as a real Power—a Power that could move mountains. Such as had it had the greatest gift that Heaven offered to mankind. It was a gift that was offered freely—all could have it, if they so willed; and this being so, how great would be the condemnation of those who refused to accept it!

And the people who had eagerly drunk in all that he had to say of the mystery of the backwoods were even more interested when he talked of this other mystery. There had been no dividing line in his subject; the Faith of which he was now speaking with all the eloquence of simple language that fell like soft music on their ears, was a natural part—the most actual part of his story of the great half-known West.

They listened to him while he discoursed for that marvellous half-hour, and the prayer that followed seemed also a part—the suitable closing part of that story of trial and trouble and danger rendered impotent by Faith. Surely, when such a gift could be had for the asking, they should ask for it. He prayed that the hearts of all who were kneeling might be opened to receive that saving grace of Faith.

"Hal, my friend," said the miller, when they stood together at the entrance to the lane, having seen Mr. Wesley drive off with Jake. "Hal, for the first time these sixteen years I have seen thee rise from thy supper without searching about for thy pipe!"

"My pipe? List, old friend, while I tell thee that to pass another such evening I would break my pipe into a hundred pieces and never draw a whiff of 'bacca between my teeth," said Hal. "Moreover, a word in thy ear: I would not have it made public; I'll smoke no more 'bacca that comes to me by a back way. I believe that why I didn't smoke this evening was by reason of the feeling that was in me that 'twould be a solemn sin for me to let him have even a sniff of 'bacca that had been run."

The miller laughed.

"Why, Hal, he did not preach to us to give the Preventive men their due," he said.

"No, no. If he had I might ha' been the less disposed to do the right thing. But now—well, no more smuggled 'bacca for me."

"Good: — good — but wherefore this honest resolve, Hal Holmes?"

"I know not. Only I seem somehow to look at some things in a new light."

"And that light will not let your tinder be fired over a pipe o' 'bacca that has paid no duty? That's right enough, but what I need to learn from you is the reason of all this."

"Ah, there you have me, friend. I can give you no reason for it; only the notion came over me quite sudden like, that for ten year I had been doing what I should ha' turned from, and I made the resolve now to turn now before it was too late. That's all, and so, good-night to you, Mat, and God bless you. I be to get that shoe on before he starts from Jake's house i' the morn, and he said he would start betimes."

The miller laughed again, but very gently, and held out his hand to the other without a word. It was not until the blacksmith had disappeared down the lane that his friend said in a low voice:

"It beats me clean. There must be a sort of magic in the man's tongue that it works those wonders. All the time that he was telling us his story o' the woods I was making up my mind to be a better man — to have more charity at heart for my fellows — to be easier on such as cannot pay all that they have promised to pay. And now here's Hal that confesses to the same, albeit he has never gone further out of the straight track than to puff a pipe that has paid nothing to King George's purse. And the man gave no preacher's admonition to us, but only talked o' the forest and such-like wild things.... Now, how did he manage to bring Faith into such a simple discourse?... Oh, 'tis his tongue that has the magic in it! Magic, I say; for how did it come that when he spoke I found myself gazing like a child at a picture — a solid, bright picture o' woods and things?... Oh, 'tis true magic, this — true!"

CHAPTER V

Oh, that a man could speak to men in the language of the Spring!" cried Mr. Wesley, when his horse stopped unbidden and unchidden and looked over the curved green roof of the hedge across the broad green pasturage beyond. "Oh, that my lips could speak that language which every ear can understand and every heart feel! What shall it profit a man to understand if he does not feel—feel—feel? The man who understands is the one who holds in his hand the doctor's prescription. The man who feels is the one who grasps the healing herbs; and 'tis the Spring that yields these for all to gather who will."

And then, automatically he took his feet out of the stirrups for greater ease, and his eyes gazed across the meadow-land which sloped gently upward to the woods where the sunbeams were snared among the endless network of the boughs, for the season was not advanced far enough to make the foliage dense; the leaves were still thin and transparent—shavings of translucent emerald—a shade without being shadowy.

Everything that he saw was a symbol to him. He looked straight into the face of Nature herself and saw in each of its features something of the Great Message to man with which his own heart was filled to overflowing. He was a poet whose imagination saw beneath the surface of everything. He was a physician who could put his finger upon the pulse of Nature and feel from its faintest flutter the mighty heart which throbbed through the whole creation.

What man was there that failed to understand the message of Nature as he understood it? He could not believe that any should be so dense as to misinterpret it. It was not a book written in a strange tongue; it was a book made up of an infinite number of pictures, full of colour that any child could appreciate, even though it had never learned to read. There was the meadow beyond the hedgerow. It was full of herbs, bitter as well as sweet. Could anyone doubt that these were the symbols of the Truth; herbs for the healing of the nations, and if some of them were bitter to the taste, were their curative properties the less on this account? Nay, everyone knew that the bitterest herbs were oftentimes the most healing. What a symbol of the Truth! It was not the dulcet truths that were purifying to the soul of man, but the harsh and unpalatable.

"God do so to me and more also if ever I should become an unfaithful physician and offer to the poor souls of men only those Truths that taste sweet in their mouths and that smell grateful to their nostrils!" he cried.

And he did not forget himself in the tumult of his thought upon his message. He was not the physician who looked on himself as standing in no need of healing.

"I have tasted of the bitter medicine myself and know what is its power. Oh, may I be given grace to welcome it again should my soul stand in need of it!"

A lark rose from the grass of the sloping meadow and began its ecstatic song as it climbed its ærie ladder upward to the pure blue. He listened to the quivering notes—a bubbling spring of melody babbling and wimpling and gurgling and flitting and fluttering as it fell through the sweet morning air.

"Oh, marvel of liquid melody!" cried the man, letting his eyes soar with the soaring bird. "What is the message that is thine! What is that message which fills thy heart with joy and sends thee soaring out of the sight of man, enraptured to the sky? Is it a message from the sons of men that thou bearest to the heavens? Is it a message from Heaven that thou sendest down to earth?"

A butterfly fluttered up from beyond the hedge, carrying with it the delicate scent of unseen primroses. It hovered over the moss of the bank for a moment and then allowed itself to be blown like a brown leaf in the breeze in a fantastic course toward the group of harebells that made a faint blue mist over a yard of meadow.

He watched its flight. The butterfly had once been taken as an emblem of the immortality of the soul, he remembered. Was it right that it should be thought such a symbol, he wondered. In latter years it was looked on as an example of all that is fickle and frivolous. Was it possible that the ancients saw more deeply into the heart of things—more deeply into the spirit of these forms of Nature?

"Who can say what wise purpose of the Creator that gaudy insect may fulfil in the course of its brief existence?" said he. "We know that nothing had been made in vain. It may be that it flutters from flower to flower under no impulse of its own, but guided by the Master of Nature, whose great design would not be complete without its existence. That which we in our ignorance regard as an emblem of all that is vain and light may, in truth, be working out one of the gravest purposes of the All Wise."

He remained under the influence of this train of thought for some time. Then his horse gave a little start that brought back his rider from the realm into which he had been borne by his imagination. He caught up the rein, slipped his feet into his stirrups, and perceived that it was the fluttering dress of a girl, who had apparently sprung from the primrose hollow beyond the hedge, that had startled the animal. It seemed that the girl herself was also startled; she stood a dozen yards away, with her lips parted, and gave signs of flight a moment before he recognised her as one of the girls who had been at the Mill the night before—the girl who had been the central figure in the game which his entrance had interrupted.

"Another butterfly—another butterfly!" he said aloud, raising his hand to salute Nelly Polwhele, who dropped him a curtsey with a faint reply to his "Good-morning."

He pushed his horse closer to her, saying:

"A fair morning to you, my child! You are not a slug-a-bed. Have you come for the gathering of mushrooms or primroses? Not the latter; the borders of the Mill stream must be strewn with them to-day."

"I am on my way to my home, sir," she replied. "I set out on my return to the village an hour ago. I should be back in less than another—'tis scarce four mile onward."

"I remember that you told me you had come from Porthawn—my destination also. I wished for a chat with you, but somehow we drifted a long way from Porthawn—we drifted across the Atlantic and got lost in the backwoods of America."

"Ah, no, sir, not lost," said the girl.

"I was a poor guide," said he. "I have only had a glimpse of the backwoods, and so could only lead you all a rood or two beyond their fringes of maple. The true guide is one that hath been on every forest track and can tell by the tinges on the tree trunk in what direction his feet tend. What a pity 'tis, my dear, that we cannot be so guided through this great tangled forest of life that we are travers-. ing now on to the place of light that is far beyond—a place where there is no darkness—a shelter but no shadow! There, you see, I begin to preach to the first person whom I overtake. That is the way of the man who feels laid upon him the command to preach."

"It does not sound like preaching, sir," said the girl. "I would not tire listening to words like that."

"That is how you know preaching from—well, from what is not preaching: you tire of the one, not of the other?" said he, smiling down at her.

She hung her head. Somehow in the presence of this man all her readiness of speech—sharpness of reply—seemed to vanish.

"I do not say that you have not made a very honest and a very excellent attempt to convey to me what is the impression of many people," he resumed. "But there is a form of preaching of which you can never grow weary. I have been listening to it since our good friend Hal Holmes helped me to mount the horse that he had just shod."

"Preaching, sir?" she said. "There are not many preachers hereabouts. Parson Rodney gives us a good ten minutes on Sunday, but he does not trouble us on week-days."

"Doth his preaching trouble you on Sunday, child? If so, I think more highly of your parson than I should be disposed to think, seeing that I have heard nothing about him save that he is the best judge of a game-cock in Cornwall. But the sermon that makes a listener feel troubled in spirit is wholesome. Ah, never mind that. I tell you that I have been listening to sermons all this lovely morning—the sermon of that eminent preacher, the sun, to the exhortation of the fields, the homily of the bursting flowers, the psalm of the soaring lark, the parable of the butterfly. I was thinking upon the butterfly when you appeared."

"You are different from Parson Rodney, if it please you, sir."

"It does please me, my child; but, indeed, I am sure that there are worse parsons than those who take part in the homely sports of their parish, rude though some of these sports may be. I wonder if your ears are open to the speech—the divine music of such a morn as this."

"I love the morning, sir—the smell of the flowers and the meadows— the lilt of the birds."

"You have felt that they bring gladness into our life? I knew that your child's heart would respond to their language—they speak to the heart of such as you. And for myself, my thought when I found myself drinking in of all the sweet things in earth and air and sky—drinking of that overflowing chalice which the morning offered to me—my thought—my yearning was for such a voice as that which I heard come from everything about me on this Spring morning. 'Oh, that a man might speak to men in the language of this morn!' I cried."

There was a long pause. His eyes were looking far away from her. He seemed to forget that he was addressing anyone.

She, however, had not taken her eyes off his face. She saw the light that came into it while he was speaking, and she was silent. It seemed to her to speak just then would have been as unseemly as to interrupt at one's prayers.

But in another moment he was looking at her.

"You surely are one of the sweet and innocent things of this dewy morn," said he. "And surely you live as do they to the glory of God. Surely you were meant to join in creation's hymn of glory to the Creator!"

She bent her head and then shook it.

"Nay," said he, "you will not be the sole creature to remain dumb while the Creator is revealing Himself in the reanimation of His world after the dark days of Winter, when the icy finger which touched everything seemed to be the finger of Death!"

His voice had not the inflection of a preacher's. She did not feel as if he were reading her a homily that needed no answer.

But what answer could she make? She was, indeed, so much a part of the things of Nature that, like them, she could only utter what was in her heart. And what was in her heart except a consciousness of her own unworthiness?

"Ah, sir," she murmured, "only last night had I for the first time a sense of what I should be."

His face lit up again when she spoke. His hands clasped, mechanically as it seemed.

"I knew it," he said in a low voice, turning away his head. "I was assured of it. When my horse cast his shoe I felt that it was no mischance. I heard the voice of a little child calling to me through the night. No doubt crossed my mind. I thank Thee—I thank Thee abundantly, O my Master!"

Then he turned to Nelly, saying:

"Child, my child, we are going the same way. Will you give me permission to walk by your side for the sake of company?"

"Nay, sir, will not you be weary a-walking?" she said. "'Tis a good three mile to the Port, and the road is rough when we leave the valley."

"Three miles are not much," said he, dismounting. "The distance will seem as nothing when we begin to talk."

"Indeed that is so, sir," said she. "Last night fled on wings while you were telling us the story of the backwoods."

"It fled so fast that I had no time to fulfil my promise to ask you about your friends at Port-hawn," said he. "That is why I am glad of the opportunity offered to me this morning. I am anxious to become acquainted with all sorts and conditions of people. Now, if I were to meet one of your neighbours to-day I should start conversation by asking him about you. But is there any reason why you should not tell me about yourself?"

She laughed, as they set out together, Mr. Wesley looping his horse's bridle over his arm.

"There is naught to be told about myself, sir; I am only the daughter of a fisherman at Porthawn. I am the least important person in the world."

"'Tis not safe, my child, to assign relative degrees of importance to people whom we meet," said he. "The most seemingly insignificant is very precious in the sight of the Master. Who can say that the humblest of men or women may not be called upon some day to fulfil a great purpose? Have you read history? A very little knowledge of history will be enough to bear out what I say. When the Master calls He does not restrict Himself to the important folk; He says to the humblest, 'Follow Me and do My work—the work for which I have chosen thee.' God forbid that I should look on any of God's creatures as of no account. What is in my thought just now is this: How does it come that you, who are, as you have told me, the daughter of a fisherman in a small village far removed from any large city—how does it come that you speak as a person of education and some refinement? Should I be right to assume that all the folk at your village are as you in speech and bearing?"

The little flush of vanity that came to her face when he had put his question to her lasted but a few seconds.

She shook her head.

"I have had such advantages—I do not know if you would look on them as advantages, sir; but the truth is that the Squire's lady and her daughters, have been kind to me. My father did the Squire a service a long time ago. His son, Master Anthony, was carried out to sea in his pleasure boat and there was a great gale. My father was the only man who ventured forth at the risk of his life to save the young gentleman, and he saved him. They were two days in the channel in an open boat, and my father was well-nigh dead himself through exhaustion. But the young squire was brought back without hurt. The Squire and his lady never forgot that service. My father was given money to carry out the plans that he had long cherished of making the port the foremost one for fishing on our coast, and the ladies had me taught by their own governess, so that I was at the Court well nigh every day. I know not whether or not it was a real kindness."

"It was no real kindness if you were thereby made discontented with your home and your friends."

"Yes, Mr. Wesley; that is just what came about. I thought myself a deal better than anyone in the village—nay, than my own father and mother. I had a scorn of those of my neighbours who were ignorant of books and music and the working of embroidery, and other things that I learned with the young ladies. I was unhappy myself, and I knew that I made others unhappy."

"Ah, such things have happened before. But you seemed on good terms with the miller's family and the others who supped last evening at the Mill. And did not you walk all the way from your village carrying that heavy fish for their entertainment?—our entertainment, I may say, for I was benefited with the others."

The girl turned her head away; she seemed somewhat disturbed in her mind. She did not reply at once, and it was in a low voice that she said: "A year ago I—I—was brought to see that—that—I cannot tell you exactly how it came about, sir; 'tis enough for me to say that something happened that made me feel I was at heart no different from my own folk, though I had played the organ at church many times when Mr. Havlings was sick and though the young ladies made much of me."

Mr. Wesley did not smile. He was greatly interested in the story which the girl had told to him. Had she told him only the first part he would have been able to supply the sequel out of his own experience and knowledge of life. Here was this girl, possessing the charms of youth and vivacity, indiscreetly educated, as people would say, "above her station," and without an opportunity of mingling on equal terms with any except her own people—how should she be otherwise than dissatisfied with her life? How could she fail to make herself disagreeable to the homely, unambitious folk with whom she was forced to associate?

He had too much delicacy to ask her how it was that she had been brought to see the mistake that she had made in thinking slightingly of her own kin who remained in ignorance of the accomplishments which she had acquired? He had no difficulty in supplying the details which she omitted. He could see this poor, unhappy girl being so carried away by a sense of her own superiority to her natural surroundings as to presume upon the good nature of her patrons, the result being humiliation to herself.

"I sympathise with you with all my heart, dear child," he said. "But the lesson which you have had is the most important in your education—the most important in the strengthening of your character, making you see, I doubt not, that the simple virtues are worthy of being held in far higher esteem than the mere graces of life. Your father would shake his head over a boat that was beautifully painted and gilded from stem to stern. Would he be satisfied, do you think, to go to sea in such a craft on the strength of its gold leaf? Would he not first satisfy himself that the painted timbers were made of stout wood? 'Tis not the paint or the gilding that makes a trustworthy boat, but the timber that is beneath. So it is not education nor graceful accomplishments that are most valuable to a man or woman, but integrity, steadfastness of purpose, content These are the virtues that tend to happiness. Above all, the most highly cultivated man or woman is he or she that has cultivated simplicity. I thank you for telling me your story in answer to my enquiry. And now that you have satisfied my curiosity on this point, it may be that you will go so far as to let me know why it was that you were filling the room in the Mill with shrieks last evening when I entered."

CHAPTER VI

Nelly Polwhele gave a little jump when Mr. Wesley had spoken. It had come at last. She had done her best to steal away from the explanation which she feared she would have to make to him. But somehow she did not now dread facing it so greatly as she had done in the Mill. She had heard that the Reverend Mr. Wesley was severe, as well as austere. She had heard his Methodism mocked by the fashionable folk at Bath, story after story being told of his daring in rebuking the frivolities of the day. She had believed him to be an unsympathetic curmudgeon of a man, whose mission it was to banish every joy from life.

But now that she had heard his voice, so full of gentleness—now that his eyes had rested upon her in kindliness and sympathy—now that she had heard him not disdain to spend an hour telling her and her friends that romance of the backwoods, thrilling them by his telling of it, her dread of being rebuked by him for her levity was certainly a good deal less than it had been. Still she looked uneasily away from him, and they had taken a good many steps in silence together before she made an attempt to answer him. And even then she did not look at him.

"'Twas a piece of folly, I am afraid, sir," she said in a low tone. "At least you may esteem it folly, though it did not fail to amuse the good people at the Mill," she added in an impulse of vanity not to be resisted.

"I had no doubt that it was a domestic game," said he. "They were all roaring with laughter. Had you heard, as I did, from without, the loud laughter of the men and above it the wild, shrill shrieks, you would, I am sure, have been as amazed as I was."

She laughed now quite without restraint.

"Bedlam—Bedlam—nothing less than Bedlam it must have seemed to you, Mr. Wesley," she said.

"I will not contend with you as to the appropriateness of your description," said he, smiling, still kindly.

"The truth is, sir, that I have just returned from paying my first visit to the Bath," said she. "'Twas the greatest event in my simple life. I went to act as dresser to the Squire's young ladies, and they were so good as to allow me to see mostly all that there was to be seen, and to hear all that there was to be heard."

"What—all? That were a perilous permission that your young ladies gave to you."

"I know not what is meant by all, but I heard much, sir; singers and preachers and players. I was taken to the Cave of Harmony for lovely music, and to the playhouse, where I saw Mistress Woffington in one of her merry parts. I was busy telling of this when you entered the Mill. I was doing my best to shriek like Mistress Woffington."

She spoke lightly and with a certain assurance, as though she were determined to uphold her claim to go whithersoever she pleased.

She was in a manner disappointed that he did not at once show himself to be shocked. But he heard her and remained silent himself. Some moments passed; but still he did not speak; he waited.

Of course she began to excuse herself; he knew that she would do so. The uneasily confident way in which she had talked of the playhouse had told him that she would soon be accusing herself by her excuses without the need for him to open his lips.

"You will understand, sir, I doubt not, that I was but in the position of a servant, though my ladies treated me graciously; I could not but obey them in all matters," she said.

"Does your saying that mean that you had some reluctance in going to the playhouse?" he asked her.

"I was not quite—quite—sure," she replied slowly. "I had heard that the playhouse was a wicked place."

"And therefore you were interested in it—is that so?"

"But I asked myself, 'Would my young ladies go to the playhouse— would the Squire, who surely knows a good deal about wickedness, having lived for so many years in London—would the Squire and his lady allow them to go to the playhouse if there was anything evil in it?'"

"And so you went and you were delighted with the painted faces on both sides of the stage, and you have remained unsettled ever since, so that you must needs do your best to imitate an actress whose shamelessness of living is in everybody's mouth? I know that you imitated this Woffington woman to your young ladies when you returned warm and excited from the playhouse, and they laughed hugely at your skill."

Nelly stood still, so startled was she at the divination of her companion.

"How came you to hear that?" she cried.

"Were we not alone in the bedroom? Who could have told you so much?"

"And when you returned to your home you were not many hours under its roof before you were strutting about feeling yourself to be decked out in the fine clothes which you had seen that woman wear in the playhouse?"

"You have been talking to someone—was it Jake Pullsford? But how could he have known? Oh, sir; you seem to have in yourself a power equal to that of the water-finder's wand, only surer by a good measure."

"And you saw no evil in the playhouse?" he said gently.

"I do not want to go again, Mr. Wesley," she said. "But indeed I dare not say that I saw any of the wickedness that I have heard of, in the theatre."

"What, are you not in yourself an example of the evil?" said he.

"What—I, sir? Surely not, Mr. Wesley. Whatever you may have heard you could hear nothing against me," she cried, somewhat indignantly.

Her indignation lent her boldness and she turned to him, saying:

"I affirm, sir, and I am not ashamed to do so, that I saw nothing of evil in the playhouse, and I made up my mind that instead of spending my days hidden away in a lonely village far from all the pleasures of life, I would try my fortune as an actress. I believe that I have some gift of mimicry—my ladies told me so. Why, sir, you allowed that my shrieks frightened you outside the Mill."

"Child, your feet are on a path perilous," said he. "You were indignant when I said that you were in yourself an example of the evil of going to the playhouse. Every word that you have spoken since has gone to prove the truth of my assertion. Do you say that the unsettling of your mind is no evil due to your visits to the playhouse—the unsettling of your mind, the discontent at your homely and virtuous surroundings, the arousing of a foolish vanity in your heart and the determination to take a step that would mean inevitable ruin to such as you—ruin and the breaking of your father's heart?"

He spoke calmly, and in his voice there was more than a suggestion of sorrow.

She had become pale; she made an attempt to face him and repel his accusations, but there was something in his face that took all the strength out of her. She covered her face with her hands and sobbed bitterly. He watched her for some moments, and then he put a soothing hand upon her arm.

"Nay, dear child, be not overcome," said he. "Have you not said to me that you have no wish ever to enter the playhouse again? Let that be enough. Be assured that I will not upbraid you for your possession of that innocence which saved you from seeing aught that was wrong in the play or the players. Unto the pure all things are pure. Unto the innocent all things are harmless. You were born for the glory of God. If you let that be your thought day and night your feet will be kept in the narrow way."

She caught his hand and held it in both her own hands.

"I give you my promise," she cried, her eyes upon his face; they were shining all the more brightly through her tears.

"Nay, there is no need for you to give me any promise," he said. "I will have confidence in your fidelity without any promise."

"You will have to reckon with me first, you robber!"

"You will have to reckon with me first, you robber!"

They both started at the sound of the voice. It came from a scowling man who, unperceived by them, had come through a small plantation of poplars on the slope at one side of the road, and now leaped from the bank, high though it was, and stood confronting them.

The girl faced him.

"What do you here, John Bennet?" she cried. "Have you been playing the spy as usual?"

"You are one of them that needs to be watched, my girl," said he. "You know that I speak the truth and that is why you feel it the more bitterly. But rest sure that I shall watch you and watch you and watch you while I have eyes in my head."

He was a lank man, who wore his own red hair tied in a queue. He had eyes that certainly would make anyone feel that the threat which he had uttered to the girl was one that he was well qualified to carry out; they were small and fierce—the eyes of a fox when its vigilance is overstrained.

He kept these eyes fixed upon her for some moments, and then turned them with the quickness of a flash of light upon Wesley.

"I heard what she said and I heard what you said, my gentleman," said he. "You will have faith in her fidelity—the fidelity of Nelly Polwhele. I know not who you are that wears a parson's bands; but parson or no parson I make bold to tell you that you are a fool—the biggest fool on earth if you have faith in any promise made by that young woman."

"Sir," said Wesley, "you called me a thief just now. My knowledge of the falsehood of that accusation enables me to disregard any slander that you may utter against this innocent girl."

"I called you a thief once and I shall call you so a second time," cried the man. "You have stolen the love of this girl from me—nay, 'tis no use for you to raise your hand like that. I know you are ready to swear that you said nothing except what a good pastor would say to one of his flock—swear it, swear it and perjure yourself, as usual—all of your cloth do it when the Bishop lays his hands upon their wigs, and they swear to devote their lives to the souls of their parishes and then hasten to their rectories to get on their hunting boots—their hunting boots that are never off their legs save when they are playing bowls or kneeling—kneeling—ay, in the cock-pit."

"Silence, sir!" cried Wesley. "Pass on your way and allow us to proceed on ours."

"I have told your reverence some home truths; and as for yonder girl, who has doubtless tricked you as she did me——"

"Silence, sir, this instant! You were coward enough to insult a man who you knew could not chastise you, and now you would slander a girl! There is your way, sir; ours is in the other direction."

He had his eyes fixed on the man's eyes, and as he faced him he pointed with his riding whip down the road. The man stared at him, and then Nelly saw all the fierceness go out of his eyes. He retreated slowly from Mr. Wesley, as though he were under the influence of a force upon which he had not previously reckoned. Once he put his hands quickly up to his face, as if to brush aside something that was oppressing him. His jaw fell, and although he was plainly trying to speak, no words came from his parted lips. With a slow indrawing of his breath he followed with his eyes the direction indicated by the other's riding whip. A horseman was trotting toward them, but in the distance.

Then it was that the man recovered his power of speech.

"You saw him coming—that emboldened you!" he said. "Don't fancy that because I was a bit dazed that 'twas you who got the better of me. I'll have speech with you anon, and if you still have faith in that girl——"

The sound of the clattering hoofs down the road became more distinct. The man took another quick glance in the direction of the sound, and then with an oath turned and leapt up to the green bank beside him. He scrambled up to the top and at once disappeared among the trees.

Wesley and the girl stood watching him, and when he had disappeared their eyes took the direction that the man's had taken. A gentleman, splendidly mounted on a roan, with half a dozen dogs—a couple of sleek spaniels, a rough sheep dog and three terriers—at his heels, trotted up. Seeing the girl, he pulled up.

"Hillo, Nelly girl!" he cried cheerily, when she had dropped him a curtsey. "Hillo! Who was he that slunk away among the trees?"

"'Twas only John Bennet, if you please, parson," said she.

"It doth not please me," said he. "The fellow is only fit for a madhouse or the county gaol. He looked, so far as I could see, as if he was threatening you or—I ask your pardon, sir; your horse hid you."

When he had pulled up Mr. Wesley had been on the off side of his horse and half a dozen yards apart from the girl; so that the stranger had no chance of seeing the bands that showed him to be a clergyman.

"You arrived opportunely, sir," he said. "I fear if the man had not perceived you coming in the distance, we might have found ourselves in trouble."

"What, did the fellow threaten you? Shall I set the dogs upon his track? Say the word and I'll wager you *King George* against your sorry skewbald that he'll find himself in trouble before many minutes are over," cried the stranger.

"Nay, sir; the man hath gone and we are unharmed," said Wesley.

"The scoundrel! Let me but get him within reach of my whip!" said the other. "But the truth is, Nelly, that the fellow is more than half demented through his love for you. And i' faith, I don't blame him. Ah, a sad puss you are, Nelly. There will not be a whole heart in the Port if you do not marry some of your admirers."

Then he turned to Wesley, saying:

"You are a brother parson, sir, I perceive, though I do not call your face to mind. Are you on your way to take some duty—maybe 'tis for Josh Hilliard; I heard that he had a touch of his old enemy. But now that I think on't 'twould not be like Josh to provide a substitute."

"I have come hither without having a church to preach in, sir; my name is Wesley, John Wesley."

"What, the head of the men we christened Methodists at Oxford?"

"The same, sir. I believe that the name hath acquired a very honourable significance since those days. I hope that we are all good churchmen, at any rate."

"I don't doubt it, Mr. Wesley; but you will not preach in my church, sir, of that you may rest assured."

"You are frank, sir; but pray remember that I have not yet asked your permission to do so."

The other laughed, and spoke a word or two to his horse, who was becoming impatient and was only controlled with difficulty.

"A fair retort, Mr. Wesley—a fair retort, sir," he said. "I like your spirit; and by my word, I have a sort of covert admiration for you. I hear that none can resist your preaching—not even a Bishop. You have my hearty sympathy and good will, sir, but I will not go to hear you preach. The truth is that you are too persuasive, Mr. Wesley, and I cannot afford to be persuaded to follow your example. I find the Church a very snug nest for a younger son with simple country tastes and a rare knowledge of whist; I am a practical man, sir, and my advice upon occasion has healed many a feud between neighbours. I know a good horse and I ride straight to hounds. In the cockpit my umpiring is as good law as the Attorney General could construe for a fee of a thousand guineas. Ask anyone in this county what is his opinion of Parson Rodney and you will hear the truth as I have told it to you. I wish you luck, Mr. Wesley, but I will not countenance your preaching in my church; nor will I hear you, lest I should be led by you to reform my ways, as I suppose you would say; I am a younger son, and a younger son cannot afford to have doubts on the existing state of things, when the living that he inherits is of the net value of eight hundred pounds per annum. So fare you well, sir, and I beg of you not to make my flock too discontented with my ten-minute sermons. They should not be so, seeing that my sermons are not mine; but for the most part Doctor Tillotson's—an excellent divine, sir—sound—sound and not above the heads of our gaffers. Fare thee well, Nelly; break as few hearts as thy vanity can do with."

And Parson Rodney, smiling gallantly, and waving his whip gracefully, whistled to his dogs, and put his roan to the trot for which he was eager.

"An excellent type," murmured Wesley. "Alas! but too good a type. Plain, honest, a gentleman; but no zeal, no sense of his responsibility for the welfare of the souls entrusted to his keeping."

He stood for some time watching the man on the thoroughbred. Then he turned to Nelly Polwhele, saying:

"We were interrupted in our pleasant chat; but we have still three miles to go. Tell me what the people think of Parson Rodney."

"They do not think aught about him, Mr. Wesley; they all like him: he never preaches longer than ten minutes."

"A right good reason for their liking of him—as good a reason as he had for liking the Church; it doth not exact overmuch from him, and it saves him from sponging on his friends. The Church of England has ever been an indulgent mother."

CHAPTER VII

Such a sight had never been seen in Cornwall before: on this Sunday morning an hour after sunrise every road leading to the village of Porthawn had its procession of men, women, and children, going to hear the preacher. The roads became dusty, as dry roads do when an army of soldiers passes over them; and here was an army of soldiers along, with its horse and foot and baggage-waggons—such an army as had never been in the West since the days of Monmouth's Rebellion; and this great march was the beginning of another rebellion, not destined to fail as the other had failed. Without banners, without arms, with no noise, with no shoutings of the captains, this great force marched to fight—to take part in an encounter that proved more lasting in its effects than any recorded in the history of England since the days of the Norman Invasion.

The Cornish crowds did not know that they were making history. The people had heard rumours of the preacher who had awakened the people of Somersetshire from their sleep of years, and who, on being excluded from the churches which had become Sabbath dormitories, had gone to the fields where all was wakefulness, and had here spoken to the hearts of tens of thousands.

The reports that spread abroad by the employment of no apparent agency must have contained some element that appealed with overwhelming power to the people of the West. The impulse that drove quiet folk from their homes and induced them to march many miles along dusty roads upon the morning of the only day of the week that gave them respite from toil was surely stronger than mere curiosity. They did not go into the wilderness to see a reed shaken by the wind. There was a seriousness of purpose and a sincerity about these people which must have been the result of a strong feeling among them that the existing order of things was lacking in some essentials—that the Church should become a stimulating force to them who were ready to perish, and not remain the apathetic force that it was when at its best, the atrophying influence that it was when at its worst.

That the ground was ready for the sowing was the opinion of Wesley, though few signs had been given to him to induce this conclusion, but that he had not misinterpreted the story of the Valley of Dry Bones was proved by the sight of the multitudes upon the roads—upon the moorland sheep-tracks—upon the narrow lanes where the traffic was carried on by pack-horses. There they streamed in their thousands. Farmers with their wives and children seated on chairs in their heavy waggons, men astride of everything that was equine—horses and mules and asses—some with their wives or sisters on the pillion behind them, but still more riding double with a friend.

On the wayside were some who were resting, having walked seven or eight or ten miles, and had seen the sun rise over the hills on that scented Spring morning. Some were having their breakfast among the primroses under the hedges, some were smoking their pipes before setting forth to complete their journey. Mothers, were nursing their infants beneath the pink and white coral of the hawthorns.

"'Tis a fair," said Hal Holmes to his friend, Dick Pritchard, who was seated by his side in a small pony cart made by himself during the winter.

"Salvation Fair," hazarded the water-finder. "Salvation Fair I would call it if only I was bold enough."

The smith shook his head.

"That is how it will be styled by many, I doubt not," he said. "And being as it must be, a strange mixture of the two—a church-going and a fairgoing—I have my fears that 'twill fall 'twixt the two. If the thing was more of a failure 'twould be a huge success. You take me, Dick?"

"Only vague, Hal—only vague, man," replied the water-finder, after a long cogitating pause. "When you spake the words there came a flash upon me like the glim from the lanthorn when 'tis opened sudden. I saw the meaning clear enough like as 'twere a stretch of valley on an uneven night of moonlight and cloud. Seemed as if there was a rift in your discourse and the moon poured through. But then the clouds fled across and I walk in the dark. Say 't again, Hal, and it may be that 'twill be plain. I have oft thought that your speech lit up marvellous well."

The blacksmith grinned.

"Maybe that is by reason of my work with the forge," he said. "The furnace is black enough until I give it a blast with the bellows and then 'tis a very ruby stone struck wi' lightning."

"Maybe—ay, very likely," said the little man doubtfully.

The smith grinned again.

"You don't altogether see it with my eyes, friend," he said. "How could you, Dick, our trades being natural enemies the one to t'other? My best friend is fire, yours is water. But what was on my mind this moment was the likelihood that the light-hearted may be fain to treat this great serious field gathering as though it were no more than a fair. Now, I say still that if 'twas no more than a gathering together of two or three parishes none would think of it in light of a fair, but being as 'tis—a marvel of moving men and women—why, then, there may be levity and who knows what worse."

"Ay, it looks as if the carcase of the hills was alive and moving with crawling maggots," remarked Dick. The summit of the hill on the road had been reached, and thus a view was given him and his companion of the hollow in the valley beyond, which was black with the slow-moving procession.

And there were many who, while anxious for the success of the meeting, shared Hal Holmes's fears and doubts as to its result. What impression could one man make upon so vast an assembly in the open air, they asked of each other. They shook their heads.

These were the sober-minded people who sympathised with the aims of the preacher—God-fearing men and women to whom his hopes had been communicated. They knew that hundreds in that procession on the march to the meeting-place were no more serious than they would be had they been going to a fair. They were going to meet their friends, and they were impelled by no higher motives than those which were the result of the instinct of the gregarious animals. Many of them lived far away from a town or even a village, in the wilder parts of the Duchy, and they laid hold on an opportunity that promised to bring them in contact with a greater crowd than they had ever joined before. The joy of being one of the crowd was enough for them; the preaching was only an insignificant incident in the day's proceedings. The sober-minded, knowing this, were afraid that in these people the spirit of levity might be aroused, especially if they could not hear the words of the preacher, and the consequences would be disastrous.

And doubtless there were hundreds of the dwellers along the coast who would have been pleased if grief came to an enterprise that threatened their employment as smugglers or the agents of smugglers. Smuggling and wrecking were along the coast, and pretty far inland as well, regarded as a legitimate calling. Almost everyone participated in the profits of the contraband, and the majority of the clergy would have been very much less convivial if they had had to pay the full price for their potations. Preaching against such traffic would have been impolitic as well as hypocritical, and the clergy were neither. The parson who denounced his congregation for forsaking the service on the news of a wreck reaching the church was, probably, a fair type of his order. His plea was for fair play. "Let us all start fair for the shore, my brethren."

Such men had a feeling that the man who had come to preach to the multitude would be pretty sure to denounce their fraud; or if he did not actually denounce it he might have such an influence upon their customers as would certainly be prejudicial to the trade. This being so, how could it be expected that they should not look forward to the failure of the mission?

And there was but a solitary man to contend against this mixed multitude! There was but one voice to cry in that wilderness—one voice to awaken those who slept. The voice spoke, and its sound echoed round the wide world.

He stood with bared head, with a rock for his pulpit, on a small plateau overlooking a long stretch of valley. On each side there was an uneven, sloping ground—rocks overgrown with lichen, and high tufts of coarse herbage between, with countless blue wild flowers and hardy climbing plants. The huge basin formed by the converging of the slopes made a natural amphitheatre, where ten thousand people might be seated. Behind were the cliffs, and all through the day the sound of the sea beating around their bases mingled with the sound of many voices. A hundred feet to the west there hung poised in its groove the enormous rocking stone of Red Tor.

Perhaps amongst the most distant of his hearers there was one who might never again have an opportunity of having the word that awakens spoken in his hearing. There might be one whose heart was as the ground in Summer—waiting for the seed to be sown that should bring forth fruit, sixtyfold or an hundredfold. That was what the man thought as he looked over the vast multitude. He felt for a moment overwhelmed by a sense of his responsibility. He felt that by no will of his own he had been thrust forward to perform a miracle, and he understood clearly that the responsibility of its performance rested with him.

For a moment the cry of the overwhelmed was in his heart.

"It is too much that is laid upon me."

For a moment he experienced that sense of rebellion which in a supreme moment of their lives—the moment preceding a great achievement for the benefit of the world—takes possession of so many of the world's greatest, and which has its origin in a feeling of humility. It lasted but for a moment. Then he found that every thought of his mind—every sense of his soul— was absorbed by another and greater force. He had a consciousness of being possessed by a Power that dominated every sensation of his existence. That Power had thrust him out from himself as it were, and he felt that he was standing by wondering while a voice that he did not know to be his own went forth, and he knew that it reached the most remote of the people before him. It was like his own voice heard in a dream. For days there had been before his eyes the vision that had come to the prophet—the vision of the Valley of Dry Bones. He had seemed to stand by the side of the man to whom it had been revealed. He had always felt that the scene was one of the most striking that had ever been depicted; but during the week it was not merely its mysticism that had possessed him. He felt that it was a real occurrence taking place before his very eyes.

And now he was standing on his rock looking all through that long valley, and he saw—not the thousands of people who looked up to him, but ranks upon ranks and range upon range of dead men's bones, bleaching in the sunshine—filling up all the hollows of the valley forsaken of life, overhung by that dread legend of a battle fought so long ago that its details had vanished. There they stretched, hillocks of white bones—ridges of white bones—heaps upon heaps. The winds of a thousand years had wailed and shrieked and whistled, sweeping through the valley, the rains of a thousand years had been down upon them—hail and snow had flung their pall of white over the whiteness of the things that lay there, the lightnings had made lurid the hollow places in the rocks, and had rent in sunder the overhanging cliffs—there was the sign of such a storm—the tumbled tons of black basalt that lay athwart one of the white hillocks—and on nights of fierce tempest the white foam from the distant sea had been borne through the air and flung in quivering flakes over cliffs and into chasm—upon coarse herbage and the blue rock flowers. But some nights were still. The valley was canopied with stars. And there were nights of vast moonlight, and the white moonlight spread itself like a great translucent lake over the white deadness of that dreary place....

The man saw scene after scene in that valley as in a dream. And then there came a long silence, and out of that silence he heard the voice that said: "Can these dead bones live?"

There was another silence before the awful voice spoke the command:

"Let these bones live!"

Through the moments of silence that followed, the sound of the sea was borne by a fitful breeze over the cliff face and swept purring through the valley.

Then came the moment of marvel. There was a quivering here and there—something like the long indrawing of breath of a sleeper who has slept for long but now awakens—a slow heaving as of a giant refreshed, and then in mysterious, dread silence, with no rattling of hollow skeleton limbs, there came the great moving among the dry bones, and they rose up, an exceeding great army.

Life had come triumphant out of the midst of

Death. That was what the voice said. The whole valley, which had been silent an hour before, was now vibrating, pulsating with life—the tumult of life which flows through a great army—every man alert, at his post in his rank—waiting for whatever might come—the advance of the enemy, the carrying out of the strategy of the commander.

Life had come triumphant out of the midst of death, and who would dare now to say that the deepest spiritual life might not lie hidden from sight among the bleaching heaps of dead bones that strewed the valley from cliffy to cliffs—hidden but only waiting for the voice to cry aloud:

"Let these bones live!"

"Oh, that that Dread Voice would speak through me!" cried the preacher.

That was the first time he became conscious of the sound of his own voice, and he was startled. He had heard that other voice speaking, carrying him away upon the wings of its words down through the depths of that mystic valley, but now all was silent and he was standing with trembling hands and quivering lips, gazing out over no valley of mystery alive with a moving host, but over a Cornish vale of crags; and yet there beneath his eyes were thousands of faces, and they looked like the faces of such as had been newly awakened after a long sleep—dazed—wondering—waiting....

He saw it. The great awakening had come to these people, and now they were waiting—for what?

He knew what he had to offer them. He knew what was the message with which he had been entrusted—the good news which they had never heard before.

And he told it with all simplicity, in all humility, in all sincerity—the evangel of boundless love—of illimitable salvation, not from the wrath to come—he had no need to speak of the Day of Wrath—his theme wras the Day of Grace—salvation from the distrust of God's mercy—salvation from the doubts, from the cares of the world, from the lethargy that fetters the souls of men, from the gross darkness and from the complacency of walking in that darkness.

He let light in upon their darkness and he forced them to see the dangers of the dark, and, seeing, they were overwhelmed. For the first time these people had brought before their eyes the reality of sin—the reality of salvation. They had had doctrines brought before them in the past, but the tale of doctrines had left them unmoved. They had never felt that doctrines were otherwise than cold, impassioned utterances. Doctrines might have been the graceful fabrics that clothed living truths, but the truth had been so wrapped up in them that it had remained hidden so far as they were concerned. They had never caught a glimpse of the living reality beneath.

But here was the light that showed them the living thing for which they had waited, and the wonder of the sight overwhelmed them.

The voice of the preacher spoke to them individually. That was the sole mystery of the preaching—the sole magnetism (as it has been called) of the preacher.

And that was the sole mystery of the manifestation that followed. Faces were streaming with tears, knees were bowed in prayer; but there were other temperaments that were forced to give expression to their varied feelings—of wonder, of humiliation, of exultation. These were not to be controlled. There were wild sobbings, passionate cries, a shout or two of thanksgiving, an outburst of penitence—all the result of the feelings too strong to be controlled, and all tokens of the new life that had begun to pulsate in that multitude—all tokens that the Valley which had been strewn with dry bones had heard the voice that said:

"Let these dry bones live."

There was a great moving among the dry bones, and they stood up, an exceeding great army.

CHAPTER VIII

His preaching had ceased, but the note that he had struck continued to vibrate through the valley. He had spoken with none of the formality of the priest who aims at keeping up a certain aloofness from the people. This Mr. Wesley had spoken as brother to brother, and every phrase that he uttered meant the breaking down of another of the barriers which centuries had built up between the pulpit and the people.

They proved that they felt this to be so when he came among them. Warm hands were stretched out to meet his own—words of blessing were ejaculated by such as were able to speak; but infinitely more eloquent were the mute expressions of the feeling of the multitude. Some there were who could not be restrained from throwing themselves upon his shoulders, clasping him as if he had indeed been their brother from whom they had been separated for long; others caught his hands and kissed them. Tears were still on many faces, and many were lighted up with an expression of rapture that transfigured their features.

He made no attempt to restrain any of the extravagances to which that hour had given birth. He knew better than to do so. He had read of the extravagant welcome given by the people of a town long besieged to the envoys who brought the first news of the approach of the relieving force, and he knew that he was there as an envoy to tell the people about him of their release. He had himself witnessed the reception given to the King's Posts that brought the tidings of the last peace, and he knew that he himself was a King's Messenger, bearing to these people the tidings of Peace and Goodwill.

He had a word of kindness and comfort and advice to all. He was an elder brother, talking to the members of his own family on equal terms. But soon he left the side of these new-found brethren, for his eyes had not failed to see some who were sitting apart among the low crags—some in silent dejection, bearing the expression of prisoners for whom no order of release has come, though they had seen it come for others. But all were not silent: many were moaning aloud with ejaculations of despair. In the joy that had been brought to their friends they had no share. Nay, the message that had brought peace to others had brought despair to them. They had been happy enough before, knowing nothing of or caring nothing for, the dangers that surrounded them in the darkness, and the letting in of the light upon them had appalled them.

He was beside them in a moment, questioning them, soothing their fears, removing their doubts, whispering a word or two of prayer in their ears. Jake, the carrier, had been right: the preacher had balm for the wounds of those who suffered. He went about among them for hours, not leaving the side of any who doubted until their doubts had been removed and they shared the happiness that the Great Message brought with it. But the evangel had arisen upon that valley as the Daystar, with healing in its wings.

When the multitude dispersed, the church bells were making melody over the hills and through the dales. The Reverend Mr. Wesley was a good churchman, and he took care that his preaching did not interfere with the usual services. His object was to fill the churches with devout men, and not merely the body of the churches, but the pulpits as well.

For himself, he withdrew from his friends and walked slowly up one of the tracks leading to the summit of the cliffs a few miles beyond the village of Porthawn. He wished to be alone, for amid all his feelings of thankfulness for the good which he knew had been done through his preaching, there came to him a doubt. Had he been faithful in his delivery of the Message? Had he yielded up everything of self to the service of the Master? Had he said a word that might possibly become a stone of stumbling to the feet that had just set out upon the narrow way?

That was the fear which was ever present with him—the possibility that the Message had failed in its power by reason of his frailty in delivering it—the possibility that he might attribute to himself some of the merit of the Message.

The hours which he passed in loneliness almost every day of his life, the solitary rides covering thousands of miles, his long walks without a companion, were devoted to self renunciation. He was more afraid of himself than of any enemy from without. He sometimes found himself in such a frame of mind as caused him to admire the spirit that led the priests of the heathen beliefs in the East to torture and mutilate themselves in the attainment of what appeared to them to be holiness. He knew that their way was not the right way, and the object which they strove to achieve was not a worthy one; but he could not deny the self-sacrifice and its value.

Yes, but was it not possible that self-sacrifice might, if performed ostentatiously, become only another form of self-glorification?

It was only now that this thought flashed upon him. He had walked along the cliff path for a mile or two, and soon became aware of the pangs of hunger. It was nothing for him to set out to preach without having more than a bite or two of bread, and to go fasting until the afternoon. He had never regarded this as an act of self-sacrifice. But how had he felt when some of his friends had made much of these facts, entreating him to be more mindful of his health? Had he not felt a certain pride in thinking that his health was regarded as important?

And now, when he should return to the house where he was a guest— it was the house of a Mr. Hartwell, the owner of a mine in the tin district some distance from Porthawn—would not his hours of fasting preceding and following the exertion of preaching to so great a multitude in the open air make him appear akin to a martyr in the eyes of the people with whom he might come in contact?

Nay, could he deny that he felt some vanity in the reflection that here again he would be seriously remonstrated with for his disregard of himself?

Even his orderly mind was unable to differentiate between the degrees of self-sacrifice and self-satisfaction involved in this simple question of fasting and eating, and he was troubled that his attempts to do so were not wholly successful. It was like the man that, in his hours of exhaustion, he should be dissatisfied with what was really the result of his exhaustion. This trivial self-examination was, though he did not know it, only the result of his neglect of the wants of his body. Yes, but this fact did not make it the less worrying to him.

He had been led by the charm of the day to walk farther than he had intended, and he was so exhausted that he found it necessary to rest in a dip of the cliffs above the little bay. On each side of him stretched the broken shore, a short crescent patch of sand at every dip in that long, uneven wall, and marking the outline of its curve was the white floss of the lazy ripples. Behind him was the coarse sand-herbage of the broken shore, and in front of him stretched the sea. A white bird or two hovered between the waters and the cliff summit, and far away a revenue cutter showed its white sails. Sunlight was over all. The warm air seemed imbued with the presence of God, which all might breathe and become at peace with all the world.

It came over the face of the waters, upon the face of the man who reclined upon a cushion of springy herbage that quite hid the shape of the rock at whose base it found root. The feathery touch upon his brow soothed him as a mother's hand soothes her child and banishes its distrust. He lay there and every doubt that had oppressed him vanished. He was weary and hungry, but he felt that the grace of heaven was giving him food in the strength of which he might wander in the wilderness for forty days.

He closed his eyes and with the faint hum of the little bees that droned among the blue cliff-flowers,—with the faint wash of the ripples upon the unnumbered pebbles of the beach—a sweet sleep crept over him.

When he awoke it was not with a start, but as gently as he had fallen asleep. For a moment he had a fear that he had overslept himself. He turned to look at the sun and saw standing only half a dozen yards away the girl by whose side he had walked a few mornings before to the village.

The picture that she made to his eyes was in keeping with the soothing sights and sounds of this placid day. She wore a white kirtle and cap, but the latter had failed to restrain the abundant hair which showed itself in little curls upon her forehead, and in long strands of sunshine over her ears and behind them. She was pleasant to look at—as pleasant as was everything else of nature on this day; and he looked at her with pleased eyes for some time before speaking.

As for Nelly, she was not watching him; but he could see that she had seen him; she had only turned away lest he should have a man's distaste to be caught sleeping in the daytime. He perceived this the moment that he spoke and she turned to him. The little start that she gave was artificial. It made him smile.

"I am at your mercy; but you will not betray my weakness to anyone," he said, smiling at her.

"Oh, sir!" she cried, raising her hands.

"You saw me sleeping. I hope that 'twas not for long," he said.

"I did not come hither more than five minutes agone, sir," she replied. "You cannot have slept more than half an hour. I came to seek you after the preaching."

"You have not been at your church, girl?" he said.

"I was at your church, Mr. Wesley. I like Parson Rodney. I did not go to his church."

He shook his head.

"I like not such an answer, child.'Twould grieve me to learn that there were many of my hearers who would frame the same excuse."

She hung her head.

"I am sorry, sir," she said. "It was my intent to go to Parson Rodney's church, if only to see how vast a difference there was 'twixt—that is—I mean, Mr. Wesley, that—that my intention was to be in church, only when I saw that you had wended your way alone through the valley, not going in the direction of Mr. Hartwell's house, but far away from it—what could one do, sir, who knew that you could not have had a bite to eat since early morning—and after such a preaching and an after-meeting that filled up another fasting hour? 'He has no one to look after him,' said my mother in my ear. 'He is a forlorn man who thinks that he is doing God's service by forgetting that his body must be nourished if his soul is to remain sound.'"

"That is what your mother said—'tis shrewd enough. And what did you reply? Mind that the answer hath a bearing upon your staying away from church, Nelly."

"I said naught, Mr. Wesley; but what I did was to hurry to our home and pack you a basket of humble victuals and—here it is."

She picked up a reed basket from the grass and brought it beside him. Kneeling then on a stone she raised the lid and showed him a dish of cooked pilchards, some cakes of wheat bread and a piece of cream cheese laid on a pale green lettuce.

She had spread the coarsest and whitest napkin he had ever seen on the face of the crag at his elbow, and with the air of a bustling housewife laid a plate and knife and fork for him, talking all the time—reproving him quite gravely and even severely for his inattention to his stomach—there was no picking and choosing of words in Cornwall or elsewhere during that robust century. She gave him no chance of defending himself, but rattled on upbraiding him as if he had been a negligent schoolboy, until she had laid out his picnic for him, and had spread the butter on one of the home-made cakes, saying:

"There, now, you must not get upon your feet until you have put down all that is before you. If you was to make the attempt to do so your long fast would make you so faint that you would run a chance of tottering over the cliff."

He saw that there was no need for him to say a word. What could he say in the face of such attention to his needs as the girl was showing?

"I submit with a good grace, my dear," he said when her work was done and she paused for breath. "Why should not I submit? I am, as you said, weak by reason of hunger, and lo, a table is spread for me with such delicacies as would tickle the appetite of a man who has just partaken of a heavy meal, and I am not that man. Happier than the prophet, I am fed not by ravens, but by a white dove."

"Oh, sir," she said, her face shining with pleasure. "Oh, sir, I protest that even in the genteelest society at the Bath, I never had so pretty a compliment paid to me."

He had paid his compliment to her in a delicate spirit of bantering, so as to make no appeal to her vanity, and he saw that her pleasure was not the result of gratified vanity.

"But concerning yourself, my dear," he cried when he had his fork in his hand, but had as yet touched nothing. "If I was fasting you must be also."

"What, sir, did I omit to say that I returned to my home after your preaching?" she said. "Oh, yes; I got the basket there and the pilchards. My father despises pilchards, but I hope that you——"

"I am a practical man, Nelly, and I know, without the need to make a calculation on paper, that you could not be more than a few minutes in your cottage, and that all that time was spent by you over my basket. I know such as you—a hasty mouthful of cake and a spoonful of milk and you say, 'I have dined.' Now I doubt much if you had so much as a spoonful of milk, and therefore I say that unless you face me at this table of stone, I will eat nothing of your store; and I know that that would be the greatest punishment I could inflict upon you. Take your place, madam, at the head of the table."

She protested.

"Nay, sir, I brought not enough for two—barely enough to sustain one that is a small feeder until he has the opportunity of sitting down to a regular meal."

"I have spoken," he said. "I need but a bite! Oh, the long fasting journeys that I have had within the year!"

She still hesitated, but when, at last, she seated herself, she did not cause him to think that he had made her feel ill at ease; she adapted herself to the position into which he had forced her, from the moment she sat opposite to him. She forgot for the time that he was the preacher on whom thousands of men and women had hung a couple of hours before, and that she, if she had not been with him, would have been eating in a fisherman's cottage.

She had acquired, through her association with the Squire's young ladies, something of their manners. Her gift of quick observation was allied to a capacity to copy what she observed, and being, womanlike, well aware of this fact, she had no reason to feel otherwise than at ease while she ate her share of the pilchards, and made him feel all the time that she was partaking of his hospitality.

As for the preacher, he felt the girl's thoughtfulness very deeply. It seemed that she was the only one of the thousands who had stood before him that had thought for his needs. Her tact and the graceful way in which she displayed it, even down to her readiness to sit with him lest he should feel that she was remaining hungry, pleased him; and her chat, abounding with shrewdness, was gracefully frank. He felt refreshed beyond measure by her freshness, and he rose to walk to the house where he was a guest, feeling that it was, indeed, good for him to have changed the loneliness of his stroll for the companionship which she offered him.

CHAPTER IX

The question had often been discussed by him to the furthest point possible (as he thought) for its consideration to be extended; and how was it that he found himself debating it at this time in its crudest form? He had long ago settled it to his own satisfaction, that his life was to be a lonely one through the world. Not for him were to be the pleasant cares of home or wife or child. Not for him was the tenderness of woman—not for him the babble of the little lips, every quiver of which is a caress. His work was sufficient for him, he had often said, and the contemplation of the possibility of anything on earth coming between him and his labours, filled him with alarm. He felt that if he were to cease to be absorbed in his work, he should be unfaithful to his trust. The only one that was truly faithful was the one who was ready to give up all to follow in the footsteps of the Master.

But being human and full of human sympathy, he had often felt a moment's envy entering the house of one of his friends who was married and become the father of children. The hundred little occurrences incidental to a household, where there was a nursery and a schoolroom, were marked by him—the clambering of little chubby legs up to the father's knee—the interpretation of the latest phrase that fell from baby lips—the charm of golden silk curls around an innocent child's face—all these and a score of other delights associated with the household had appealed to him, giving him an hour's longing at the time, and a tender recollection at intervals in after years.

"Not for me—not for me," he had said. So jealous was he of his work that, as has been noted, the possibility of his becoming absorbed—even partially—by anything that was not directly pertaining to his work, was a dread to him. He set himself the task of crushing down within him every aspiration that might tend to interfere with the carrying out of the labour of his life, and he believed that, by stern and strict endeavour, he had succeeded in doing so.

Then why should he now find himself considering the question which he believed he had settled forever? Why should he now begin to see that the assurance that it was not good for a man to be alone was based upon a knowledge of men and was wise?

He found an apt illustration of the wisdom of the precept in the conduct of the girl who had shown such thoughtfulness in regard to him. "Mentem mortalia tangunt," was the *sors Virgiliana* which came to his mind at the moment. He recognised the truth of it. A man was affected by the material conditions of his life. If the girl had not shown such thought for his comfort, he would well-nigh have been broken down by his exhausting labours of the day, followed up by an exhausting walk along the cliffs. He might not have returned to the house at which he was staying in time to dine, before setting out for a long drive to another place for an afternoon's meeting. So absorbed was he apt to be in his preaching that he became oblivious to every consideration of daily life. What were to him such trivial matters as eating and drinking at regular intervals? He neglected the needs of his body, and only when he had suffered for so doing did he feel that his carelessness was culpable. On recovering from its' immediate effects, however, he fell back into his old habits.

But now the thought that came to him was that he had need for someone to be by his side as (for example) Nelly Polwhele had been. He knew quite well, without having had the experience of married life, that if he had had a wife, he would not have been allowed to do anything so unwise as to walk straight away from the preaching to the cliffs, having eaten nothing since the early morning, and then only a single cake of bread. A good wife would have drawn him away from the people to whom he was talking, to the house where he was a guest, and when there have set about providing for him the food which he lacked and the rest which he needed to restore him after his arduous morning's work, so that he might set out for the afternoon's preaching feeling as fresh as he had felt in the morning.

He was grateful to the girl, not only for her attention to him, but also for affording him an illustration favourable to his altered way of looking at a question which he fancied had long ago been settled forever in his mind. (He had long ago forgiven the woman, who, in America, had taught him to believe that a life of loneliness is more conducive to one's peace of mind than a life linked to an unsympathetic companion.)

And having been led to such a conclusion, it was only reasonable that he should make a resolution that, if he should ever be so fortunate as to meet with a virtuous lady whom he should find to possess those qualities which promised most readily to advance the work which he had at heart, he would not be slow to ask her to be his companion to such an end.

This point settled to his satisfaction (as he thought), he mounted his horse, after a week's stay in the valley of the Lana, and made his way to the tinners of Camlin, twenty miles further along the coast Here he was received with open arms, and preached from his rock pulpit to thousands of eager men and women an hour after sunrise on a summer morning.

On still for another fortnight, in wilder districts, among people who rarely entered a church, and whom the church made no attempt to reach. These were the people for him. He was told that he was going forth to sow the seed in stony ground, but when he came and began to sow, he found that it fell upon fruitful soil. Here it was impossible for him to find a huge congregation, so scattered were the inhabitants. But this was no obstacle to him: he asked for no more than a group of hearers in every place, and by the time that night came he found that he had preached to thousands since sunrise. Beginning sometimes at five o'clock in the morning, he would preach on the outskirts of a village and hold a second service before breakfasting six miles away. It was nothing for him to preach half a dozen times and ride thirty miles in one of these days.

But as he went further and further on this wonderful itinerary of his, that sense of loneliness of which he had become aware at Porthawn seemed to grow upon him. During those intervals of silence which he spent on horseback, his feeling of loneliness appeared to increase, until at last there came upon him a dread lest he should affect his labours. He had a fear that a despondent note might find its way into his preaching, and when under such an influence he made a strong effort in the opposite direction, he was conscious of an artificial note; and, moreover, by the true instinct of the man who talks to men, he was conscious that it was detected by his hearers.

He was disappointed in himself—humiliated. How was it that for years he had been able to throw off this feeling of walking alone, through the world, or making no effort to throw it off, to glory in it, as it were—to feel all the stronger because of it, inasmuch as it could not come without bringing with it the reflection that he—he alone—had been chosen to deliver the message to the multitudes—the message of Light to the people that walked in darkness?

He could not understand how the change had come about in him, and not being able to understand it, he felt the more humiliated.

And then, one day, riding slowly along the coach road, he saw a young woman standing waiting for a change of horses for her post chaise at the door of a small inn.

He started, for she had fair hair and a fresh face whose features bore some resemblance to those of Nelly Polwhele—he started, for there came upon him, with the force of a revelation, the knowledge that this was the companionship for which he was longing—that unconsciously, she had been in his thoughts—some way at the back of his thoughts, to be sure, but still there—that, only since he had been her companion had his need for some sweet and helpful companionship become impressed upon him..

He rode on to his destination overwhelmed by the surprise at the result of this glimpse which had been given to him into the depths of his own heart. The effect seemed to him as if with the sight of that stranger—that young woman on the roadside—a flash of lightning had come, showing him in an instant what was in the depths of his heart.

He tried to bring himself to believe that he was mistaken.

"Impossible—impossible!" he cried. "It is impossible that I should be so affected—a village girl!... And I did not talk with her half a dozen times in all!... Kind, thoughtful, with tact—a gracious presence, a receptive mind.... Ah, it was she undoubtedly who set me thinking—who made me feel dissatisfied with my isolation, but still.. . oh, impossible—impossible!"

And, although a just man, the thoughts that he now believed himself to have in regard to Nelly Polwhele were bitter rather than sweet. He began to think that it was too bold of her—almost immodest—to make the attempt to change the whole course of the life of such a man as he was. He had once courted the lonely life, believing it to be the only life for such as he—the only life that enabled him to give all his thoughts—all his strength—oh, all his life—all his life—to the work which had been appointed for him to do in the world of sinners; but lo! that child had come to him, and had made him feel that he was not so different from other men.

Under the influence of his bitterness, he resented her intrusion, as it were. Pshaw! the girl wras nothing. It was only companionship as a sentiment that he had been longing for; he had a clear idea of the companionship that he needed; but he had never thought of the companion. It was a mere trick of the fancy to suggest that, because the young woman had sent his thoughts into a certain groove, they must of necessity be turned in the direction of the young woman herself.

He soon found, however, that it is one thing for a man to prove to the satisfaction of his own intelligence that it would be impossible that he should set his heart on a particular young woman, but quite another to shut her out from his heart. He had his heart to reckon with, though he did not know it.

Before the day had passed he had shut the doors of his heart, and he believed that he had done right. He did not know that he had shut those doors, not against her, but upon her.

Like all men who have accomplished great things in the world, he was intensely human. His sympathy flowed forth for his fellow-men in all circumstances of life. But he did not know himself sufficiently well to understand that what he thought of with regret as his weaknesses, were actually those elements wherein lay the secret of his influence with men.

He had just succeeded, he fancied, in convincing himself that it was impossible he could ever have entertained a thought of Nelly Polwhele as the one who could afford him the companionship which he craved, when a letter came to him from Mr. Hartwell, whom he had appointed the leader of the class which he had established at Porthawn, entreating him to return to them, as they were in great distress and in peril of falling to pieces, owing to the conduct of one of their members, Richard Pritchard by name.

Could he affirm that the sorrow which he felt on receiving this news was the sum of all the emotions that filled his heart at that moment?

He laid down the letter, saying,

"It is the Lord's doing."

And when he said that, he was thinking, not of the distress in which his children at Porthawn found themselves by reason of Richard Pritchard, but of the meaning of the summons to himself.

"It is the trial to which my steadfastness is to be put," he said. "I am not to be allowed to escape without scathe. Why should I expect to do so when others are tried daily? There can be no victory without a battle. The strength of a man is developed by his trial. I am ready. Grant me grace, O Lord, to sustain me, and to keep my feet from straying!"

He prepared himself for this journey back to Porthawn, and he was presently amazed (having been made aware of his own weakness) to find himself thinking very much less about himself and scarcely at all about Nelly Polwhele, nor that the chance of seeing her again had, without the least expectation on his part, came to him. He found himself giving all his thoughts to the question of his duty. Had he been over-hasty in accepting the assurances of all these people at Porthawn to whose souls peace had come through his preaching? Was he actuated solely by a hope to spread abroad the Truth as he had found it, or had a grain of the tares of Self been sown among the good seed? Had there been something of vanity in his desire to increase the visible results of his preaching?

These were his daily questionings and soulsearching, and they had been ever present with him since he had put his hand to the plough. He was ever apt to accuse himself of vainglory—of a lack of that spirit of humility which he felt should enter into every act—every thought of his life. He thought of himself as the instrument through which his Master spake to His children. Should the harp vaunt itself when a hand sweeps over its strings, making such music as forces those who hear to be joyful or sad? Should the trumpet take credit to itself because through its tubes is blown the blast that sends an army headlong to the charge?

After his first preaching in the valley of the Lana, hundreds of those who heard him had come to him making a profession of the Faith that he preached. He asked himself now if it was not possible that he had been too eager to accept their assurance. He had had his experiences of the resultat the emotions of his listeners being so stirred by his preaching that they had come to him with the same glad story; but only to become lukewarm after a space, and after another space to lapse into their former carelessness. The parable of the Sower was ever in his mind. The quick upspring-ing of the seed was a sign that it had fallen where there was no depth of earth. And this sowing was more hopeless than that on stony ground—than that among thorns.

He feared that he had been too hasty. He was a careless husbandman who had been too ready to assume that a plentiful harvest was at hand, because he had sown where there was no depth of earth. He should have waited and watched and noted every sign of spiritual growth before leaving the field of his labours.

These were some of his self-reproaches which occupied all his thoughts while making his return journey to Porthawn, thus causing all thought of Nelly Polwhele to be excluded from his mind. He had caught a glimpse of the Lana winding its way through the valley before he had a thought of her, and then it was with some bitterness that he reflected that, all unknown to himself, he had shortened his stay in this region because he had had an instinct that a danger would threaten him if he were to remain. Instinct? Now he was dealing with a force that was wholly animal—wholly of the flesh, and the flesh, he knew, was waging perpetual war with the things that appertained to the spirit.

He urged his horse onward. Whatever danger might threaten himself by his returning to this region, he would not shrink from it; what was such a danger compared with that threatening the edifice of Faith which he had hoped had been built up in the midst of the simple people of the land?

He urged his horse forward, and on the afternoon of the second day of his journey he was within a few hours' journey of Ruthallion Mill. He meant to call at the Mill, feeling sure that he would get from the miller a faithful and intelligent account of all that had happened during the three weeks of his absence from this neighbourhood. Miller Pendelly, once the champion of the old system of lifeless churchgoing, had become the zealous exponent of the new. He was the leader of the little band that formed the nucleus of the great organisation of churchmen who, under the teaching of Wesley, sought to make the Church the power for good among the people that it was meant to be. Jake Pullsford, who had spread the story of Wesley's aims among his friends before the preacher had appeared in Cornwall, had given evidence of the new Light that had dawned upon him when he had heard Wesley at Bristol. Both these were steadfast men, not likely to cause offence, and if Wesley had heard any report of their falling short of what was expected of them he would have been more than disappointed.

It was through Richard Pritchard, the professional water-finder, that offence had come or was likely to come, Mr. Hartwell's letter had told him. He remembered the man very clearly. He had had some conversation with him, and Jake had satisfied him as to the sincerity of his belief. He had never been otherwise than a clean-living man, and he had studied many theological works. But he had not impressed Mr. Wesley as being a person of unusual intelligence. His remarkable calling and the success with which he practised it all through the West had caused Him to appear in the eyes of the people of the country as one possessing certain powers which, though quite legitimate, being exercised for good, were bordering on the supernatural. Wesley now remembered that he had had some doubt as to the legitimacy of the man's calling. Believing, as he did, so fully in the powers of witchcraft, he had a certain amount of uneasiness in accepting as a member of the little community which he was founding, a man who used the divining rod; but the simplicity of Pritchard and his exemplary character, were in his favour, so much as to outweigh the force of. Wesley's objection to his mode of life.

Now, as he guided his horse down the valley road, he regretted bitterly that he had allowed his misgivings to be overcome so easily. Like all men who have accomplished great things in the world, the difficulties which occasionally beset him were due to his accepting the judgment of others, putting aside his own feelings or tendencies, in certain matters. The practice of the virtue of humility, in regard to his estimation of the value of his own judgment, had cost him dearly upon occasions.

It was all the more vexatious to reflect that the man through whom the trouble (whatever it might be) was impending, was the last one in the world from whom any trouble might reasonably be looked for. This was probably the first time in his life that he had reached any prominence in the little circle in which he lived. To be allowed to remain in the background, seemed to be his sole aspiration. His fear of giving offence to anyone seemed to be ever present with him, and his chief anxiety was to anticipate an imaginary offence by an apology. How a man who was so ludicrously invertebrate should become a menace to the stability of a community that included such robust men as the miller, the carrier, and the smith, to say nothing of Farmer Tregenna and Mr. Hartwell, the mine owner, was more than Wesley could understand. It was this element of mystery that caused him to fear that Pritchard had all along been an agent of the Enemy—that his noted successes with the divining rod were due to his connection with the Powers of Darkness, and that his getting within the fold of the faithful was, after all, only what might have been expected from one whose tactics were devised for him by the Old Serpent—the origin of every evil since the expulsion from Paradise.

CHAPTER X

He spent an hour at the Old Waggoner Inn at the corner of the River Road, and while his horse was getting a feed in the stable he had some bread and cheese in the inn parlour—a large room built to accommodate the hungry coach passengers, who, accustomed to break their journey to or from Plymouth, were at this house.

The room was not crowded when he arrived, but in the course of the next half-hour two additional parties entered, and while tankards were filled and emptied, and pewter platters of underdone beef laden with pickles were passed round, there was a good deal of loud talk, with laughter and an interchange of friendly, if rude, humour. Wesley had had a sufficient experience of inn parlours to prevent his being greatly interested by the people here or their loud chat.

This was only at first, however, for it soon became clear to him that the conversation and the jests were flowing in one channel. Then he became interested.

"Come hither, friend Thomas, and pay all scores," cried one jovial young fellow to an elderly stout farmer who had been standing in the bar.

"Not me, lad," cried the farmer. "By the Lord Harry, you've the 'impidence'!".

"What, man, pay and look joyous. What will all your hoard of guineas be to you after Monday?" cried the younger man.

"'Twill be worth twenty-one shillings for every guinea, if you must know," replied the farmer.

"Nay, sir, you know well that there will be no use for your guineas at the Day of Judgment, which, as surely as Dick Pritchard is a prophet, will happen on Monday," said the other.

"I'm ready to run the chance, i' the face o' the Prophet Pritchard," said the farmer. "Ay, and to show what's in me, I am ready 'twixt now and Sunday to buy any property at a reasonable discount rate that any believer in Dick Pritchard may wish to sell."

"Good for you, farmer—good for you!" shouted a dozen voices, with the applause of rattling pewters on the table.

"Let Dick stick to his trade—water and not fire is his quality; he'd best leave the Day of Judgment in subtler hands," growled a small, red-faced man, who was cooling himself this Summer day with Jamaica rum.

There was some more laughter, but it was not of a hearty sort; there was a forced gaiety in it that Wesley easily detected.

"By my troth, the fellow's prophecy hath done a good turn to the maltster; there hath been more swilling, hot and cold, since he spoke a week ago yesterday, than in any month of ordinary calm weather, without a sniff of brimstone in it," said Mr. Hone, the surgeon of the revenue men, who was in the act of facing a huge beef-steak with onions and a potato baked with a sauce of tansy.

"Small blame to the drouthy ones; they know full well that by this day week they will be ready to pay Plymouth prices for a mugful o' something cooling," remarked a traveller.

"Gentlemen and friends, all, I make bold enough to affirm that this matter is too grave an one to be jested on or to be scoffed at," said a tall, pale-faced young man. "I tell you, sirs, that there may be more in this thing than some of us suspect."

"What, Mr. Tilley, are you feeble enough to believe that an event of such considerable importance to the Government as the Day of Judgment would be announced through such an agent? This Dick Pritchard is a common man, as full of ignorance as a young widow is of tricks," said the surgeon, looking up from his plate.

"Ignorant? ay, doubtless, Mr. Hone; but how many ignorant men have yet won an honourable place in the book of the prophets, sir?" asked the young man. "Seems to any natural man, sir, that ignorance, as we call ignorance, was the main quality needful for an ancient old prophet that spake as he was moved."

"That was in the Antique Dispensation, Mr. Tilley; you must not forget that, sir," cried the surgeon.

"Ay, that's sure; 'tis a different age this that we live in," said an acquiescent voice behind the shelter of a settle.

"I'd as lief credit a Christian as a Jew in such a matter: the Jews seem to have had this business of prophecy as exclusive in their hands as they have the trade of money now," said the traveller. "The Jewish seers busied themselves a good deal about the Day of Judgment, why should not a humble Christian be permitted a trifle of traffic on the same question, since it is one that should be of vital interest to all—especially innkeepers in hot weather?"

There was only a shred of laughter when he had spoken. It was clear that in spite of some of the jeers against the water-finder that had taken place in the room, there was a feeling that whatever he had taken it upon him to say—it seemed to Wesley that it had reference to the Day of Judgment on the next Monday—should not be treated with levity. The jocular tone of a few men who were present was distinctly forced. Upon several faces Wesley perceived an expression that reminded him of that upon the faces of some of the prisoners under sentence of death whom he had visited in his young days at Oxford.

"Say what you will, gentlemen," resumed the young man called Tilley, "this Dick Pritchard is no ordinary man. I have seen him at work with his wizard's wand', and inside five minutes o' the clock he had shown us where to bore for water in a meadow slope that was as deeply pitted before with borings as if it had an attack of smallpox. Ay, sirs, a hole had been dug here and another there—and there—and there—" he indicated with his finger on the floor the locality of the diggings to which he referred—"but not a spoonful of water appeared. Then in comes our gentleman with a sliver of willow between his palms, and walks over the ground. I was nigh to him, and I affirm that I saw the twig twist itself like a snake between his fingers, jerking its tip, for all the world like the stumpy head of an adder, first in one direction, anon in another—I'll swear that it turned, wicked as any snake, upon Dick himself at one time, so that he jerked his hands back and the thing fell on the grass, and if it did not give a kind of writhe there, my eyes played me false. But he picked it up again and walked slowly across the ground, not shunning in the least as an ordinary man would have done, if he had his wits about him, the parts that showed the former borings that had come to naught. 'Twas in full boldness, just between two of the old holes, that he stopped short, and says he, 'There's your spring, and 'tis not six foot from the surface. I'll wait to have a mugful, if I don't make too bold,' says he, 'for 'tis strangely drying work, this waterfinding.' And by my faith, sirs, the fellow had a pitcher of the softest spring water from that spot before an hour had gone and the rude scum of the field had been rinsed away."

The silence that followed the man's story was impressive. It seemed as if the cloud which had been overhanging the company had become visible. No man so much as glanced at his neighbour, but every one of them stopped eating or drinking at that moment, and stared gloomily straight in front of him. Only one man, however, uttered a groan.

"Lord have mercy on us!—the rocks and the mountains—the great and terrible day of the Lord!" he murmured.

Then it was that a couple of men passed their hands over their foreheads.

"I would sooner see my cattle die of drouth than call in a water-finder," said the farmer. "I've oft-times said that he has a partner in his trade. In my young days, a water-finder was burnt at the stake, for 'twas clearly proven that he was in league with the Fiend: after drinking o' the water that he drew from the bowels o' th' earth the husbandman's son was seized wi' a fit and down he fell like a log and was only saved by the chance of the curate passing near the farm. Though but a young man, he saw at once that the boy had been tampered with.'Twas by good luck that he had with him a snuffbox made of the cedar wood of Lebanon at Jerusalem, where King Solomon built his temple, and 'tis well known that neither witch nor warlock can stand against such. Before you could say 'Worm,' the young parson had made a circle o' snuff around the poor victim, and with a deadly screech the fiend forsook the boy and 'twas said that it entered into a young heifer of promise, for she went tearing out of her byre that same night and was found all over a lather wandering on Dip-stone Sands in the morning. Ay, they burnt the water-finder at the next 'Sizes, the testimony being so clear as I say."

"'Tis time they burnt Dick Pritchard," said someone else in a low voice. "Though I'm not sure that 'tis in the Book that mere water-finding is heinous."

"Maybe not, but sure a proof o' the gift o' prophecy is burnable in the New Dispensation," suggested another.

A big man sprang to his feet. His face was pale and his hands were nervous. He clapped his palms together.

"Every man in the room has a tankard with me," he cried. "I'll pay the score for all. What use is the blunt to me after Monday? But now is our time, lads. Let us eat and drink, for to-morrow we die!"

The sentiment was greeted with a loud and harsh laugh by some men, but by a serious shake of the head by others. A young man started a ribald song.

"Shame, sir, shame, a parson's present in the room," cried an elderly man, who was seated near Wesley.

The lilt was interrupted, and two or three fingers were pointed toward Wesley, who was half hidden from most of the people in the room. Now he stood up and faced them all.

"Hey, 'tis Wesley the preacher himself!" cried the surgeon, and expressions of surprise were uttered in various directions.

"You have come in good time to superintend the winding up of the world, Mr. Wesley. Nay, don't be over modest; 'tis one of your own children hath said it," said another. "What, sir; would you disown your own offspring?"

Wesley had held up his hand twice while the man was speaking.

"Friends, I am John Wesley," he said. "I have come sixty miles and better, having heard from Mr. Hartwell that I was needed in regard to this same Pritchard, but having been made acquainted with no points of detail. Sirs, since I entered this room I have, I believe, learned all that Mr. Hartwell forbore to tell me, and now I hasten to give you my assurance that I cannot countenance aught that this man Pritchard said. I deplore most heartily that he should be so far misled as to take upon him to utter a statement of prophecy touching the most awful event that our faith as believers takes a count of. Brethren, we are told that we know not the day nor the hour when that dread shall fall upon the world. That is the written Word of the Most High, and any man who, whether under the impulse of vanity or in the sincere belief that he possesses the gift of prophecy, is presumptuous, is likely to become a stumbling block and a rock of offence. That is all that I have to say at this time. I have said so much in the hope that all who hear me will refrain from attributing to the influence of my preaching or teaching, an act or a statement which I and my associates repudiate and condemn."

He inclined his head slowly, and then, picking up his hat, left the room. But before he reached the door every man in the room had risen respectfully, though no word was spoken by anyone present. Even after his departure there was a silence that lasted for several minutes. Everyone seemed to have drawn a long breath as of relief.

"Gentlemen, I think you may breathe freely once more: the world will last over Monday after all," said the surgeon.

"Ay, the master has spoken and disowned his pupil," said another.

"Maybe that's because he feels chagrined that he lost the chance that Dick Pritchard grappled with," suggested the pale youth.

"Boy," said the traveller, with a contemptuous wave of the hand. "Boy, Mr. Wesley is a man of learning and a man of parts, not a charlatan in a booth at a fair."

"Or one with the duck's instinct of seeking for water with a quack—ay, a quack with a quack," said the surgeon.

"Well, if the world is not to expire on Monday, we would do well to drink her health, so hey for a gallon of old ale so far as it goes," cried the man with the shaking head.

The opinion seemed to be all but general, that some sign of hilarity would not now be so much out of place as it seemed to be a quarter of an hour earlier, and the landlord was zealous in support of this view. He promised them a tipple worthy of the name, even if the world were to break up in a day or two!

But long before the company were satisfied Wesley was on his horse riding slowly down to Ruthallion Mill.

He felt deeply pained by his experience in the inn parlour. So this was what Mr. Hartwell had hinted at in his letter—this assumption of the divine gift of the prophet by Pritchard. And the subject of his prophecy was one that every charlatan who had existed had made his own! He himself could remember more than one such prediction being made by men who were both ignorant and vain. One of them had afterwards stood in the pillory and another—the more sincere—had gone to a mad-house. It seemed to him strange that they should have had a following, but beyond a doubt their prediction had been widely credited, and the men themselves had achieved a notoriety which was to them the equivalent to fame. They had had their followers even after the date which they named in their prophecies had gone by without any disaster to the world. It seemed that the people were so glad at escaping that they had no room in their thoughts for any reproach for the false prophet.

He knew, however, that in the case of Richard Pritchard, the same leniency would not be shown. He knew that his own detractors—and they were many who regarded his innovations as a direct menace to the Church—would only be too glad of the chance which was now offered to them of ridiculing him and his out-of-doors preaching, pointing out, as they most certainly would, that Richard Pritchard represented the first fruit of his preaching, and that his assumption of the authority of a prophet was the first fruit of his Methodism.

But it was not only by reason of the possible injury that would be done to the movement which he had inaugurated in Cornwall that he was vexed.

He had been greatly pained to observe the spirit in which the most awful incident on which the mind of man could dwell was referred to by the men in the inn parlour—men fairly representative of the people of the neighbourhood. The Day of Wrath had been alluded to with levity by some, in a spirit of ridicule by others; while one man had made it the subject of a wager, and another had made it an excuse for drunkenness!

He was grieved and shocked to reflect that it was Pritchard's connection with his mission that had produced this state of things. He felt certain that if the man had remained outside the newly founded organisation, he would not have taken it upon himself to speak as a prophet.

But he felt that he could not lay the blame for what had occurred at the door of anyone whom he had appointed to help him in his work, and who had advanced the claims of Pritchard, for who could have foreseen that a man who seemed abnormally modest and retiring by nature should develop such a spirit? Beyond a doubt the man's weak head had been turned. He had become possessed of a craving after notoriety, and now that he had achieved it, he would be a very difficult person to deal with. This Wesley perceived when he began to consider how to deal with the source of the affair.

The most difficult point in this connection was his feeling that the man was quite sincere in his belief, that upon him the spirit of prophecy had descended. He felt sure that the man was unaware of the existence of any motive in his own heart apart from the desire to utter a warning and a call to repentance to the people of the world, as Jonah the prophet, had done to the people of Nineveh.

That fact, Wesley perceived, made it a matter of great difficulty both to silence Pritchard, and to hold him up as a charlatan.

He was indeed greatly perplexed in mind as he rode down the valley path leading to the Mill.

CHAPTER XI

Wesley could not, of course, know that Pritchard was at that time in the Mill awaiting his arrival. But it was the case that the water-finder, learning that the coming of Mr. Wesley was looked for during the afternoon, had gone to the Mill early and had rejected the suggestion made by the blacksmith and Jake Pullsford, that he should not appear in the presence of Mr. Wesley until he was sent for. He was almost indignant at the hint conveyed to him in an ambiguous way by Hal Holmes, that it would show better taste if he were to remain away for the time being.

"Take my word for 't, Dick, you'll be brought face to face with him soon enow," said Hal. "You'll be wishful that you had ne'er been born or thought of. Mr. Wesley is meek, but he isn't weak, and 'tis the meek ones that's the hardest to answer when the time comes, and it always comes too soon. Before your Monday comes you'll be wishful to hide away and calling on the mountains to cover ye."

"List to me, Hal; there's naught that will say nay to me when my mind is made up, and go to face Mr. Wesley I shall," Dick had replied.

The blacksmith folded his big bare arms and looked at him with curiosity from head to foot.

"A change has come o'er a good many of us since Mr. Wesley began to preach, but what's all our changes alongside yours, Dick Pritchard?" he said, shaking his head as though he relinquished this task of solving the problem which had been suggested to him. "Why, you was used to fear and tremble at the thin noise of your own voice, Dick Pritchard. With these ears I have heard you make an apology for saying 'Thank ye,' on the score that you were too bold. But now you are for rushing headlong to meet the man that you scarce dare lift your hat to a month or two agone."

"I hadn't learned then all that there's in me now, Hal," replied the water-finder. "I always did despise myself, being unmindful that to despise myself was to do despite to Heaven. Doesn't it stand to reason, Hal, that the greater a man thinks himself, the greater is the honour he does to his Maker? I think twice as much of God since I came to see what a man He made in me."

"That's a square apology for conceit, Dick, and I don't think aught the better of you for putting it forward at this time and in such a case as this. What, good fellow, would you be at the pains to magnify a man's righteousness pace for pace with his conceit? At that rate, the greater the coxcomb the more righteous the man."

Dick was apparently lost in thought for some time. At last he shook his head gravely, saying:

"Not for all cases, Hal, not for all cases. You be a narrow-souled caviller, I doubt; you cannot comprehend an argyment that's like a crystal diamond, with as many sides to it as a middling ignorant man would fail to compute."

"That may be, but I've handled many a lump of sea-coal that has shown as many sides as any diamond that was ever dug out of the earth, and it seems to me that your talk is more like the sea-coal than the crystal, Dick, my friend," said the blacksmith. "Ay, your many-sided argyments are only fit to be thrust into the furnace, for all, their sides."

"Mr. Wesley will comprehend," said Pritchard doggedly; "though even Mr. Wesley might learn something from me. Ay, and in after years you will all be glad to remember that you once dwelt nigh a simple man by name Richard Pritchard."

"In after years?" cried Hal Holmes. "Why, where are your after years to come from, if the end of all things is to be on us on Monday?"

"Don't you doubt but that 'twill come to an end on Monday," said the water-finder, "however you may twist and turn. Be sure that you be prepared, Hal Holmes. You have been a vain-living blacksmith, I am feared, and now you side with them that would persecute the prophets. Prepare yourself, Hal, prepare yourself."

This was the style in which the man had been talking for some time, astonishing everyone who had known his extreme modesty in the past; and this was the strain in which he talked when he had entered the Mill, and found the miller, Jake Pulls-ford and Mr. Hartwell seated together awaiting the arrival of Wesley.

The man's entrance at this time surprised them. They knew he was aware that Mr. Wesley was returning in haste, owing solely to his, Pritchard's, having put himself forward in a way that his brethren could not sanction, and it never occurred to them that he would wish to meet Mr. Wesley at this time. They were, as was Hal Holmes, under the impression that when Wesley arrived Pritchard's former character might show itself once more, causing him to avoid even the possibility of meeting the preacher face to face.

They were soon undeceived. The water-finder was in no way nervous when he came among them.

When he had in some measure recovered from his surprise, the miller said: "We looked not for thy coming so soon, Dick, but maybe 'tis as well that thou 'rt here."

"How could I be away from here unless I had hastened to meet Mr. Wesley on his way hither?" said Pritchard. "I have been trembling with desire to have his ear for the past week. It is laid on me to exhort him on some matters that he neglected. These matters can be neglected no longer."

The miller looked at Jake Pullsford, and the latter sat aghast. He was so astounded that he could only stare at Pritchard, with his hands on his knees and his head in its usual poise, craning forward. Some moments had passed before he succeeded in gasping out, after one or two false starts:

"You—you—you—Dick Pritchard,—you talk of exhorting Mr. Wesley? Oh, poor fellow! poor fellow! Now, indeed, we know that you are mad!"

"Mr. Wesley should ha' found out the gift that is mine," said Pritchard, quite ignoring the somewhat frank utterance of the carrier. "I suspected myself during several months of having that great gift of prophecy.'Twas no more than a suspicion for some time, and I dare not speak before I was sure."

"And what made thee sure, Dick?" asked the miller.

"'Twas reading how the great prophet, Moses, made water flow from the rock," replied Pritchard. "'What,' said I to my own self. 'What, Richard Pritchard, hath not all thy life been spent in performing that great miracle of Moses, and hast not known the greatness of thy gift?' And then I made search and found that water-finding has been the employment of most of the great prophets, Elijah being the foremost. Like to a flash from a far-off cannon gun, that reaches the eyes before ever the sound of the boom comes upon the ear, the truth was revealed to me. I knew then that the gift of the Tishbite was mine."

It was Jake Pullsford who now looked at the miller. The miller shook his head.

"'Twould not matter much what you thought of yourself, Dick," said the miller, "if only you had not been admitted to our fellowship; but things being as they be—-"

He shook his head again.

"What overcomes me is the thought of thy former habit of life, Dick," said the carrier. "Why, up to a month agone, a man more modest, shy and tame speaking, wasn't to be found in all the West Country. Why, man, I've seen thee sweat at the sound of thine own voice, like as if thou hadst been a thief a-hearing o' the step of an officer! Meek! Meek is no name for it! I give thee my word that it oft made me think shame of all manhood in the world to hear thee make apology for a plain truth that, after all, thou wast too bashful to utter!"

"You could not see my heart, Miller," said Pritchard. "'Twas only that I was humble in voice; I know now that in spirit I was puffed up with pride, so that I could hardly contain myself. But even after the truth came upon me in that flash, I was ready to treat the likes of you, Miller—ay, even the likes of thee, Jake Pullsford, as mine equal, so affable a heart had I by birth."

"You promoted yourself a bit, Dick," remarked the miller. "But I've always observed that when a man tells another in that affable way that he regards the other as his equal, he fancies in the inwardness of his heart, that he is far above the one he gives such an assurance to."

"I feel a sort of light of knowledge within me ready to break forth and tell me a wonderful reply to that remark of yours, Miller," said Pritchard. "Tarry a while, and give me time for the light to-break forth with fulness, and you'll be rewarded; friends, you will hear a reply that will make you all stand back in amaze, and marvel, as I have done, how noble a thing is the gift of speech—saying a phrase or two that makes the flesh of man tingle. All I ask is time. It may not come to me within the hour, but— —"

"Here's one that hath come to thee, my man, and he will listen to all you have to say: I hear the sound of his horse on the lane," cried the miller.

Jake Pullsford sprang from the settle, and strained himself to look out of the window.

"Right; 'tis Mr. Wesley, in very deed," he said.

"That's as should be," cried Pritchard, with an air of satisfaction that made the others feel the more astonished.

And when Wesley had entered and greeted his-friends, including the water-finder, they were a good deal more astonished at the attitude taken by Pritchard. Without wasting time over preliminaries, he assumed that Wesley had come to the Mill in order not to admonish him, but to be admonished by him. Before Mr. Wesley had time to say more than a word, Pritchard had become fluent on the subject of the preacher's responsibilities. It was not for Mr. Wesley to go wandering in the uttermost parts of Cornwall, he said; he should have remained at Porthawn to consolidate the work that he had begun; had he done so until he had gathered in every soul, the Lord might have been as merciful to the world as He had been to Nineveh in the days of Jonah. But Mr. Wesley had, like Jonah, fled from his duty, and the next Monday was to be the Day of Judgment.

Wesley listened gravely until the man got upon his feet and with an outstretched finger toward him, cried:

"I have been mocked by some, and held in silent despite by others — all of them professing to be of the Household of Faith, because the Spirit of prophecy came upon me, and I announced the truth. Nor, Mr. Wesley, will you dare to join with the disbelievers and say straight out that the first Monday will not be the Last Day that will dawn on this world?"

"No," said Wesley, "I would not be so presumptuous as to lay claim to any knowledge that would entitle me to speak on a subject of such awful import. 'Ye know not the day nor the hour' — those were the words of our Lord, and anyone who makes profession of knowing either, commits a grievous sin."

"Ay, anyone but me," said Pritchard. "But the revelation was made to me — I take no glory to myself. The great and terrible Day of the Lord cometh next Monday, and they shall cry unto the rocks to fall on them and the mountains to cover them. What other place could that refer to if not Ruthallion and Porthawn; is't not that Buthallion is in the heart of the hills and Porthawn the place of rocks?"

With all gentleness Wesley spoke to the man of the great need there was for caution on the part of anyone venturing to assign times and seasons to such prophecies as had been uttered respecting the mystery of the Last Judgment. He tried to show him that however strong his own conviction was on the subject of the Revelation, he should hold his peace, for fear of a mistake being made and enemies being afforded a reason for railing against the cause which they all had at heart. The interpretation of prophecy, he said, was at all times difficult and should certainly not be lightly attempted even by those men who had spent all their lives dealing with the subject, with the light of history to guide them. Nothing could exceed the tact, patience and gentleness with which the pastor pleaded with this erring one of his flock — the miller and Jake Pullsford were amazed at his forbearance; they learned a lesson from him which they never forgot. He was patient and said no word of offence all the time that they were waxing irritable at the foolishness of the man who sat shaking his head now and again, and pursing out his lips after the manner of pig-headed ignorance when objecting to the wisdom of experience.

It was all to no purpose that Wesley spoke. The man listened, but criticised with the smile of incredulous superiority on his face almost all the time that Wesley was speaking—it varied only when he was shaking his head, and then throwing it back defiantly. It was all to no purpose.

"You are right, Mr. Wesley, in some ways," he cried. "But you talk of the interpretation of prophecy. Well, that is within your sphere, and I durstn't stop you so far. Ay, but I am not an interpreter of prophecy—I am the very prophet himself. Friends, said not I the truth to you this hour past—how I felt as it were a burst of flame within me, whereby I knew that I had been possessed of the spirit of prophecy? The gift of water-finding, which has been mine since my youth, was only bestowed upon the major prophets, Moses being the chief; and when I read of Elijah, who in the days of the grievous water famine was enabled by the exercise of his gift, and guided by the hand of the Lord, to find water—even the running brook Chereth—in the midst of a land that was dusty dry, all unworthy doubt was set at rest. Is it not written that Elijah, the prophet, was to come back to earth to warn the people of the Great Day being at hand?"

"Dear friend, stay thy tongue for a moment—say not words that might not be forgiven thee even by the Most Merciful," cried Wesley.

"You are a great preacher and a faithful servant—up to a certain point, Mr. Wesley; but you are not as I am," replied Pritchard firmly, but not without a tone of tenderness. "You are a preacher; I am the prophet. I have spoken as Jonah spoke to the men of Nineveh: 'Yet forty days and Nineveh shall be overthrown.' 'In eleven days the world shall be overthrown,' said I, feeling the flame within me."

"The people of Nineveh repented and the destruction was averted," said Wesley. "Have there been signs of a great repentance among the people who got tidings of your prediction?"

"My prophecy has everywhere been received with ridicule," replied the man proudly.

"I can testify to that," said Jake Pullsford. "I travel about, as you know, and I hear much of what is talked over from here to Devon, and only for a few light-headed women—ready to believe that the moon was the sun if they were told so from the pulpit—only for these, it might be said that Dick's foolishness would ha' fallen on ears as deaf as an adders."

"I, myself, can bear witness to the evil effect that has been produced among a people who were, I hoped, ready for the sowing of the good seed," said Wesley. "It was a great sorrow to me to hear the lightness of talk—the offer of wagers—the excuse of drunkenness—all the result of Richard Pritchard's indiscretion."

"And everywhither it has been received as coming from us—from us whom you have instructed in the Truth, sir," said Jake. "'Tis not Dick Pritchard that has been ridiculed, but we whom they call Methodists. That is the worst of it."

"And now that I have paved the way for you, the preacher, Mr. Wesley, you will be able for three days to exhort the people to repentance," said Pritchard, with the air of a man accustomed to give advice on grave matters, with confidence that his advice would be followed.

"My duty is clear," said Wesley. "I shall have to disclaim all sympathy with the statements made by Richard Pritchard. Souls are not to be terrorised to seek salvation. I am not one of those ministers who think that the painting of lurid pictures of the destruction of the earth and all that is therein the best way of helping poor sinners. Nay, there have come under mine own eyes many instances of the very temporary nature of conversions brought about by that paradox of the gospel of terror. But need we look for guidance any further away than the history of Jonah and the Ninevites? The prophet preached destruction, and the people repented. But how long did the change last? The fire and brimstone had to be rained down upon them before the sackcloth that they assumed was worn out."

"On Monday the fire and brimstone will overwhelm the whole world, and woe be to him that preacheth not from that text till then!" cried Pritchard. He was standing at one end of the table facing the window that had a western aspect, and as he spoke, the flaming beams of the sinking sun streamed through the glass and along the table until they seemed to envelop him. In spite of the smallness of his stature he seemed, with the sunbeams striking him, to possess some heroic elements. The hand that he uplifted was thin and white, and it trembled in the light. His face was illuminated, not from without only; his eyes were large and deep, and they seemed staring at some object just outside the window.

Watching him thus, everyone in the room turned toward the window—Wesley was the only exception; he kept his eyes fixed upon the man at the foot of the table. He saw his eyes move as if they were following the movements of someone outside, and their expression varied strangely. But they were the eyes of a man who is the slave of his nerves—of a visionary who is carried away by his own ill-balanced imagination—of the mystic who can see what he wishes to see.

Wesley was perplexed watching this man whose nature seemed to have completely changed within the month. He had had a good deal of strange experience of nervous phases, both in men and women who had been overcome by his preaching, but he had never before met with a case that was so strange as this. The man was no impostor; an impostor would have been easy to deal with. He was a firm believer in his own mission and in his own powers, and therein lay the difficulty of suppressing him.

And while Wesley watched him, and everyone else seemed striving to catch a glimpse of the object on which the man's eyes were fixed, the light suddenly passed out of his eyes and they became like those of a newly dead man, staring blankly at that vision which comes before the sight of a soul that is in the act of passing from the earth into the great unknown Space. There he stood with his hand still upraised, and that look of nothingness in his staring eyes..

Wesley sprang up from the table to support him when he fell, and he appeared to be tottering after the manner of a man who has been shot through the heart while on his feet; and Wesley's movement caused the others to turn toward the man.

In a second the miller was behind him with outstretched arms ready to support him. Pritchard did not fall just then, however. Breathlessly and in a strained silence, the others watched him while he swayed to the extent of a hand's breadth from side to side, still with his hand upraised and rigid. For some minutes—it might have been five—he stood thus, and in the end he did not collapse. He went slowly and rigidly backward into Wesley's arms, and then down into his own chair, his eyes still open—still blankly staring, devoid of all expression.

"Dead—can he be dead?" whispered Jake, slipping a hand under his waistcoat.

Wesley shook his head.

"He is not dead, but in a trance," he replied.

CHAPTER XII

For half an hour the four men in that room sat watching with painful interest the one who sat motionless in the chair at the end of the table. There was not one of them that had not a feeling of being a watcher by the side of a bed on which a dead body was lying. Not a word was exchanged between them. In the room there was a complete silence—the silence of a death chamber. The sound of the machinery of the mill—the creaking of the wooden wheels, and the rumbling of the grindstones—went on in dull monotony in the mill, and from the kitchen, beyond the oaken door, there came the occasional clink of a pan or kettle; and outside the building there was the clank of the horses of a waggon, and the loud voices of the waggoners talking to the men in one of the lofts, and now and again directing the teams. A cock was crowing drowsily at intervals in the poultry run, and once there was a quacking squabble amongst the ducks on the Mill race. And then, with the lowing of the cows that were being driven to the milking shed, came the laughter of a girl, passing the waggoners.

But in the room there was silence, and soon the dimness of twilight.

And then John Wesley prayed in a low voice.

Enough light remained in the room to allow those watchers to see when consciousness returned to the man's eyes: he was facing the window. But before the expression of death changed to that of life, his arm, that was still stiffly outstretched, and seeming all the more awkward since he had ceased to be on his feet, fell with a startling thud upon the edge of the table. It was as if a dead man had made a movement. Then his eyes turned upon each in the room in turn. He drew a long breath.

"You are among friends, Dick; how feel you, my man?" said Jake Pullsford, laying his hand upon Pritchard's that had fallen upon the table.

"I saw it again—clear—quite clear, Jake," said Pritchard.

"What saw ye, friend Dick?" asked Jake.

"The vision—the Vision of Patmos. The heavens rolled together like a scroll—blackness at first—no mind o' man ever conceived of such blackness—the plague of Egypt was snow-white to compare. And then 'twas all flame—flame—flame. The smith's furnace hath but a single red eye of fire, but its sharp brightness stings like a wasp. But this—oh, millions upon millions of furnace eyes, and every eye accusing the world beneath. Who can live with everlasting burning?—that was what the Voice cried—I know not if it was the strong angel, or him that rode upon the White Horse, but I heard it, and all the world heard it, and the most dreadful and most unusuallest thing of all was the sight of that White Horse, plunging and pawing with all the fiery flames around it and above and below! And the Voice said, 'There shall be no more sea,' and forthwith all the tide that had been flowing in hillocks into Porthawn and teasing the pebbles where the shallows be, and lapping the Dog's Teeth reef, wimpling around the spikes—all that tide of water, I say, began to move out so that every eye could see it move, and the spikes o' the reef began to grow as the water fell, till the bases of the rocks appeared with monstrous weeds, thick as coiled snakes, and crawling shells, monstrous mighty that a man might live in; and then I saw the slime of the deep, thick as pitch and boiling and bubbling with the heat below, even as pitch boils over the brazier when the boats lie bottom up on the beach. And then I saw a mighty ship lying in the ooze—a ship that had become a wreck, maybe a hundred years agone, half the timbers rotted from the bends so that she was like some monster o' the deep with its long ridges of ribs showing fleshless as a skeleton. And then the Voice cried, 'The Sea gave up its Dead.'... You shall see it for yourselves on Monday—ay, all that came before mine eyes.'Twas Mr. Wesley preached on the great moving among the dry bones—they were dry in that valley, but in the dread secret depths where the sea had been these were damp with the slime of ages, and they crawled together, bone unto bone, throwing off the bright green seaweeds that overlaid them like shrouds of thin silk. They stood up together all in the flesh, and I noted that their skin was the yellow pale skin of the drowned, like the cheeks of a female who holds a candle in her hands and shades the flame with one of her palms. Flame—I saw them all by the light of the flaming sky, and some of them put up their saffron hands between their faces and the flame, but the light shone through their flesh as you have seen the sun shine through a sere leaf of chestnut in the autumn."

He stopped suddenly and drew a long breath. For some moments he breathed heavily. No one in the room spoke. A boy went past the door outside whistling.

When the man spoke again it was in a whisper. He turned to Wesley.

"Mr. Wesley, I knew not that I had the gift until I heard you preach," he said. "I only suspected now and again when I felt the twitchings of the twig between my hands when I was finding the water, that I was not as other men; but when I heard you preach and saw how you carried all who listened away upon your words as though they were not words, but a wave of the sea, and the natural people the flotsam of the waste, I felt my heart swell within me by reason of the knowledge that I had been chosen to proclaim something great beyond even all that you could teach. And now 'tis left for you to stand by my side and tell all that have ears to hear to prepare for the Great Day. It is coming—Monday. I would that we had a longer space, Sir, for, were it so, my name would go forth through all the world as yours has done—nay, with more honour, for a prophet is ahead of the mere preacher. But you will do your best for the world in the time allowed to us, will you not, Mr. Wesley?"

He laid his hand on one of Wesley's, firmly and kindly.

"My poor brother!" said Wesley gently. "God forgive me if I have been the means of causing hurt to even the weakest of my brethren. Let us live, dear brother, as if our days in the world were not to be longer than this week, giving our thoughts not to ourselves, but to God; seeking for no glory to attach to our poor names, but only to the Name at which every knee must bow. Humility—let us strive after humility. What are we but dust?"

The man looked at him—there was still some light in the room—and after the lapse of a few moments he said:

"You have spoke a great truth, Mr. Wesley. Humility is for all of us. Pray that I may attain it, brother. It should come easy enough to some that we know, but for such as you and me, especially me, dear brother, 'tis not so easy. The gift of prophecy surely raises a humble man into circumstances so lofty that he is above the need for any abject demeanour. Ay, now that I reflect on't, I am not sure that I have any right to be humble. 'Twould be like flouting a gift in the face of the giver. 'Twould be like a servant wearing a ragged coat when his master hath provided him with a fine suit of livery."

He had risen from his place, and now he remarked that the evening had come and he had far to travel. He gave Wesley his hand, nodded to the others and went through the door without another word.

The men whom he left in the room drew long breaths. One of them—the farmer—made a sound with his tongue against his teeth as one might do when a child too young to know better breaks a saucer. The miller gave an exclamation that went still further, showing more of contempt and less of pity. Mr. Hartwell, the mine-owner, who was a quiet, well-read man, said:

"I have heard of cases like to his; I have been reading of revivals, as some call such an awakening as has taken place through Mr. Wesley's preaching, and every one of them has been followed by the appearance of men not unlike Dick Pritchard in temper—men who lose themselves in their zeal—get out of their depth—become seized by an ambition to teach others before they themselves have got through the primer."

"For me, I call to mind naught but the magic men of Egypt," said Jake Pullsford. "They were able to do by their traffic with the Evil One all that Moses did by miracle. I always had my doubts about the power that Dick Pritchard professed—finding water by the help of his wand of hazel—as 'twere a wizard's wand—maybe the staves of the Egyptian sorcerers were of hazel—I shouldn't wonder. And now he falls into a trance and says he sees a vision, equalling himself to St. John at Patmos! For myself I say that I never knew of a truly godly man falling into a trance. My grandfather—you are old enough to remember him, farmer?"

"I mind him well—pretty stiff at a bargain up to the end," said the farmer with a side nod of acquiescence.

"We be talking of the same man," resumed the miller. "Well, I say that he told me of one such mystical vision seer that came from Dorset in his young days, and he saw so many things that he was at last tried for sorcery and burnt in the marketplace. Ah, those were the days when men wasn't allowed by law to go so far as they do now-a-days. Why, 'tis only rarely that we hear of a witch burning in these times."

Wesley held up his hand.

"I had my misgivings in regard to Pritchard from the first," he said. "And when I got news that he had been causing you trouble I felt that he had indeed been an agent of the Evil One. But now—God forbid that I should judge him in haste. I scarce know what to think about him. I have heard of holy men falling into trances and afterwards saying things that were profitable to hear. I am in doubt. I must pray for guidance."

"The man is to be pitied," said Mr. Hartwell.

"You heard the uplifted way he talked at the last—like a fool full of his own conceit? Have you heard yet, Mr. Wesley, what an effect his prediction has had upon the country?"

"I heard naught of it until I had entered the parlour at the inn where I dined to-day, but I think I heard enough to allow of my forming some notion of the way his prediction was received. Some were jocular over it, a few grave, and a large number ribald."

"You have described what I myself have noticed, sir," said Mr. Hartwell. "Only so far as I can see there are a large number who are well-nigh mad through fear. Now what we may be sure of is that these people, when

Monday passes, will turn out open scoffers at the truth. And you may be certain that your opponents will only be too glad of the opportunity thereby afforded them of discrediting your labours; they will do their best to make Methodism responsible for the foolishness and vanity of that man?"

"I perceived that that would be so the moment I got your letter," said Wesley. "And yet—I tell you, brethren, that I should be slow to attribute any imposture to this man, especially since I have heard him speak in this room. He believes that he has been endowed by Heaven with the gift of prophecy."

"And he only acknowledges it to boast," said Mr. Hartwell. "It is his foolish boasting that I abhor most, knowing, as I do full well, that every word that comes from him will be used against us, and tend to cast discredit upon the cause which we have at heart."

Wesley perceived how true was this view of the matter, but still he remained uncertain what course to adopt in the circumstances. He knew that it was the fervour of his preaching that had affected Pritchard, as it had others; he had heard reports of the spread of a religious mania at Bristol after he had preached there for some time; but he had always succeeded in tracing such reports to those persons who had ridiculed his services. This wras the first time that he was brought face to face with one who had been carried away by his zeal to a point of what most people would be disposed to term madness.

He had known that there would be considerable difficulty dealing with the case of Pritchard, but he had also believed that the man would become submissive if remonstrated with. It had happened, however, that, so far from becoming submissive, Pritchard had reasserted himself, and with so much effect that Wesley found himself sympathising with him—pitying him, and taking his part in the face of the others who were apparently but little affected by the impassioned account the man had given of his vision when in the trance.

It was not until the night had fallen that they agreed with Wesley that it might be well to wait for a day or two in order that he should become acquainted with some of the effects of the prediction, and thus be in a position to judge whether or not he should take steps to dissociate himself and his mission from the preaching of the man Pritchard.

He had not, however, gone further than Port-hawn the next day before he found out that the impression produced by the definite announcement that the Day of Judgment was but forty-eight hours off was very much deeper than he had fancied. He found the whole neighbourhood seething with excitement over the prophecy. It had been made by Pritchard, he learned, in the course of a service which had been held in a field on the first Sunday after Wesley's departure, and it had been heard by more than a thousand of the people whom Wesley's preaching had aroused from lethargy to a living sense of responsibility. Religious fervour had taken hold upon the inhabitants of valley and coast, and under its influence extravagance and exuberance were rife. Only at such a time would Pritchard's new-found fervour have produced any lasting impression, but in the circumstances his assumption of the mantle of the prophet and his delivery of the solemn warning had had among the people the effect of a firebrand flung among straw. He had shouted his words of fire to an inflammable audience, and his picture of the imminent terror had overwhelmed them. The shrieks of a few hysterical women completed what his prediction had begun, and before the evening the valley of the Lana was seething with the news that the world was coming to an end within the month.

All this Wesley heard before he left the Mill, and before he had ridden as far as the coast village he had ample confirmation of the accuracy of the judgment of his friends, who had assured him that the cause which they had at heart was likely to suffer through the vanity of Pritchard. He also perceived that the man had good reason for being puffed up on observing the effect of his deliverance. In a moment he had leaped into notoriety from being a nonentity. It seemed as if he had been ashamed of hearing his own voice a short time before, and this fact only made him appear a greater marvel to himself as well as to the people who had heard him assume the character of a prophet of fire and brimstone. It was no wonder, Wesley acknowledged, that the man's head had been turned.

The worst of the matter was that he was referred, to by nearly all the countryside as Wesley's deputy. Even the most devoted of Wesley's hearers seemed to have accepted Pritchard as the exponent of the methods adopted by Wesley to get the ears of the multitude. In their condition of blind fervour they were unable to differentiate between the zeal of the one to convey to them the living Truth and the excess of the other. They were in the condition of the French mob, who, fifty years later, after being stirred by an orator, might have gone to think over their wrongs for another century had not a madman lighted a torch and pointed to the Bastille.

It was only to be expected that the opponents of the great awakening begun by Wesley should point to the extravagance of Pritchard and call it the natural development of Methodism. Wesley's crusade had been against the supineness of the Church of England, they said; but how much more preferable was this supineness to the blasphemy of Methodism as interpreted by the charlatan who arrogated to himself the power of a prophet!

He was pained as he had rarely been since his American accusers had forced him to leave Georgia, when he found what a hold the prediction had got on the people. He had evidence of the extent of Pritchard's following even during his ride to Port-hawn. At the cross roads, not two miles from the Mill, he came upon a large crowd being preached to by a man whom he had never seen before, and the text was the Judgment Day. The preacher was fervid and illiterate. He became frantic, touching upon the terror that was to come on Monday; and his hearers were shrieking—men as, well as women. Some lay along the ground sobbing wildly, others sang a verse of a hymn in frenzy.

Further along the road a woman was preaching repentance—in another two days it would be too late; and in the next ditch a young woman was making a mock of her, putting a ribald construction upon what she was saying. Further on still he came to a tavern, outside which there was a large placard announcing that the world would only last till Monday, and having unfortunately a large stock of beer and rum in fine condition, the innkeeper was selling off the stock at a huge reduction in the price of every glass of liquor.

Wesley had no difficulty in perceiving the man's generosity was being appreciated. The bar was crowded with uproarious men and women, and some were lying helpless on the stones of the yard.

On the wall of a disused smithy a mile or two nearer the coast there was chalked up the inscription:

"The Methodys have bro' about the Ende of the World. Who will bring about the Ende of the Methodys? Downe with them all, I saye."

He rode sadly onward, with bowed head. He felt humiliated, feeling that the object for which he lived was humiliated.

And the worst of the matter was, he saw, that these people who were making a mock of the Truth, some consciously, others unconsciously, were not in a condition to lend an ear to any remonstrance that might come from him. The attitude assumed by Pritchard was, Wesley knew, typical of that which would be taken up by his followers, and the mockers would only be afforded a new subject for ridicule.

"Is it I—is it I who am an unprofitable servant?" he cried out of the depth of his despondency. "Is it I that have been the cause of the enemy's blasphemy? What have I done that I should be made a witness of this wreckage of all that I hoped to see accomplished through my work?"

For some time he felt as did the man who cried "It is enough! I am not better than my fellows."

He let his rein drop on his horse's neck when approaching the house where he was to be a guest. The day was one of grey mists rolling from the sea through the valley, spreading wisps of gauze over the higher slopes, which soon whirled into muslin scarfs with an occasional ostrich plume shot through with sunshine. At times a cataract of this grey sea vapour would plunge over the slopes of a gorge and spread abroad into a billowy lake that swirled round the basin of the valley and then suddenly lifted, allowing a cataract of sunshine to pour down into the hollows which were dewy damp from the mist.

It was a strange atmosphere with innumerable changes from minute to minute.

"For me the shadows of the mist—the shadows touched by no ray of sunshine," he cried when he felt the cold salt breath of the vapour upon his face.

And then he bowed his head and prayed that the shadows might flee away and the Daystar arise once more to lighten the souls of the people as he had hoped that they would be enlightened.

When he unclosed his eyes, after that solemn space in which a man stretches out weak hands, "groping blindly in the darkness," hoping that they will touch God's right hand in that darkness and be guided into a right path, he saw the tall figure of a man standing on a crag watching him.

The man had the aspect of a statue of stone looking out of a whirl of sea-mist.

Wesley saw that it was Bennet, the man by whom he had been met when he was walking through this Talley for the first time with Nelly Polwhele. He had heard a great deal about the man during the few weeks that he had sojourned in the neighbourhood. He found that he was a man of some education—certainly with a far more intimate knowledge of the classics than was possessed by most of the parsons west of Exeter. He had been a schoolmaster in Somerset, but his erratic habits had prevented him from making any position for himself. He had become acquainted with Nelly Polwhele at Bristol, and his devotion to her amounted almost to a madness. It was all to no purpose that she refused to listen to him; he renewed his suit in season and out of season until his persistence amounted to persecution. Of course Nelly found many self-constituted champions, and Bennet was attacked and beaten more than once when off his guard. When, however, he was prepared for their assault he had shown himself to be more than a match for the best of them. The fact that he had disabled for some weeks two of his assailants did not make him any more popular than he had been in the neighbourhood.

There he stood looking at Wesley, and there he remained for several minutes, looking more than ever like a grey stone figure on a rough granite pedestal.

It was not until Wesley had put his horse in motion that the man held up one hand, saying:

"Give me one minute, Mr. Wesley. I know that you are not afraid of me. Why should you be?"

"Why, indeed?" said Wesley. "I know not why I should fear you, seeing that I fear no man who lives on this earth?"

"You came hither with a great blowing of trumpets, Mr. Wesley," said the man. "You were the one that was to overthrow all the old ways of the Church—you were to make such a noise as would cause the good old dame to awake from her slumber of a century. Well, you did cause her to awake; but the noise that you made awoke more than that good mother, the Church of England—it aroused a demon or two that had been slumbering in these valleys, and they began to show what they could do. They did not forget their ancient trick—an angel of light—isn't that the wiliest sorcery of our ancient friend, the Devil, Mr. Wesley?"

"You should know, if you are his servant sent to mock me," said Wesley.

"You have taught the people a religion of emotion, and can you wonder that the Enemy has taken up your challenge and gone far beyond you in the same direction? He found a ready tool and a ready fool in your ardent disciple with the comical Welsh name—Richard Pritchard, to wit. He has shown the people that you were too tame, and the water-finder hath found fire to be more attractive as a subject than insipid water. You are beaten out of the field, Mr. Wesley. As usual, the pupil hath surpassed the master, and you find yourself in the second place."

Wesley sat with his head bent down to his horse's neck. He made no reply to the man's scoff; what to him was the scoffing of this man? When one is sitting in the midst of the ruins of his house what matters it if the wind blows over one a handful of dust off the roadside?

"John Wesley, the preacher, hath been deposed, and Pritchard, the prophet, reigns in his stead," the man went on. "Ay, and all the day you have been saying to yourself, 'What have I done to deserve this? What have I done to deserve this?' Dare you deny it, O preacher of the Gospel of Truth?"

Wesley bowed his head once more.

"Mayhap you found no answer ready," Bennet cried. "Then I'll let you into the secret, John Wesley. You are being rightly punished because you have been thinking more of the love of woman than of the Love of God."

Wesley's head remained bent no longer.

"What mean you by that gibe, man?" he cried.

"Ask your own heart what I mean," said the man fiercely. "Your own heart knows full well that you sought to win the love of the woman who walked with you on this road little more than a month ago, and who ministered to you on the day of your great preaching—you took her love from those to whom she owed it, and you have cherished, albeit you know that she can never be a wife to you."

"The Lord rebuke thee," said Wesley, when the man made a pause.

"Nay, 'tis on you that the rebuke has fallen, and you know it, John Wesley," cried Bennet, more fiercely than ever. "Nelly Polwhele would have come to love me in time had not you come between us—that I know—I know it, I tell you, I know it—my love for her is so overwhelming that she would not have been able to hold out against it. But you came, and—answer me, man: when it was written to you that you were to return hither in hot haste to combat the folly of Pritchard, did not your heart exult with the thought singing through it, 'I shall see her again—I shall be beside her once more'?"

Wesley started so that his horse sprang forward and the man before him barely escaped being knocked down. But Bennet did not even pretend that he fancied Wesley intended riding him down. He only laughed savagely, saying:

"That start of yours tells me that I know what is in your heart better than you do yourself. Well, it hath made a revelation to you now, Mr. Wesley, and if you are wise you will profit by it. I tell you that if you think of her again you are lost—you are lost. The first rebuke has fallen upon you from above.'Tis a light one. But what will the second be? Ponder upon that question, sir. Know that even now she is softening toward me. Come not between us again. Man, the love of woman is not for such as you, least of all the love of a child whose heart is as the heart of the Spring season quivering with the joy of life. Now ride on, sir, and ask your reason if I have not counselled you aright."

He had spoken almost frantically at first; but his voice had fallen: he had become almost calm while uttering his last sentences.

He took off his hat, stepped to one side, and pointed down the road. He kept his arm stretched out and his fingers as an index, while Wesley looked at him, as if about to make a reply.

But if Wesley meant to speak he relinquished his intention. He looked at the man without a word, and without breaking the silence, urged his horse forward and rode slowly away.

CHAPTER XIII

John Wesley had ample food for thought for the remainder of his journey. He knew that the man who had appeared to him so suddenly out of the mist had for some time been on the brink of madness through his wild passion for Nelly Pol-whele, which brought about a frenzy of jealousy in respect of any man whom he saw near the girl. The fierceness of his gibes was due to this madness of his. But had the wretch stumbled in his blindness over a true thing? Was it the truth that he, Wesley, had all. unknown to himself drawn that girl close to him by a tenderer cord than that which had caused her to minister to his needs after he had preached his first great sermon?

The very idea of such a thing happening was startling to him. It would have seemed shocking to him if it had not seemed incredible. How was it possible, he asked himself, that that girl could have been drawn to love him? What was he to attract the love of such a young woman? He was in all matters save only one, cold and austere. He knew that his austereness had been made the subject of ridicule—of caricature—at Oxford and Bath and elsewhere. He had been called lugubrious by reason of his dwelling so intently on the severer side of life, and he had never thought it necessary to defend himself from such charges. He was sure that they were not true.

That was the manner of man that he was, and this being so, how was it possible that he should ever draw to himself the love of such a bright creature as Nelly Polwhele? What was she? Why, the very opposite to him in every respect. She was vivacious—almost frivolous; she had taken a delight in all the gaieties of life—why, the first time he saw her she had been in the act of imitating a notorious play-actress, and, what made it worse, she was playing the part extremely well. To be sure she had taken his reproof with an acknowledgment that it was deserved, and she had of her own free will and under no pressure from him promised that she would never again enter a playhouse; but still he knew that the desire for such gaieties was not eradicated from her nature. It would be unnatural to suppose' that it was. In short, she had nothing in common with him, and to fancy that she had seen anything in him to attract her love would be to fancy the butterfly in rapture around a thistle.

Oh, it was incredible that such a thing should happen. The notion was the outcome of the jealousy of that wretch. Why, the first time that the man had seen them together had he not burst out on them, accusing him of stealing away the child's affection, although he had not been ten minutes by her side?

Of course the notion was preposterous. He felt that it was so, and at the same moment that this conviction came to him, he was conscious of a little feeling of sadness to think that it was so. The more certain he became on the matter the greater was the regret that he felt.

Was it curious that he should dwell upon what the man had said last rather than upon what he had said first? But some time had passed before he recalled the charge that Bennet had brought against him almost immediately after they had met—the charge of having Nelly Polwhele in his thoughts rather than the work with which he had been entrusted by his Maker. The man had accused him of loving the girl, and declared that his present trouble was the rebuke that he had earned.

He had been startled by this accusation. Was that because he did not know all that was in his own heart? Could it be possible that he loved Nelly Polwhele? Once before he had asked himself this question, and he had not been able to assure himself as to how it should be answered, before he received that letter calling him back to this neighbourhood; and all thoughts that did not bear upon the subject of that' letter were swept from his mind. He knew that he heard in his ear a quick whisper that said:

"*You will be beside her again within four days;*" but only for a single second had that thought taken possession of him. It had come to him with the leap up of a candle flame before it is extinguished. That thought had been quenched at the moment of its exuberance, and now he knew that this accusation brought against him was false; not once—not for a single moment, even when riding far into the evening through the lonely places of the valley where he might have looked to feel cheered by such a thought, had his heart whispered to him:

"*You will be beside her again within four days.*"

She had not come between him and the work which he had to do.

But now the man had said to him all that brought back his thoughts to Nelly Polwhele; and having, as he fancied, answered the question which he put to him respecting her loving him, he found himself face to face with the Question of the possibility of his loving her.

It came upon him with the force of a blow; the logical outcome of his first reflections:

"If I found it incredible that she could have any affection for me because we have nothing in common, is not the same reason sufficient to convince me that it is impossible I could love her?"

He was exceedingly anxious to assure himself that the feeling which he had for her was not the love which a man has for a woman; but he did not feel any great exultation on coming to this logical conclusion of his consideration of the question which had been suggested to him by the accusations of Bennet; on the contrary, he was conscious of a certain plaintive note in the midst of all his logic—a plaintive human note—the desire of a good man for the love of a good woman. He felt very lonely riding down that valley of sea-mist permeated not with the cold of the sea, but with the warmth of the sunlight that struck some of the highest green ridges of the slopes above him. His logic had led him only into his barren loneliness, until his sound mental training, which compelled him to examine an argument from every standpoint, asserted itself and he found that his logic was carrying him on still further, for now it was saying to him:

"If you, who have nothing in common with that young woman, have been led to love her, what is there incredible in the suggestion that she has been led to love you?"

Then it was that he was conscious of a feeling of exultation. His own heart seemed to be revealed to him in a moment. Only for a moment, however; for he gave a cry, passing his hand athwart his face as if to sweep away a film of mist from before his eyes.

"Madness—madness and disaster! The love of woman is not for such as I—the man spoke the truth. The love of woman is not for me. Not for me the sweet companionship, the fireside of home, the little cradle from which comes the little cry—not for me—not for me!"

He rode on, and so docile had his mind become through the stern discipline of years, not once did his thoughts stray to Nelly from the grave matter which he had been considering when he encountered bennet—not once did he think even of Bennet. What he had before him was the question of what steps he should take to counteract the mischief which had been done and was still being done by the man who had taken it upon him to predict the end of the world.

A change seemed to have come over his way of looking at the matter. Previously he had not seen his way clearly; the mist that was sweeping through the valley seemed to have obscured his mental vision. He had been aware of a certain ill-defined sympathy in regard to the man since he had shown himself to be something of a mystic; his trance and, his account of the vision that he had seen had urged Wesley's interest into another channel, as it were; so that he found himself considering somewhat dreamily the whole question of the trustworthiness of visions, and then he had been able to agree with his friends at the Mill who had certainly not taken very long to make up their minds as to how Pritchard should be dealt with.

Now, however, Wesley seemed to see his way clearly. He became practical in a moment. He perceived that it was necessary for him to dissociate himself and his system from such as Pritchard—men who sought to play solely upon the emotions of their hearers, and who had nothing of the Truth to offer them however receptive their hearers' hearts had become. He did not doubt that Pritchard would take credit to himself for the non-fulfilment of his prophecy. He would bring forward the case of Jonah and Nineveh. Jonah had said definitely that Nineveh would be destroyed on a certain day; but the inhabitants had been aroused to repent, and the city's last day had been deferred. He would take credit to himself for arresting the Day of Judgment, his prophecy having brought about the repentance of his neighbours at Porthawn and Ruthallion, and thus the fact of his prophecy not being realised would actually add to the fame which he had already achieved, and his harmfulness would be proportionately increased.

Wesley knew that not much time was left to him and his friends to take action as it seemed right to him. The day was Friday, and he would preach on Sunday and state his views in respect of Pritchard and his following, so that it should be known that he discountenanced their acts. He had seen and heard enough during his ride through the valley to let him know how imminent was disaster to the whole system of which he was the exponent.

He had succeeded in banishing from his mind every thought which he had had in regard to Nelly Polwhele; so that it was somewhat disturbing for him to come upon her close to the entrance gates to the Court. She was carrying a wicker bird cage containing two young doves; he heard her voice talking to the birds before he recognised her. For a moment lie felt that he should stop his horse and allow her to proceed so far in front of him that she should reach the village without his overtaking her; but a moment's reflection was enough to assure him that to act in this way would be cowardice. He had succeeded in banishing her from his mind, and that gave him confidence in his own power to abide by the decision to which he had come respecting her. To avoid her at this time would have been to confess to himself that he was not strong enough to control his own heart; and he believed that he was strong enough to do so. Therefore he found himself once more beside her and felt that he was without a trouble in the world.

Of course she became very red when he spoke her name and stooped from his saddle to give her his hand. She had blushed in the same way an hour before when old Squire Trevelyan had found her with his daughters and said a kindly word to her.

"I have been to my young ladies," she said, "and see what they have given to me, sir." She held up the cage and the birds turned their heads daintily in order to eye him. "They were found in a nest by one of the keepers, and as my ladies are going to London they gave the little birds to me. I hope they will thrive under my care."

"Why should they not?" he said. "You will be a mother to them and they will teach you."

She laughed with a puzzled wrinkle between her eyes.

"Teach me, sir?"

"Ay, they will teach you, I would fain hope, how becoming is a sober shade of dress even to the young."

"Do I need to be taught such a lesson, Mr. Wesley?" she cried, and now her face was in need of such a lesson. She spoke as if hurt by his suggestion.

"I have never seen you dressed except modestly and as is becoming to a young woman," he replied. "Indeed I meant not what I said to be a reproach. I only said what came first to mind when I saw those dainty well-dressed creatures. My thought was: 'Her association with such companions will surely prevent her from yielding to the weakness of most young women. She will see that the dove conveys gentleness to the mind, whereas the peacock is the type of all that is to be despised.' Then, my dear child, the pair of turtle doves is an emblem of sacrifice."

"Is that why they were chosen as the symbols of love?" said the girl, after a pause.

He looked at her curiously for some time. He wondered what was in her mind. Had she gone as far as her words suggested in her knowledge of what it meant to love?

"I think that there can be no true love without self-sacrifice," said he. "'Tis the very essence—the spiritual part of love."

"Is It so in verity, sir?" she cried. "Now I have ever thought that what is called love is of all things the most selfish. Were it not so why should it provoke men to quarrel—nay, the quarrelling is not only on the side of the men. I have seen sisters up in arms simply because the lover of one had given a kindly glance to the other."

"To be ready to sacrifice one's self to save the loved one from disaster—from trouble in any shape or form—that is the love that is true, he assured of that, Nelly," said he. "Love, if it be true, will help one to do one's duty—to our Maker as well as to our fellow-men, and to do that duty without a thought of whatever sacrifices it may demand. Love, if it be true, will not shrink from the greatest sacrifice that can be demanded of it—separation from the one who is beloved—a dividing asunder forever. That is why it is the noblest part of a man's nature, and that is why it should not be lightly spoken of as is done daily."

"Ah, sir," she said, "that may be the love that poets dream of; I have read out of poetry books to my ladies at the Court, when they were having their hair brushed. There was the poet Waller, whom they liked to have read to them, and Mr. Pope, in places. Mr. Marlowe they had a great regard for. They all put their dreams of love into beautiful words that would make the coldest of us in love with love. But for the real thing for daily life I think that simple folk must needs be content with the homelier variety."

"There is only one sort of love, and that is love," said he. "'Tis a flower that blooms as well in a cottage garden as in the parterres of a palace—nay, there are plants that thrive best in a poor soil, becoming stunted and losing their fragrance in rich ground, and it hath oft seemed to me that love is such a growth."

"And yet I have heard it said that love flies out at the window when poverty comes in by the door," she said.

"That never was love; 'twas something that came in the disguise of love."

"I do believe that there are many such sham things prowling about, and knocking at such doors as they find well painted. Some of them have heard of silver being stored away in old jugs, and some have gone round to the byres to see exactly how many cows were there before knocking at the door."

He smiled in response to her smiling. And then suddenly they both became grave.

"Have you had recent converse with that man Bennet?" he asked suddenly.

She swung the bird cage so quickly round that the doves were well-nigh jerked off their perch. She had flushed at the same moment, and a little frown was upon the face that she turned up to him.

"Why asked you that question? Is it because you were speaking of the sham loves, sir?" she asked.

"I ask your pardon if I seem somewhat of a busybody, Nelly Polwhele," he said. "But the truth is that I—I find myself thinking of you at times—as a father—as an elder brother might think of—a sweet sister of tender years."

Now she was blushing rosier than before, and there was no frown upon her forehead. But she did not lower her eyes or turn them away from his face. There was about her no sign of the bashful country girl who has been paid a compliment by one above her in rank. She did not lower her eyes; it was he who lowered his before her.

"'Tis the truth, dear child, that I tell you: I have been strangely interested in you since the first day I saw you, and I have oft wondered what your future would be. I have thought of you in my prayers."

"I do not deserve so much from you, sir," she said softly, and now her eyes were on the ground, and he knew by the sound of her voice that they were full of tears. She spoke softly—jerkily. "I do not deserve so much that is good, though if I were asked what thing on earth I valued most I should say that it was that you should think well of me."

"How could I think otherwise, Nelly?" he asked. "You gave me your promise of your own free will, not to allow any further longing after the playhouse to take possession of you, and I know that you have kept that promise. You never missed a preaching and you were ever attentive. I do not doubt that the seed sown in your heart will bear good fruit. Then you were thoughtful for my comfort upon more than one occasion and—Why should you not dwell in my thoughts? Why should you not be associated with my hopes? Do you think that there is any tenderer feeling than that which a shepherd has for one of his lambs that he has turned into the path that leads to the fold?"

"I am unworthy, sir, I have forgotten your teaching even before your words had ceased to sound in mine ears. I have not scrupled to deceive. I led on John Bennet to believe that I might relent toward him, when all the time I detested him."

"Why did you do that?" he asked gravely.

"It was to induce him to come to hear you preach, Mr. Wesley," she replied. "I thought that it was possible if he heard you preach that he might change his ways as so many others have changed theirs, and so I was led to promise to allow him to walk home with me if he came to the preaching. I felt that I was doing wrong at the time, though it did not seem so bad as it does now."

"But you did not give him any further promise?"

"None—none whatsoever. And when I found that he was unaffected by your preaching I refused him even the small favour—he thought it a favour—which I had granted him before. But I knew that I was double-dealing, and indeed I have cried over the thought of it, and when I heard that you were coming back I resolved to confess it all to you."

"I encountered the man not more than half an hour ago," said he.

She seemed to be surprised.

"Then he has broken the promise which he made to me," she cried. "He gave me his word to forsake this neighbourhood for two months, at least, and I believed that he went away."

"By what means were you able to obtain such a promise from him?" asked Wesley.

She was silent for some time—silent and ill at ease. At last she said slowly:

"I fear that I was guilty of double dealing again. I believe he went away with the impression that I would think with favour of him."

"I fear that you meant to convey such an impression to him, Nelly."

"I cannot deny it sir. I admit it. But I got rid of him. Oh, if you knew how he persecuted me you would not be hard on me."

"My poor child, who am I that I should condemn you? I do not say that you were not wrong to deceive him as you did; the fact that your own conscience tells you that you were wrong proves that you were."

"I do not desire to defend myself, sir; and perhaps it was also wrong for me to think as I have been thinking during the past week or two that just as it is counted an honourable thing for a general in battle to hoodwink his enemy, so it may not be quite fair to a woman to call her double dealing for using the wits that she has for her own protection. Were we endowed with wits for no purpose, do you think, Mr. Wesley?"

Mr. Wesley, the preacher of austerity, settled his countenance—not without difficulty—while he kept his eyes fixed upon the pretty face that looked up innocently to his own. He shook his head and raised a finger of reproof. He began to speak with gravity, his intention being to assure her of the danger there was trying to argue against the dictates of one's conscience. If cunning was the gift of Nature, Conscience was the gift of God—that was in his mind when he began to speak.

"Child," he began, "you are in peril; you

"A woman," she cried. "I am a woman, and I know that there are some—they are all men—who assert that to be a woman is to be incapable of understanding an argument—so that——"

"To be a woman is to be a creature that has no need of argument because feeling is ever more potent than argument," said he. "To be a woman is to be a creature of feeling; of grace, of tenderness—of womanliness. If your conscience tells you that you were wrong to deceive John Bennet, be sure that you were wrong; but Heaven forbid that I should condemn you for acting as your womanly wit prompted. And may Heaven forgive me if I speak for once as a man rather than a preacher. 'Tis because I have spoken so that I—I—oh, if I do not run away at once there is no knowing where I may end. Fare thee well, child; and be sure—oh, be sure that your conscience is your true director, not your woman's wits—and least of all, John Wesley, the preacher."

He laid his hand tenderly upon her head; then suddenly drew it back with a jerk as if he had been stung upon the palm. His horse started, and he made no attempt to restrain it, even when it began to canter. In a few seconds he had gone round the bend on the road beneath the trees that overhung the wall of the Trevelyan demesne.

He had reached the house where he was to lodge before he recollected that although he had been conversing with Nelly Polwhele for close upon twenty minutes—although they had touched upon some topics of common interest, neither of them had referred even in the most distant way to the matter which had brought about his return to the neighbourhood; neither of them had so much as mentioned the name of Pritchard, or referred to his prophecy of the End of all things.

As a matter of fact a whole hour had passed before John Wesley remembered that it was necessary for him to determine as speedily as possible what form his protest against the man and his act should take.

His sudden coming upon Nelly Polwhele had left a rather disturbing impression upon him—at first a delightfully disturbing impression, and then one that added to the gravity of his thoughts—in fact just such a complex impression as is produced upon an ordinary man when coming out of the presence of the woman whom he loves, he knows not why.

The sum of his reflections regarding their meeting was that while he had an uneasy feeling that he had spoken too impulsively to her at the moment of parting from her, yet altogether he was the better of having been with her. A cup of cool water in the desert—those were the words that came to him when he was alone in his room. After the horrible scenes that he had witnessed while riding through the valley—after the horrible torture to which he had been subjected by the gibes of John Bennet—she had appeared before his weary eyes, so fresh, so sweet, so gracious! Truly he was the better for being near her, and once more he repeated the word:

"A cup of cool water in the desert land."

CHAPTER XIV

Wesley lost no time in announcing to his friends the decision to which he had come. He was to preach on Sunday at the place where his first meeting had been held, and he felt sure that his congregation would be sufficiently large for his purpose, which was to let it be known throughout the country that he and all those who were associated with him in his work in Cornwall discountenanced Pritchard in every way. To be sure there was very little time left to them to spread abroad the news that Mr. Wesley had returned and would preach on Sunday. Only a single day remained to them, and that was not enough to allow of the announcement being made outside an area of twenty-five or thirty miles from Porthawn; but when Mr. Hartwell and Jake Pullsford shook their heads and doubted if this preaching would bring together more than a few hundred people, these being the inhabitants of the villages and hamlets within a mile or two of Porthawn, Wesley explained that all that was necessary to be done would be accomplished even by a small congregation. All that should be aimed at was to place it on record that Pritchard had done what he had done on his own responsibility and without any previous consultation with the leader of the movement with which he had been associated. But, of course, the more people who would be present the more fully his object would be accomplished, and Wesley's friends sent their message with all speed and in every direction.

"I would fain believe that the news of this distressing folly of Pritchard's has not spread very far abroad," said Wesley. "I travelled, as you know, through a large portion of the country on my return, and yet it was not until I had reached the head of the valley that the least whisper of the matter reached me; I would fain hope that the trouble will be only local."

"Those who are opposed to us will take the best of care to prevent it from being circumscribed," said Mr. Hartwell. "The captain of my mine tells me that there is excitement as far away as Falmouth and Truro over the prediction. In some districts no work has been done for several days. That news I had this morning."

"'Tis more serious than I thought possible it could be," said Wesley. "Our task is not an easy one, but with God's help it shall be fulfilled." Going forth through the village in the early afternoon, he was surprised to find so much evidence of the credence which the people had given to the prediction and so pronounced a tendency to connect it with the movement begun by Wesley in the early Summer. It seemed to be taken for granted that Wesley had come back to urge upon them the need for immediate repentance. This Pritchard had done with great vehemence ever since he had prophesied the Great Day.

Wesley found his old friends agitated beyond measure—even those who had professed to have received the Word that he had preached. No boats except those owned by Nelly Polwhele's father had put off to the fishing ground for some days, and, strange to say, although Isaac Polwhele held that Pritchard had gone too far in all that he had said, he returned on Friday morning from his night's fishing with a strange story of lights seen in the depths of the Channel—something like fires seething beneath the surface—of wonderful disturbances of the waters, although only the lightest of breezes was hovering round the coast; and of a sudden sound, thunderous, with the noise as of a cataract tumbling in the distance, followed by the rolling of large waves in spite of the fact that for the time there was not a breath stirring the air.

The old fisherman told his story of these things without any reserve; but while he was still disposed to give a contemptuous nod when anyone mentioned Pritchard's name, his experience through that night had done much to widen Pritchard's influence until at last there seemed to be neither fisherman nor boat-builder that did not dread the dawning of Monday.

And yet Nelly had not spoken one word about the prophecy when he had talked with her a few hours before!

This circumstance caused Wesley no little surprise. He asked himself if Polwhele's girl was the only sensible person in the neighbourhood. While the other people were overwhelmed at the prospect of a catastrophe on Monday, she had gone to visit her young ladies and brought back with her a pair of young doves.

He began to feel that he had never given the girl credit for some of those qualities which she possessed—qualities which certainly are not shared by the majority of womankind.

Her father told him before he had reached the village something of the marvels which had come under his notice only two nights before. But he tried to make it plain that he did not attach any great importance to them: he did not regard them as portents, however other people might be disposed to do so. The old fisherman was shrewd enough to guess that Mr. Wesley's sympathies were not with Pritchard. Still he could not deny that what he had seen and heard surpassed all his experience of the Channel, although he allowed that he had heard of the like from the lips of mariners who had voyaged far and wide, and had probably been disbelieved in both hemispheres, by the best judges of what was credible. He had heard, for instance, of parallels where through long sultry nights the ocean had seemed one mass of flame. But he himself was no deep-sea sailor.

"A sea of flame is common enough in some quarters," said Wesley. "I myself have seen the Atlantic palpitating like a furnace, and our ship dashed flakes of fire from the waters that were cloven by her cut-water. But the sounds which you say you heard—think you not that they came from a distant thunderstorm?"

"Likely enough, sir, likely enough," replied the man after a pause; but he spoke in a way that assured Mr. Wesley that he knew very well that the sounds had not come from a thunderstorm, however distant. He had had plenty of experience of thunderstorms, near at hand as well as far off.

"Or Admiral Hawke's ships—might not some of the Admiral's fleet have come within a mile or two of the coast and discharged their carronades?" Wesley suggested.

"Ay, sir, the boom of a ship's gun carries a long way on the water," said the fisherman, but in a tone that suggested graver doubt than before.

"'Tis clear you are convinced that what you heard was stranger than either thunder or gunpowder," said he.

"Nay, sir, what I am thinking of is the sudden uprise of the sea," said Polwhele. "Without warning our smack began to sway so that the mast well-nigh went by the board, albeit there was ne'er a draught o' wind. And there was summat besides that I kept back from all the world."

"A greater mystery still?" said Wesley.

"The biggest of all, sir; after the last rumblings my mates thought that we had been long enough anchored on the fishing bank; so we got in the grapple and laid out sweeps to pull the smack to the shore."

He made another pause, and looked into the face of his auditor and then out seawards. He took a step or two away and stood thoughtfully with pursed out lips.

"And then?" said Wesley.

"And then, sir, then—sir, the oar blades refused to sink. They struck on something hard, though not with the hardness of a rock or even a sand bank. 'Twas like as if they had fallen on a floating dead body—I know what the feel is, sir. When the *Gloriana*, East Indiaman, went ashore forty years agone, and broke up on the Teeth—you know the reef, sir—we were coming on the bodies o' the crew for weeks after, as they came to the surface, as bodies will after eight days—some say ten, but I stick to eight."

"But if you came upon the body of a drowned man the night before last you would surely have reported it, Polwhele," said Wesley.

"It were dead bodies that we touched wi' our blades, but they was the dead bodies of fishes. There they floated, sir, thick as jelly bags after a Spring tide—hundreds of them—thousands of them—all round the boats— big and little—mackerel and cod and congers and skates and some monsters that I had never seen before, with mighty heads. They held the boat by their numbers, blocking its course till we got up a flare o' pitch and held it out on an oar and saw what was the matter. That was how it came about that we landed with fish up to the gunwale, though we had hauled in empty seines—or well-nigh empty half an hour before. And if all the other boats had been out that night they would have been filled likewise. I tell you, sir, all we picked up made no difference to the shoals that was about us. But I said no word to mortal man about this event nor e'en to my own wife. What would be the good? I asks you, sir. The poor folk be troubled enow over Dick Pritchard, as no doubt you heard. I would that Tuesday was safe o'er us. List, you can hear the voice o' Simon Barwell baying the boys into the fold like a sheep dog. Simon was a sad evil liver before he heard you preach, sir, and now he's telling the lads that they have only another day and half to repent, so they'd best not put it off too long."

Wesley looked in the direction he indicated and saw a young fellow mounted on a fish barrel, haranguing a group of men and women. He was far off, but his voice every now and again reached the place where Wesley and the old man stood.

"There be some that holds that Simon himself would ha' done well to begin his repentance a while back," resumed Polwhele. "And there's some others that must needs scamp their penitence, if I have a memory at all; howsomever, Dick Pritchard——"

"Ah, friend," said Wesley, "if I could think that the repentance which is being brought about through fear of Monday will last, I would take joy to stand by the side of Pritchard and learn from him, but alas, I fear that when Monday comes and goes——"

"But will it come and go?" cried the old man eagerly.

"I cannot tell—no man living can tell if to-morrow will come and go, or if he will live to see the day dawn. We know so much, but no more, and I hold that any man who says that he knows more is tempting the Lord."

"And I hold with you, Mr. Wesley; only not altogether so fast since those happenings I have rehearsed to you. What was it slew them fish, sir?"

"I cannot tell you that. I have heard that some of your mines are pierced far below the sea, and that for miles out. Perhaps we shall hear that a store of gunpowder exploded in one of them, throwing off the roof and killing the fish in the water over it—I do not say that this is the only explanation of the matter. I make no pretence to account for all that you saw and heard. I have heard of earthquakes beneath the water."

"Earthquakes in divers places, Mr. Wesley, 'twas from that text Dick Pritchard preached last Sunday." The man's voice was lowered, and there was something of awe in his whisper. "He prophesied that there would be an earthquake in divers places—meaning the sea—before the coming of the terrible day, Monday next. Now you know, sir, why I said naught that was particular—only hazy like—that none could seize hold upon about Thursday's fishing. But I've told you, Mr. Wesley, whatever may happen."

He took off his hat and walked away, when he had looked for some moments into Wesley's face, and noted the expression that it wore.

And, indeed, Wesley was perturbed as he turned and went up the little track that led to the summit of the cliffs, and the breezy space that swept up to the wood. He was greatly perturbed by the plain statement of the fisherman. He had been anxious to take the most favourable view of Pritchard and his predictions. He had believed that the man, however foolish and vain he might be, had been sincere in his conviction that he was chosen by Heaven to prophesy the approaching end of all things; but now the impression was forced upon him that the man was on a level with the soothsayers of heathendom.

Even though he had taken a ludicrously illiterate view of the text, "There shall be earthquakes in divers places," he had made it the subject of another prediction, and it seemed as if this prediction had actually been realised, although only a single fisherman, and he a friend of Pritchard's, was in a position to testify to it.

Wesley had heard it said more than once that the finding of water by the aid of a divining rod was a devil's trick; but he had never taken such a view of the matter; he affirmed that he would be slow to believe that a skill which had for its object so excellent an object as the finding of a spring of the most blessed gift of water, should be attributed to the Enemy. He preferred to assume that the finding of water was the result of a certain delicacy of perception on the part of the man with the hazel wand, just as the detection of a false harmony in music is due to a refinement of the sense of hearing on the part of other men.

But was he to believe that any man possessed such a sense as enabled him to predict an earthquake?

It was impossible for him to believe it. And what then was he to think of the man who had foretold such an event—an event which had actually taken place within a week of his prediction?

The man could only be a soothsayer. The very fact of his corrupting the text out of the Sacred Word was a proof of this. If he were in the service of God, he would never have mistaken the word in the text to mean the sea. The man was a servant of the Evil One, and Wesley felt once more that he himself had been to blame in admitting him to his fellowship, without subjecting him to such tests as would have proved his faith.

And then he found himself face to face with the further question: If the man had, by reason of his possession of a certain power, achieved success in his forecast of one extraordinary event, was it to be assumed that the other event—the one of supreme importance to the world, and all that dwell therein—would also take place?

What, was it possible that the Arch Enemy had been able to get possession of the secret which not even the angels in heaven had fathomed, and had chosen this man to communicate it to some people in the world?

What, was it possible that Satan, if he acquired that secret, would allow it to be revealed, thereby losing his hold upon as many of the people of the world as became truly repentant, and there was no doubt that Pritchard had urged repentance upon the people?

It was a tangled web that Wesley found in his hand this day. No matter which end of it he began to work upon, his difficulties in untangling seemed the same. He was fearful of doing the man an injustice; but how could he, as a faithful servant, stand by and see the work with which he had been entrusted, wrecked and brought to naught?

And then another point suggested itself to him: what if this prediction became the means of calling many to repentance—true repentance—how dreadful would be his own condemnation if he were to oppose that which had been followed by blessing!

It was the flexibility and the ceaseless activity of his mind that increased the difficulties of his position. He, and he only, could look at the matter from every standpoint and appreciate it in all its bearings. If he had not had the refuge of prayer, having faith that he would receive the Divine guidance, he would have allowed the vanity—if it was vanity—of Pritchard to be counteracted in the ordinary—in what seemed to be the natural way—namely, by the ridicule which would follow the nonfulfilment of his prophecy.

He prayed.

CHAPTER XV

He had seated himself on the trunk of a fallen tree on the edge of the wood, and he had a feeling that he was not alone. The Summer ever seemed to him to be a spiritual essence—a beautiful creature of airy flashing draperies, diffusing perfumes a& she went by. He had known the joy of her companionship for several years, for no man had ampler opportunities of becoming acquainted with the seasons in all their phases.

There was the sound of abundance of life in the woods behind him, and around the boles of the scattered trees in front of him the graceful little stoats were playing. At his feet were scattered all the wild flowers of the meadow. Where the earth was brown under the trees, myriads of fairy bells were hanging in clusters, and in the meadow the yellow buttercups shone like spangles upon a garment of green velvet. He was not close enough to the brink of the cliffs to be able to see the purple and blue and pink of the flowers scattered among the coarse herbage of the rocks. But the bank of gorse that flowed like a yellow river through the meadow could not be ignored. In the sunlight it was a glory to see.

The sky was faintly grey, but the sea was of the brightest azure—the pure translucent blue of the sapphire, and it was alive with the light that seemed to burn subtly within the heart of a great jewel. But in the utter distance it became grey until it mingled imperceptibly with the sky.

The poet-preacher saw everything that there was to be seen, and his faith was upheld as it ever was, by the gracious companionship of nature, and he cried now:

"Oh, that a man could speak to men in the language of the Summer!"

Why could not all eyes of men look forth over that sea to where the heaven bowed down and mingled with it? Why could not men learn what was meant by this symbol of the mystic marriage of heaven and earth? Why should they continue to refuse the love which was offered them from above?

Everything that he saw was a symbol to him of the love of which he was the herald—the love which is followed by a peace that passeth all understanding. He was conscious of this peace leaning over him with outstretched wings, and he felt that the answer to his prayer had come. He would make no further attempt to solve the difficulties which had perplexed him. The voice that breathed the message that soothed him was the same that Elijah heard, and it said:

"Rest in the Lord, and He shall direct thy ways."

He remained there for another hour, and then rose and made his way slowly toward the village.

The meadow track led to a broad gap in the hedge of gorse, and just as he had passed through, he was aware of the quick pattering of a galloping horse on the short grass behind him, and before he had time to turn, the horseman had put his mount to the hedge, making a clear jump of it.

"What, ho!" cried the man, apparently recognising Wesley before the horse's feet had reached the ground. "What, ho!" and he pulled the animal to its haunches.

Wesley saw that he was Parson Rodney, the good-humoured Rector who had spoken to him when he had been on the road with Nelly six weeks before.

"Ho, Mr. Wesley, I had heard that you were returning to us," he cried. "Is it your thought that at Monday's Assize you will run a better chance if you are found in good company? What, sir, never shake your head in so gloomy a fashion. The Prophet Pritchard may be wrong. I was thinking of him when I came upon a clump of guzzlers reeling along the road an hour ago—reeling along with the buttercups as yellow as gold under their feet, and the sunlight bringing out all the scents of the earth that we love so well—I thought what a pity 'twould be if the world should come to an end when all her creatures are so happy!"

"Pardon me, Reverend sir," said Wesley. "But I have at heart too much sorrow to enjoy any jest, least of all one made upon a matter that seems to me far too solemn for jesting."

"Pshaw! Mr. Wesley, what is there serious or solemn in the vapourings of a jackanapes?" cried the other. "What doth a parson of our church— and a learned parson into the bargain—a Fellow of his College—not a dunce like me—what, I say, doth such an one with the maunderings of a vain and unlettered bumpkin whom his very godfathers and godmothers made a mark for ridicule when they had him christened Richard—Richard Pritchard?"

"Ah, sir," said Wesley, "you witnessed what you did an hour ago on the roadside—you saw what I saw, and yet you can ask me why I should be troubled. Were not you troubled, Mr. Rodney?"

"Troubled? Oh, ay; my horse became uneasy when one of the drunken rascals yelled out a ribald word or two across the hedge—I am very careful of my horse's morals, sir; I never let him hear any bad language. When we are out with the hounds I throw my kerchief over his ears when we chance to be nigh the Master or his huntsmen. That is why I laid over the rascal's shoulders with my crop, though the hedge saved them from much that I intended. Trust me, Mr. Wesley, that is the way such fellows should be treated, and as for this Pritchard—faugh! a horsewhip on his back would bring him to his senses, though as a Justice of the Peace, I would be disposed to let this precious water-finder find what the nature of a horse-pond is like. Why, in Heaven's name, do you trouble yourself about him?"

"It was I who gave him countenance at first, sir. He made profession to me and I trusted him. I fear that the work on behalf of which I am very jealous may suffer through his indiscretion."

"His indiscretion? *your* indiscretion, you surely mean, Mr. Wesley."

"I accept your correction, sir."

"Look ye here, Mr. Wesley, I have more respect for you, sir, than I have for any man of our cloth—ay, even though he may wear an apron and lawn sleeves. I know that as a clergyman I am not fit to black your shoes, but I am equally sure that as a man of the world, with a good working knowledge of human nature, I am beyond you; and that is why I tell you that this movement of yours has—well, it has too much movement in it to prove a lasting thing. You have never ridden to hounds or you would know that 'tis slow and steady that does it. If you keep up the pace from the start, you will be blown before the first half-hour is over, and where will you be when you have a double ditch to hop over? Why, you'll be up to your neck in the mire of the first. Mr. Wesley, there are a good many ditches to be got over in the life of a beneficed clergyman of your Church and mine; and, my word for it, you would do well to take them slowly, and reserve your strength. You want to go too fast ahead—to rush your hedges—that's how the thorns in the flesh thrive, and this Pritchard is only one of the many thorns that will make your life wearisome to you, and bring your movement to an end. You have never said a hard word about me, Mr. Wesley, though you had good reason to do so; and I have never said aught but what is good about you."

"I know it, sir. Others have called me a busybody—some a charlatan."

"They were fools. You are the most admirable thing in the world, sir—a zealous parson; but a thoroughbred horse is not the best for daily use; a little blood is excellent, but not too much. Your zeal will wear you out—ay, and it will wear your listeners out sooner. You cannot expect to lead a perpetual revival, as people call it, and that's why I am convinced that the humdrum system, with a stout woollen petticoat here and a bottle of sound port there, is the best for the parsons and the best for the people."

"Your views are shrewd, and I dare not at this moment say that they are not justifiable. But for myself—sir, if God gives me strength, I shall not slacken the work with which I believe He hath entrusted me—until our churches are filled with men and women eager in their search after the Truth."

"If all your friends were like you, the thing might be accomplished, Mr. Wesley; but the breakdown of your methods—your Methodism—will come through your introduction of the laity as your chief workers. You will find yourself face to face with Pritchards, and the last state of the people will be, as it is now, worse than the first. You may have done some good since you came here to preach a month ago, but you have—unwittingly, I say—done great mischief. My parishioners were heretofore living quite comfortably, they were satisfied with my ministrations, such as they were. I have heard it said that a healthy man does not know that he has any liver or spleen or vitals within his body: 'tis only the sick that have that knowledge. Well, the same is true in respect to their souls. Sir, there was not a man of my flock that knew he had a soul. There was a healthy condition of things for you!"

"Sir, I entreat of you not to mock!"

"I am not mocking, friend Wesley. What have people in the state of life to which the majority of my parishioners have been called, to do with the state of their souls? There should be a law that no man below the Game Law qualification shall assume that he has a soul."

"I cannot listen further to you, Mr. Rodney."

"Nay, Mr. Wesley, whatever you be, I'll swear that you are no coward: you will not run away by reason of not agreeing with an honest opponent— and I am not an opponent—I am only an honest friend. I say that my people were simple, homely people who respected me because I never wittingly awoke a man or woman who went asleep in my church, and because I never bothered them with long sermons, when they could hear their Sunday dinners frizzling in their cottages—they respected me for that, but more because they knew I had a sound knowledge of a horse, a boat, a dog and a game-cock."

"Mr. Rodney——"

"Pshaw, Wesley, have you not eyes to see that the Church of England exists more for the bodies than the souls of the people? I would rather see a good, sturdy lot of Englishmen in England—good drinkers of honest ale, breeders of good fat cattle, and growers of golden wheat—honest, hard swearers of honest English oaths, and with selfrespect enough to respect their betters—I would rather have them such, I say, than snivelling, ranting Nonconformists, prating about their souls and showing the whites of their eyes when they hear that an educated man, who is a gentleman first and a parson afterwards, follows the hounds, relishes a main in the cockpit, and a rubber of whist in the rectory parlour and preaches the gospel of fair play for ten minutes in his pulpit, and the rest of the twenty-four hours out of it."

"And I, Mr. Rodney, would rather hear of the saving of a sinner's soul by a Nonconformist ranter, Churchman though I be, than see the whole nation living in comfortable forgetfulness of God."

Parson Rodney laughed.

"I will give you another year of riding to and fro and telling the peasantry that they have souls," he said. "You will not make us a nation of spiritual hypochondriacs, Mr. Wesley. For a while people will fancy that there is something the matter with them, and you'll hear a deal of groaning and moaning at your services; but when the novelty of the thing is gone, they will cease to talk of their complaints. Englishmen are stronger in their bodies than in their souls, and the weaker element will go to the wall, and your legs will be crushed against that same wall by the asses you are riding. Why, already I know that you have suffered a bruise or two, through the shambling of that ass whose name is Pritchard. The unprofitable prophet Pritchard. A prophet? Well, 'tis not the first time that an ass thought himself a prophet, and began to talk insolently to his master. But Balaam's animal was a hand or two higher than his brother Pritchard; when he began to talk he proved himself no ass, but the moment the other opens his mouth, he stands condemned. Lay on him with your staff, Mr. Wesley; he has sought to make a fool of you without the excuse that there is an angel in your way. I have half a mind to give his hide a trouncing myself to-morrow, only I could not do so without giving a cut at you, who are, just now, holding on by his tail, hoping to hold him back in his fallow, and, believe me, sir, I respect you with all my heart, and envy your zeal. Good-day to you, Mr. Wesley; I hope I may live to see you in good living yet; if you worry to a sufficient degree the powers that be, they will assuredly make you a Dean, hoping that in a Cathedral Close, where everything slumbers, you will fold your hands and sleep comfortably like the rest. I doubt if you would, sir. But meantime if you will come to my humble rectory this evening, I can promise you a Tubber with a good partner, and a bottle of Bordeaux that the King of France might envy, but that has paid no duty to the King of England."

"I thank you for your invitation, sir; but you know that I cannot accept it."

"I feared as much, sir. But never mind, I hope that I shall live until you are compelled to accept my offer of hospitality to you as my Bishop."

He waved his hand, and gave his horse, who had never heard his master talk for so long a time at a stretch and whose impatience had for some time given way to astonishment, a touch with the spur. Wesley watched him make a beautiful jump over the gate that led into the park, beyond which the rectory nestled on the side of a hill among its orchards.

He turned with a sigh to the cliff path leading beyond the village to where Mr. Hartwell's house stood, separated from the beach only by a wall of crags, and a few rows of weather-beaten trees, all stretching rather emaciated arms inland.

CHAPTER XVI

Wesley had preached under varying conditions in different parts of England, but never under such as prevailed on this Sunday, when he set out in the early morning with his friend, Mr. Hartwell, for the pulpit among the crags which he had occupied several times during his previous stay at Porthawn.

When he set out from the Hartwells' house the grey sea-mist, which had been rolling round the coast and through the valley of the Lana for several days past, was as thick as a fog. It was dense and confusing to one who faced it for the first time. It was so finely grey that one seemed to see through it at first, and boldly plunged into its depths; but the instant that one did so, its folds closed over one as the dense waters of the sea do over a diver, and one was lost. Before one had recovered, one had the feeling of being smothered in a billow of grey gauze, smooth as silk that has been dipped in milk, and gasped within the windings of its folds. It was chilly, with the taste of the salt sea in its moisture. It took the heart out of one.

"This is nothing, sir," said Mr. Hartwell. "Lay your hand upon my arm and you will have no trouble: I could find my way along our cliffs through the thickest weather. I have been put to the test before now."

"I am not thinking so much of ourselves as of our friends whom we expect to meet us in the valley," said Wesley. "How, think you, will they be able to find their way under such conditions?"

"I do not assume that this mist is more than a temporary thing—it comes from the sea well-nigh every Summer morn, but perishes as it rolls over the cliffs," said Mr. Hartwell.

"It was clinging to the ridges of the valley slopes when I rode through, almost at noon yesterday," said Wesley.

"Stragglers from the general army that we have to encounter here," said the other. "When the phalanx of sea-mist rolls inland, it leaves its tattered remnants of camp followers straggling in its wake. I believe that when we reach the place we shall find ourselves bathed in sunshine."

"May your surmise prove correct!" said Wesley.

And so they started breaking into the mist, feeling its salt touch upon their faces and hearing the sound of the waves breaking on the beach below them. It was curiously hollow, and every now and then amid the noise of the nearer waves, there came the deep boom from the distant caves, and the sob of the waters that were choked in the narrow passage between the cliffs and the shoreward limits of the Dog's Teeth.

They had not gone more than half a mile along the track that led to the pack horse road, when they heard the sound of voices, near at hand, with a faint and still fainter far-off hail. The next moment they almost ran into a mixed party of travellers on the same track.

Mr. Hartwell was acquainted with some of them. They came from a hamlet high up in the valley a mile from Ruthallion.

"We are bound for the preaching," said one of them. "What a wandering we have had for the past two hours! We lost our way twice and only recovered ourselves when we gained the horse road."

"We are going to the preaching also," said Mr. Hartwell.

"How then does it come that we meet you instead of overtaking you?" asked the other.

There was a silence. The halloa in the distance became fainter.

"One of us must be wrong," said Wesley.

"We don't match our knowledge against Mr. Hartwell's," said the spokesman of the strangers.

"I am confident that I know the way," said Mr. Hartwell. "I only left the main track once, and that was to cut off the round at Stepney's Gap."

"On we go then, with blessings on your head, sir," said the other man. "Friends, where should we ha' landed ourselves if we had fallen short of our luck in coming right on Mr. Hartwell? Would we not do kindly to give a halloa or twain to help those poor hearts that may be wandering wild?" he added, pointing in the direction whence the hail seemed to come.

"Ay, 'twould be but kind," said an old man of the party. "Oh, 'tis a dread and grisly mishap to be wandering wild in an unknown country."

Forthwith the younger ones sent out answering hails to the halloas that came to them. But when the next sounds reached their ears like echoes of their own shouts, it seemed that they came from quite another quarter.

"I could ha' taken my davy that the lost ones was off another point o' the compass," said the old man.

"No, Comyn," said another. "No, my man, they came from thither."

He pointed straight in front of him.

"From where we stand that should be the Gap," said Mr. Hartwell.

"A special comfortable place to be wandering wild in is the Gap, for if you walk straight on it carries you to the mighty ocean, and if you walk back you will reach your own home safe, if it be in that direction," said the old man with emphasis.

"Was this mist far up the valley?" Wesley enquired.

"Not more than a league, sir," replied the old man. "'Twas a sunlit morn when we made our start, and then it came down on us like a ship in full sail. There goes another hail, and, as I said, it comes from behind us. Is there one of us that has a clear throat. 'Kish Trevanna, you was a gallery choir singer in your youth, have you any sound metallic notes left that you could cheer up the lost ones withal? Come, goodman, be not over shy. Is this a time to be genteel when a parson's of the company, waiting to help and succour the vague wanderers?"

"The call is for thee, Loveday, for didst not follow the hounds oft when there was brisk work in Squire's coverts?" said the man to whom the appeal was made.

"We must hasten onward," said Mr. Hartwell, making a start. "'Tis most like that we are overtaking whomsoever it be that was shouting a hail. Forward, friends, and feel your way to the pack-horse road."

The whole party began to move, Mr. Hartwell and Wesley leading, and before they had proceeded for more than two hundred yards they heard the sound of talking just ahead of them, and the next moment a group of men loomed through the mist. Friends were also in the new party.

"Were you them that sang out?" asked one of them.

"Only in answer to your hail; we be no cravens, but always ready to help poor wanderers," replied the talkative old man.

"We did not sound a note before we heard a hail," said the questioner in the new party. "We have not strayed yet, being bound for the preaching."

"Have you been on the horse road?" asked Hartwell.

"The horse road? Why, sir, the horse road lies down the way that you came," said the other.

"Surely not, my friend. How could we have missed it?" said Hartwell.

"If 'twasn't for the fog I could walk as steady for it as a mule," said the old man. "Ay, friends, us any mule under a pack saddle, for I have traversed valley and cleft an hundred times in the old days, being well known as a wild youth, asking your pardon for talking so secular when a parson is by. I am loath to boast, but there was never a wilder youth in three parishes, Captain Hartwell."

(Mr. Hartwell had once been the captain of a mine.)

"Surely we should be guided by the sound of the sea," said Wesley. "A brief while ago I heard the boom of waters into one of the caves. If we listen closely we should learn if the sound is more distinct and thereby gather if we are approaching that part of the cliff or receding from it."

"Book-learning is a great help at times, but 'tis a snare in a streaming fog, or in such times of snow as we were wont to have in the hard years before the Queen died in her gorgeous palace," remarked the patriarch.

"One at a time, grandfather," said a man who had arrived with the last party. "There's not space enough for you and the ocean on a morn like this. Hark to the sea."

They stood together listening, but now, through one of the mysteries of a fog, not a sound from the sea reached them. They might have been miles inland.

"I have been baffled by a fog before now," said a shepherd. "Have followed the bleat of an ewe for a mile over the hills, and lo, the silly beast had never left her lamb, and when I was just over her she sounded the faintest."

"Time is passing; should we not make a move in some direction?" said Wesley. "Surely, my friends, we must shortly come upon some landmark that will tell us our position in a moment."

"I cannot believe that in trying to cut off the mile for the Gap I went grossly astray," said Mr. Hartwell. "I am for marching straight on."

"Straight on we march and leave the guidance to Heaven," said Wesley.

On they went, Wesley marvelling how it was that men who should have known every inch of the way blindfold, having been on it almost daily all their lives, could be so baffled by a mist. To be sure Mr. Hartwell had forsaken the track at one place, but was it likely that he had got upon a different one when he had made his detour to cut off a mile of their journey.

On they walked, however, their party numbering fourteen men, and then all of a sudden the voice of the sea came upon them, and at the same moment they almost stepped over the steep brink of a little chasm.

"What is this?" cried Hartwell. "As I live 'tis Gosney hollow, and we are scarcely half a mile from my house! We have walked a good mile back on our steps."

"Did not I tell you how I followed the ewe?" said the shepherd. "'Tis for all the world the same tale. Sore baffling thing is a sea-mist."

"The valley will be full o' lost men and women this day," remarked the old man.

There is no condition of life so favourable to the growth of despondency as that which prevails in a fog. The most sanguine are filled with despair when they find that their own senses, to which they have trusted for guidance and protection, are defeated. The wanderers on this Sunday morning stood draped by the fog, feeling a sense of defeat. No one made a suggestion. Everyone seemed to feel that it would be useless to make the attempt to proceed to the crags where the preaching was to be held.

"Think you, Mr. Wesley, that this state of weather is the work of the Fiend himself?" asked the talkative old man. "I know 'tis a busy question with professing Christians, as well as honest Churchmen—this one that pertains to the weather. Stands to reason, for say I have a turnip crop coming on and so holds out for a wet month or two, while a neighbour may look for sunshine to ripen his grain. Now if so be that the days are shiny my turnips get the rot, and who is to blame a weak man for saying that the Foul Fiend had a hand in prolonging the shine; but what saith my neighbour?"

"Hither comes another covey of wandering partridges," said one of the first party, as the sound of voices near at hand was heard.

"Now, for myself, I hold that 'tis scriptural natural to say that aught in the matter that pertains to the smoke of the Pit is the Devil's own work, and if such a fog as this comes not straight out the main flue of——"

The old man's fluency was interrupted by the arrival of the new party, Nelly Polwhele and her father.

"You are just setting out for the preaching, I suppose; so we are not so late as we feared," cried the girl. "Still, though we shall certainly not be late for the preaching, however far behind we may be, we would do well to haste."

Wesley surely felt less despondent at the cheery greeting of the girl. He laughed, saying:

"'Tis all very well to cry 'Haste,' child; know that it Has taken us a whole hour to get so far."

"Is't possible that you have been out for an hour, sir?" she cried. "Surely some man of you was provident to carry with him a compass on such a morn as this?"

"You speak too fast, maid; book-learning has made thee talkative; a mariner's compass is for the mariners—it will not work on dry land," said the old man.

"Mine is one of the sort that was discovered since your sensible days, friend—ay, as long agone as that; it works on land as well as on sea. If a bumpkin stands i' the north its finger will point dead to him. Wouldst like to test it thyself?" said Nelly's father. Before the old man had quite grasped his sarcasm, though it was scarcely wanting in breadth, he had turned to Mr. Hartwell, displaying a boat's compass in its wooden box.

"'Twas Nelly bade me carry it with us," he Said. "I worked out all the bearings o' the locality before we started, and I can make the Red Tor as easy as I could steer to any unseen place on the lonely ocean. Here we be, sir; west sou'west to the Gap, track or no track; then west and by nor'-west a little northerly to the lift o' the cliff, thence south-half-east to the Red Tor. Up wi' your grapples, friends, we'll be there before the sermon has begun or even sooner if we step out."

Wesley, and indeed all of the party except perhaps the pessimistic old man, whose garrulity had suffered a check, felt more cheerful. Hartwell clapped Polwhele on the back, saying:

"You are the man we were waiting for. Onward, pilot; we shall reach the Tor in good time, despite our false start and the delay it made to us." They started along the track, Polwhele at their head, and Wesley with Mr. Hartwell and Nelly immediately behind him.

"There's a whole sermon in this, child," said the preacher.

"A whole sermon, sir?" said she.

"There should be only one sermon preached by man to men, and this is it," said Wesley. "The poor wandering ones standing on a narrow causeway, with danger on every side, and the grey mist of doubt in the air. The sense of being lost—mark that, dear child,—and then the coming of the good Pilot, and a complete faith in following Him into the place of safety which we all seek. There is no sermon worth the preaching save only this." On they went, Polwhele calling out the bearings every now and again, and as they proceeded they came upon several other travellers, more or less forlorn—all were hoping to reach the Red Tor in time; so that before the abrupt turn was made from the pack-horse track, there was quite a little procession on the way.

Never had Wesley had such an experience as this.

Out from the folds of the impenetrable mist that rolled through the hollows of the low mounds that formed that natural amphitheatre, came the sound of many voices, and the effect was strange, for one could not even see that a mass of people was assembled there. The hum that the newcomers heard when still some distance away became louder as they approached, and soon they were able to distinguish words and phrases—men calling aloud to men—some who had strayed from the friends were moving about calling their names, and occasionally singing out a hail in the forlorn hope of their voices being recognised; then there came the distressed wail of a woman who had got separated from her party, and with the laughter of a group who had got reunited after many wanderings. There was no lack of sounds, but no shape of men or women could be distinguished in the mist, until Wesley and his party were among them. And even then the dimly seen shapes had suggestions of the unreal about them. Some would loom larger than human for a few moments, and then vanish suddenly. Others seemed grotesquely transfigured in the mist as if they had enwrapped themselves in a disguise of sackcloth. They seemed not to be flesh and blood, but only shadows. Coming suddenly upon them, one felt that one had wandered to another world—a region of restless shadows.

How was any man to preach to such a congregation? How was a preacher to put force into his words, when failing to see the people before him?

When Wesley found himself on the eminence where he had spoken to the multitude on his first coming to Cornwall, and several times later, he looked down in front of him and saw nothing except the fine gauze of the grey clouds that rolled around the rocks. He stood there feeling that he was the only living being in a world that was strange to him. He thought of the poet who had gone to the place of departed spirits, and realised his awful isolation. How was he to speak words of life to this spectral host?

He had never known what fear was even when he had faced a maddened crowd bent upon the most strenuous opposition to his preaching: he had simply paid no attention to them, and the sound of his voice had held them back from him and their opposition had become parched. But now he felt something akin to terror. Who was he that he should make this attempt to do what no man had ever done before?

He fell upon his knees and prayed aloud. Light—Light—Light—that was the subject of his prayer. He was there with the people who had walked in darkness—he had walked with them, and now they were in the presence of the One who had said "Let there be Light." He prayed that the Light of the World might appear to them at that time—the Light that shineth through the darkness that comprehended Him not. He prayed for light to understand the Light, as the poet had done out of the darkness of his blindness.

"So much the rather, Thou Celestial Light,
Shine inward and the mind through her way
Irradiate; there plant eyes; all mists from thence
Purge and disperse that I may see and tell
Of things invisible to mortal sight."

And after his prayer with closed eyes, he began to preach into that void, and his text was of the Light also. His voice sounded strange to his own ears.

It seemed to him that he was standing in front of a wall, trying to make his words pass through it. This was at first; a moment later he felt that he was speaking to a denser multitude than he had ever addressed before. The mist was before his eyes as a sea of sad grey faces waiting, earnest and anxious for the message of gladness which he was bringing them. His voice rose to heights of impressiveness that it had never reached before. It clove a passage through the mist and fell upon the ears of the multitude whom he could not see, stirring them as they had never been stirred before, while he gave them his message of the Light.

For close upon half an hour he spoke of the Light. He repeated the word—again and again he repeated it, and every time that it came from his lips it had the effect of a lightning flash. This was at first. He spoke in flashes of lightning, uttered from the midst of the cloud of a night of dense blackness; and then he made a change. The storm that made fitful, fiercer illumination passed away, and after an interval the reiteration of the Light appeared again. But now it was the true Light—the light of dawn breaking over a sleeping world. It did not come in a flash to dazzle the eyes and then to make the darkness more dread; it moved gradually upward; there was a flutter as of a dove's wing over the distant hills, the tender feathers of the dawn floated through the air, and fell upon the Eastern Sea, quivering there; and even while one watched them wondering, out of the tremulous spaces of the sky a silver, silken thread was spread where the heaven and the waters met—it broadened and became a cincture of pearls, and then the thread that bound it broke, and the pearls were scattered, flying up to the sky and falling over all the waters in beautiful confusion; and before the world had quite awakened, the Day itself gave signs of hastening to gather up the pearls of Dawn. The Day's gold-sandalled feet were nigh—they were shining on the sea's brim, and lo! the East was bright with gold. Men cried, "Why do those feet tarry?" But even while they spoke, the wonder of the Morn had come upon them. Flinging down his mantle upon the mountains over which he had stepped—a drapery of translucent lawn, the splendour of the new light sprung upward, lifting hands of blessing over the world, and men looked and saw each other's faces, and knew that they were blest.

And the wonder that he spoke of had come to pass. While the preacher had been describing the breaking light, the light had come. All unnoticed, the mist had been dissolving, and when he had spoken his last words the sunlight was bathing the preacher and the multitude who hung upon his words. The wonder that he told them of had taken place, and there did not seem to them anything of wonder about it. Only when he made his pause did they look into each other's faces as men do when they have slept and the day has awakened them. Then with the sunlight about them, for them to drink great draughts that refreshed their souls, he spoke of the Light of the World—of the Dayspring from on High that had visited the world, and their souls were refreshed.

And not one word had he said of all that he had meant to say—not one word of the man whom he had come so far to reprove.

No one was conscious of the omission.

CHAPTER XVII

The day became sultry when the mist had cleared away, and by noon the heat was more oppressive than had been known all the Summer. Wesley was exhausted by the time he set out with Mr. Hartwell to return to the village. They needed no mariner's compass now to tell them the way.

They scarcely exchanged a word. They seemed to have forgotten the conditions under which they had gone forth in the early morning. A new world seemed to have been created since then—a world upon which the shadow of darkness could not fall for evermore.

They had gone straight to the cliffs, hoping for a breath of air from the sea to refresh them; but they were disappointed; the air was motionless and the reflection of the sunlight from the waves was dazzling in its brilliancy.

"I should have thought that the very weight of this heavy atmosphere would make the sea like glass," said Wesley, while they rested on the summit of the cliff. "And yet there are waves such as I have never seen on this part of the coast unless when something akin to a gale was blowing."

"I daresay there was a strong breeze blowing, though we did not feel it in the shelter of the hollow of the Tor," said his companion.

"True; it would require a strong wind to sweep away the mist so suddenly," said Wesley.

"Ah, sir," said the other, "I did not think of a wind in that connection. Was it the fingers of the wind, think you, that swept that thick veil aside, or was it the Hand that rent in twain the veil of the Temple?"

"I am reproached, brother," said Wesley. "Let us give thanks unto God. May He give us grace to think of all things as coming from Him—whether they take the form of a mist which obscures His purpose, or the darkness of a tempest on which He rides. I know myself wanting in faith at all times—in that faith without reserve which a child has in his father. I confess that for a moment in the morning I had the same thought as that which was expressed by the old man who joined us: I thought it possible that that fog which threatened to frustrate our walk had been sent by the Enemy. Should I have thought so if our work had been hindered in very truth? I dare not say no to that question. But now I know that it helped rather than obstructed, us."

"There can be no doubt about that," said Hartwell. "For myself, I say that I was never so deeply impressed in my life as at that moment when I found myself looking at you; you were speaking of the world awakening, and it seemed to me that I had been asleep—listening to the sound of your voice—the voice of a dream, and then I was full awake, I knew not how. I tell you, Mr. Wesley, I was not conscious of the change that was taking place—from darkness to light."

"Nor was I," said Wesley. "My eyes were closed fast while I was preaching. I had closed them to shut out that incongruous picture of obscurity, while I thought of the picture of the breaking of light; when I opened my eyes the picture that I had been striving to paint was before me. It was the Lord's doing."

While they remained resting on the cliff the officer of the Preventive men came upon them. He knew Hartwell, and had, when Wesley had been in the neighbourhood before, thanked him for the good influence his preaching had in checking the smuggling.

He now greeted them cordially and enquired if they had come from the village, adding that he hoped the fishing boats had not suffered from the effects of the tide.

"We left the port early in the morning, and in the face of the mist. What is the matter with the tide?" said Hartwell.

"You have not been on the beach? Why, 'tis a marvel, gentlemen," cried the officer. "The like has not been seen since I took up my appointment in this neighbourhood—a tide so high that the caves are flooded to the roof. List, sirs; you can hear naught of the usual boom of the waters when the pressed air forces them back."

They listened, but although there was the usual noise of the waves breaking along the coast, the boom from the caves which had been heard at intervals through the mist was now silent.

"As a rule 'tis at high tide that the sound is loudest," said Hartwell.

"That is so," said the officer. "The higher the water is, the more the air in the caves becomes pressed, and so the louder is the explosion. But this day the water has filled the caves to the roof, leaving no air in their depths to bellow. One of my men, on his patrol an hour ago, was overtaken by the tide at the foot of the cliffs at a place high above spring tide mark. He had to climb to safety. He did so only with difficulty. Had he been at Nitlisaye, nothing would have saved him."

"What, are Nithsaye sands flooded? Impossible," cried Hartwell.

"Flooded up to Tor, sir. I tell you the thing is a marvel!"

"All the more so, since there is no wind to add to the force of the tide," said Wesley.

"True, sir; there was a strong breeze in the early morning that swept the sea-mist over the shore; but there has not been a capful since," said the officer.

"But see the waves! Are they the effects of the early wind, think you, sir?" asked Wesley.

"Maybe; but if so, this also is past my experience of this coast, sir," replied the man. "But I allow that when I was sailing with Captain Hawke in the West Indies I knew of the waters of the Caribbean Sea being stirred up like this in the dead calm before a hurricane that sent us on our beam ends, and one of our squadron on to the Palisades Reef at Port Royal."

"Do you fear for a hurricane at this time?" asked Wesley.

"A gale, maybe; but no such hurricane as wrecks the island it swoops down on in the Leewards, sir. Oh, a hurricane in very deed! Our ship's cutter—a thirty-foot boat swung in on the iron davits—and lashed down to iron stanchions on the deck—was whisked adrift as if it had been an autumn leaf. I say it went five hundred fathom through the air and no man saw it fall. I saw a road twenty foot wide shorn through the dense forest for five miles as clean as with a scythe, as you go to Spanish Town—a round dozen of planters' houses and a stone church had once stood on that cutting. They were swept off, and not a stone of any one of them was ever found by mortal after. Oh, a hurricane, indeed! We need expect naught like that, by the mercy of Heaven, gentlemen; though I care not for the look of yon sun."

They glanced upwards. The sun had the aspect of being seen through a slight haze, which made it seem of a brazen red, large and with its orb all undefined. It looked more like the red fire of a huge lighted brazier than the round sun, and all around it there was the gleam as of moving flames.

"Looks unhealthy—is't not so?" said the officer.

"There is a haze in the air; but the heat is none the less," said Hartwell.

"I like it not, sirs. This aspect of the sun is part and parcel of some disturbance of nature that we would do well to be prepared for," said the officer, shaking his head ominously.

"A disturbance of nature? What mean you? Have you been hearing of the fishing-boats that have been hauled up on the stones at the port for the past two days? Have you taken serious account of the foolishness of a man who calls himself a prophet?" asked Hartwell.

The officer laughed.

"Oh, I have heard much talk of the Prophet Pritchard," he said. "But you surely do not reckon me as one of those poor wretches whom he has scared out of their lives by threatening them with the Day of Judgment to-morrow? Nay, sir; I placed my trust in a statement that begins with soundings, the direction of the wind and its force, the sail that is set, the last cast of the log, the bearings of certain landmarks, and the course that is being steered. My word for it, without such a preface, any statement is open to doubt."

"And have you received such a statement in regard to your 'disturbance of nature,' sir?"

"That I have, sirs. Our cutter was cruising about a league off shore two nights ago, light breeze from west-nor'-west, sail set; mainsail, foresail, jib, speed three knots. Hour, two bells in the morning, Master in charge on deck, watch, larboard—names if necessary. Reports, night sultry, cloudless since second dog watch, attention called to sounds as of discharge of great guns in nor'-nor'west. Lasted some minutes, not continuous; followed by noise as of a huge wave breaking, or the fall of a cataract in same quarter. Took in jib, mainsail haul, stand by to lower gaff. No further sounds reported, but sea suddenly got up, though no change of wind, force or direction, and till four bells cutter sailed through waves choppy as if half a gale had been blowing. After four bells gradual calm. Nothing further to report till eight bells, when cutter, tacking east-nor'east, all sail set, gunner's mate found in it a dead fish. Master reports quantity of dead fish floating around. Took five aboard—namely, hake two, rock codling one, turbot two, rock codling with tail damaged. That's a statement we can trust, Mr. Hartwell. Yesterday it was supplemented by accounts brought by my men of the coast patrol, of quantities of dead fish washed ashore in various directions. And now comes this marvellous tide. Sirs, have not I some grounds for touching upon such a subject as 'a great disturbance of nature'?"

"Ample, sir, ample," said Wesley. "Pray, does your West Indian experience justify you in coming to any conclusion in regard to these things?"

"I have heard of fish being killed by the action of a volcano beneath the sea," said the officer. "I have heard it said that all the Leeward Islands are volcanos, though only one was firing broadsides the year that I was with my Lord Hawke. 'Twas at Martinique which we took from the French.

Even before the island came in sight, our sails were black with dust and our decks were strewn with cinders. But when we drew nigh to the island and saw the outburst of molten rocks flying up to the very sky itself—sir, I say to you that when a man has seen such a sight as that, he is not disposed to shudder at all that a foolish fellow who has never sailed further than the Bristol Channel may prate about the Day of Judgment."

"And to your thinking, sir, an earthquake or some such convulsion of nature hath taken place at the bottom of our peaceful Channel?" said Wesley.

"In my thinking, sir, yes. But I would not say that the convulsion was at the bottom of the Channel; it may have been an hundred leagues in the Atlantic. And more is to come, sirs; take my word for it, more is to come. Look at yonder sun; 'tis more ominous than ever. I shall look out for volcano dust in the next rain, and advise the near-, est station east'ard to warn all the fishing craft to make snug, and be ready for the worst. I should not be surprised to find that the tide is still rising, and so I wish you good-morning, sirs."

He took off his hat and resumed his patrol of the coast.

"This is a day of surprises," said Wesley.

"The story of the fish is difficult to believe, in spite of the cocoon of particulars in which it is enclosed," said Hartwell. "The greatest marvel in a mariner's life seems to me to be his imagination and his readiness of resource when it comes to a question of memory. A volcano mountain in our Channel!"

"Do not condemn the master of the revenue cutter too hastily," said Wesley. "His story corresponds very nearly to that narrated to me yesterday by Polwhele."

"Is't possible? True, Polwhele was the only fisherman who went out to the reef three nights ago," said Hartwell. "And the strange sounds——"

"He heard them also—he thought that they came from a frigate discharging a broadside of carronades."

Hartwell was silent for some time. At last he said:

"I could wish that these mysterious happenings had come at some other time. Are you rested sufficiently in this place, sir? I am longing for a cool room, where I can think reasonably of all that I have seen and heard this day."

Wesley rose from the hollow where he had made his seat and walked slowly down the sloping path toward the village. But long before they had reached the place of his sojourning, he became aware of a scene of excitement in the distance. The double row of straggling cottages that constituted the village of Porthawn they had left in the morning standing far beyond the long and steep ridge of shingle, at the base of which the wrack of high water lay, was now close to the water's edge. The little wharf alongside of which the fishing boats were accustomed to lie had been hauled up practically to the very doors of the houses. Scores of men and women were engaged in the work of hauling them still higher, not by the machinery of the capstans—the capstans were apparently submerged—but by hawsers. The sound of the sailors' "Heave ho!" came to the ear of Wesley and his companion a few seconds after they had seen the bending to the haul of all the people who were clinging to the hawsers as flies upon a thread. The shore was dark with men running with gear-tackles with blocks, while others were labouring along under the weight of spars and masts that had been hastily outstepped.

Mr. Hartwell was speechless with astonishment.

"It is indeed a day of wonder!" exclaimed Wes—ley. "A high tide? Ay; but who could have believed such an one possible? Should we not be doing well to lend them a hand in their emergency?"

He had to repeat his question before the other had recovered from his astonishment sufficiently to be able to reply.

"Such a tide! Such a tide!" he muttered. "What can it mean? Lend a hand? Surely—surely! Every hand is needed there."

They were compelled to make a detour landward in order to reach the people, for the ordinary path was submerged, but they were soon in the midst of them, and bending to the work of hauling, until the drops fell from their faces, when the heavy boat at which they laboured had her bowsprit well-nigh touching the window of the nearest house.

Wesley dropped upon a stone and wiped his forehead, and some of the fishermen did the same, while others were loosing the tackles, in readiness to bind them on the next boat.

Nelly Polwhele was kneeling beside him in an instant—her hair had become unfastened, for she had been working hard with the other women, and fell in strands down her back and over her shoulders. Her face was wet.

"Oh, sir; this is overmuch for you!" she cried.

"Far overmuch, after all that you have gone through since morning. Pray rest you in the shade. There is a jug of cider cooling in a pail of water fresh drawn from the well. You need refreshment."

He took her hand, smiling.

"I am refreshed, dear child," he said. "I am refreshed."

"Why should that man he treated different from the rest of us; tell me that," came the voice of a man who had been watching them, and now stepped hastily forward. Wesley saw that he was Bennet. "Is there a man in the village who doesn't know that 'tis John Wesley and his friends that has brought this visitation upon us? Was there anything like to this before he came with his new-fangled preaching, drawing down the wrath of Heaven upon such as have been fool enough to join themselves to him? Was there any of you, men, that thought with trembling limbs and sweating foreheads of the Day of Judgment until John Wesley turned the head of that poor man Pritchard, and made him blaspheme, wrapping himself in Wesley's old cloak, and telling you that'twas the mantle of a prophet?"

Nelly had risen to her feet before his last sentence was spoken, but a moment afterward she sprang to one side with a cry. She was just in time to avoid the charge of a man on horseback. But Bennet was not so fortunate. Before he was aware of a danger threatening him, he felt himself carried off his feet, a strong man's hands grasping the collars of his coat, so that he was swung off the ground, dangling and scrawling like a puppet. Down the horse sprang into the water, until it was surging over the pommel of the saddle. Then, and only then, the rider loosed his hold, reining in his horse with one hand, while with the other he flung the man headforemost a couple of yards farther into the waves.

"The hound! the hound! that will cool his ardour!" cried Parson Rodney, backing his horse out of the water, while the people above him roared, and the man, coming to the surface like a grampus, struck out for a part of the beach most remote from the place where he had stood.

Wesley was on his feet and had already taken a step or two down the shingle, for Parson Rodney's attitude suggested his intention of preventing the man from landing, when he saw that Bennet was a strong swimmer, and that he, too, had put the same interpretation upon the rider's raising of his hunting crop.

"Sir," said Parson Rodney, bringing his dripping horse beside him, "I grieve that any man in my parish should put such an affront upon you. Only so gross a wretch would have done so. Thank Heaven the fellow is not of Porthawn, nor a Cornishman at all. If you do not think that my simple rebuke has been enough, I am a Justice, and I promise you to send him to gaol for a month at next session."

"Sir, you mean well by me," said Wesley; "but I would not that any human being were placed in jeopardy of his life on my account."

"That is because you are overgentle, sir," said Rodney. "Thank Heaven, my fault does not lie in that direction."

"Repent, repent, repent, while there is yet time In a few more hours Time shall be no more!" came a loud voice from the high ground above the bank.

Everyone turned and saw there the figure of Richard Pritchard, standing barehead in the scorching sun, his hands upraised and his hair unkept; and a curious nondescript garment made apparently of several sacks hastily stitched together, with no sleeves. On his feet he wore what looked like sandals—he had cut down the upper portion of his shoes, so that only the sole remained, and these were fastened to his feet by crossed pieces of tape. He was the prophet of the Bible illustration. It was plain that he had studied some such print and that he had determined that nothing should be lacking in his garb to make complete the part which he meant to play.

Up again went the long, lean, bare arms, and again came the voice:

"O men of Porthawn, now is the accepted time, now is the Day of Salvation. Yet a few more hours and Time shall be no more. Repent, repent, repent, while ye have time."

CHAPTER XVIII

There could be no doubt about the depth of the impression which the strange figure and his unusual garb produced upon the people.

There he stood on the high ground above the houses, the man who had prophesied the end of the world, while beneath them tumbled the waves of a sea where they had never seen sea water before! The occurrence, being so far outside their experience, had about it the elements of the supernatural—the aspect of a miracle. Was this the beginning of the end of all? they asked themselves. To these people the daily ebb and flow of the tide, ever going on before their eyes, was the type of a regularity that nothing could change; and never once had the water been forced, even under the influence of the strongest gale from the southwest, beyond the summit of the shingle-heap—never until this day.

It was an awful thing that had come to pass before their eyes, and while their brains were reeling beneath its contemplation there rang out that voice of warning. The man who had predicted an event that was not more supernatural in their eyes than the one which had come to their very feet, was there bidding them repent.

But strange to say, there was not one among the-people assembled there who made a motion—who cried out in conviction of the need for repentance, as hundreds had done upon every occasion of John. Wesley's preaching, although it had contained no element that, in the judgment of an ordinary person, would appeal with such force to the emotions of the villagers as did the scene in which Pritchard now played a part.

They remained unmoved—outwardly, however shrinking with terror some of them may have been. Perhaps it was they felt that the man had, in a way, threatened them physically, and they had a feeling that it would show cowardice on their part to betray their fear, or it may have been that, as was nearly always the case when a prophet came to a people, they attributed to the bearer of the messages of the ill the responsibility for the ills which he foretold—however it may have been, the people only glanced up at the weird figure, and made no move.

But the appearance of the man at that moment had the effect of making them forget the scene which had immediately preceded the sound of his voice. No one looked to see whether or not John Bennet had scrambled back to the beach or had gone under the waters.

"It is coming—it is coming: I hear the sound of the hoofs of the pale Horse—yonder is the red Horse spoken of by the prophet at Patmos, but the White Horse is champing his bit. I hear the clink of the steel, and Death is his rider. He cometh with fire and brimstone. Repent—repent—repent!"

"I have a mind to make the fellow repent of his impudence," said Parson Rodney. "The effrontery of the man trying to make me play a part in his quackery. I wonder how this water-finder would find the water if I were to give him the ducking I gave to the other?"

"You would do wrong, sir," said Wesley. "But I feel that I have no need to tell you so: your own good judgment tells you that yonder man is to be pitied rather than punished."

"Oh, if that is the view you take of the matter, you may be sure that I'll not interfere," cried the other. "The fellow may quack or croak or crow for aught I care.'Twas for you I was having thought. But I've no intention of constituting my humble self your champion. I wish you well; and I know that if the world gets over the strain of Monday, we shall never see you in our neighbourhood again."

"The elements shall melt with fervent heat. You feel it—you feel it on your faces to-day: I foretold it, and I was sent to cry unto all that have ears to hear, 'Repent—repent—repent'!"

"The fellow has got no better manner than a real prophet," laughed Parson Rodney; but there was not much merriment in his laughter. "I have a mind to have him brought before me as an incorrigible rogue and vagabond," he continued. "An hour or twain in the stocks would make him think more civilly of the world. If he becomes bold enough to be offensive to you, Mr. Wesley, give me a hint of it, and I'll promise you that I'll make him see more fire and brimstone than he ever did in one of his ecstatic moods; and so good-day to you, sir."

He put his horse to a trot, and returned the salutes of the men who were standing idly watching Pritchard in his very real sackcloth.

But he had scarcely ridden past them when he turned his horse and called out:

"Wherefore are you idle, good men? Do you mean to forsake the remainder of your smacks?"

A few of the fishermen looked at one another; they shook their heads; one of them wiped his forehead.

"'Twill be all the same after Monday, Parson," said that man.

"You parboiled lobster-grabber!" cried the Parson. "Do you mean to say that you have the effrontery to believe that addle-pate up there rather than a clergyman of the Church of England? Look at him. He's not a man.'Tis a poor cut torn from, a child's picture Bible that he is! Do you believe that the world would come to an end without your properly ordained clergyman giving you a hint of it? Go on with your work, if you are men. Repent? Ay, you'll all repent when 'tis too late, if you fail to haul up your boats so that their backs get not broken on that ridge. If you feel that you must repent, do it hauling. And when you've done your work, come up to the Rectory and cool your throats with a jug of cider, cool from the cellar, mind."

"There shall be no more sea," came the voice of the man on the mound; it was growing appreciably hoarser.

"No more sea?" shouted the parson. "That's an unlucky shot of yours, my addle-pated prophet; 'tis too much sea that we be suffering from just here."

Wesley had not reseated himself. He put his hand upon Mr. Hartwell's arm. The latter understood what he meant. They walked away together.

"I have seen nothing sadder for years," said Wesley. "I have been asking myself if I am to blame. Should not I have been more careful in regard to that unhappy man?"

"If blame is to be attached to any it is to be attached to those who recommended the man to you, and I was among them," said Hartwell. "I recall how you were not disposed to accept him into our fellowship by reason of his work with the divining rod; but we persuaded you against your judgment. I, for one, shall never forgive myself."

"Was ever aught so saddening as that travesty of the most solemn event?" said Wesley. "And then the spectacle of that well-meaning but ill-balanced man! A clergyman of our Church—you saw him turn to mock the wretch? He made a jest upon the line that has never failed to send a thrill through me: 'No more sea.' Shocking—shocking!... Friend, I came hither with the full intention of administering a rebuke to Pritchard—of openly letting it be understood that we discountenanced him. But I did not do so to-day, and I am glad of it. However vain the man may be—however injuriously he may affect our aims among the people—I am still glad that I was turned away from saying a word against him."

Mr. Hartwell was too practical a man to look at the matter in the same light. But he said nothing further about Pritchard. When he spoke, which he did after a time, it was about Bennet. He asked Wesley if he could guess why the man had spoken to him so bitterly. Why should the man bear him a grudge?

Wesley mentioned that Bennet had come upon him when he was walking with Polwhele's daughter from the Mill.

"Ah, that is the form of his madness—he becomes insanely jealous of anyone whom he sees near that girl. But one might have thought that you at least—oh, absurdity could go no further! But a jealous man is a madman; he is incapable of looking at even the most ordinary incident except through green glasses. You are opposed to clergymen marrying, are you not, Mr. Wesley? I have heard of your book— —-"

"I wrote as I was persuaded at that time," replied Wesley. "But more recently—I am not confident that I did not make a mistake in my conclusions. I am not sure that it is good for a man to be alone; and a clergyman, of all men, needs the sympathy—the sweet and humane companionship of a woman."

"True, sir; but if a clergymen makes a mistake in his choice of a wife, there can be no question that his influence declines; and so many men of your cloth wreck themselves on the quicksand of matrimony. I daresay that 'tis your own experience of this that keeps you single, though you may have modified your original views on the subject. Strange, is't not, that we should find ourselves discussing such a point at this time? But this seems to be the season of strange things, and 'twould be the greatest marvel of all if we ourselves were not affected. Is it the terrible heat, think you, that has touched the heads of those two men?"

"I scarce know what I should think," said Wesley. "The case of Pritchard is the more remarkable. Only now it occurred to me that there may be a strange affinity between the abnormal in nature and the mind of such a man as he.'Twould be idle to contend that he has not been able as a rule to say where water is to be found on sinking a shaft; I have heard several persons testify to his skill in this particular—if it may be called skill. Does not his possession of this power then suggest that he may be so constituted that his senses may be susceptible of certain vague suggestions which emanate from the earth, just as some people catch ague—I have known of such in Georgia—when in the neighbourhood of a swamp, while others remain quite unaffected in health?"

"That is going too far for me, sir," said Hartwell. "I do not need to resort to anything more difficult to understand than vanity to enable me to understand how Pritchard has changed. The fellow's head has been turned—that's all."

"That explanation doth not wholly satisfy me," said Wesley. "I think that we have at least some proof that he was sensible of something abnormal in Nature, and this sensibility acting upon his brain disposed him to take a distorted view of the thing. His instinct in this matter may have been accurate; but his head was weak. He receives an impression of something strange, and forthwith he begins to talk of the Day of Judgment, and his foolish vanity induces him to think of himself as a prophet. The Preventive officer thinks that there hath been an earthquake. Now there can, I think, be no doubt that Pritchard was sensible of its coming; Pol-whele told you yesterday that he had predicted an earthquake in the sea, although it seemed that his illiteracy was accountable for this: and now there comes this remarkable tide—the highest tide that the memory of man has known."

"You have plainly been giving the case of Pritchard much of your attention," said Hartwell; "but I pray you to recall his account of the vision which he said came to him when he fell into that trance. 'Twas just the opposite to a high tide—'twas such an ebbing of the water as left bare the carcase of the East Indiaman that went ashore on the Dog's Teeth reef forty years ago."

"True; but to my way of thinking it matters not whether 'twas a prodigious ebb or a prodigious flow that he talked of so long as he was feeling the impression of the unusual—of the extraordinary. Mind you, I am only throwing out a hint of a matter that may become, if approached in a proper spirit, a worthy subject for sober philosophical thought. God forbid that I should take it upon me to say at this moment that the power shown by that man is from the Enemy of mankind, albeit I have at times found myself thinking that it could come from no other source."

"You are too lenient, I fear, Mr. Wesley. For myself, I believe simply that the man's head has been turned. Is't not certain that a devil enters into such men as are mad, and have we not proof that witches and warlocks have sometimes the perverted gift of prophecy, through the power of their master, the Old Devil?"

"I cannot gainsay it, my brother, and it is because of this you say, that I am greatly perplexed."

They had been walking very slowly, for the heat of the day seemed to have increased, and they were both greatly exhausted. Before entering Mr. Hartwell's house they stood for a short time looking seaward. There, as before, the waves danced under the rays of the sun, although not a breath of air stirred between the sea and the sky. The canopy of the heaven was blue, but it suggested the blue of hard steel rather than that of the transparent sapphire or that of the soft mass of a bed of forget-me-nots, or of the canopy of clematis which clambered over the porch.

The sun that glared down from the supreme height was like to no other sun they had ever seen. The haze on its disc, to which the Preventive officer had drawn their attention an hour earlier, had been slowly growing in the meantime, until now it was equal to four diameters of the orb itself, and it was so permeated with the rays that it seemed part of the sun itself. There that mighty furnace seethed with intolerable fire, and so singular was the haze that one, glancing for a moment upward with hand on forehead, seemed to see the huge tongues of flame that burst forth now and again as they do beneath a copper cauldron on the furnace of the artificer.

But this was not all, for at a considerable distance from the molten mass, which had the sun for its core, there was a wide ring apparently of fire. Though dull as copper for the most part, yet at times there was a glow as of living and not merely reflected flame, at parts of the brazen circle, and flashes seemed to go from the sun to this cincture, conveying the impression of an enormous shield, having the sun as the central boss of shining brass, on which fiery darts were striking, flying off again to the brass binding of the targe.

"Another marvel!" said Wesley; "but I have seen the dike more than once before. Once 'twas on the Atlantic, and the master of our ship, who was a mariner of experience, told me that that outer circle was due to the sun shining through particles of moisture. Hold up a candle in the mist and you have the same thing."

"I myself have seen it more than once; 'tis not a marvel, though it has appeared on a day of marvels," said Hartwell; and forthwith they entered the house.

They were both greatly exhausted, the fact being that before setting out for the preaching in the early morning they had taken no more than a glass of milk and a piece of bread, and during the seven hours that had elapsed they had tasted nothing, though the day had been a most exhausting one.

In a very few minutes the cold dinner, with the salad, which had been in readiness for their return, found them grateful; and after partaking of it Wesley retired to his room.

He threw himself upon a couch that stood under the window; a group of trees, though birch and not very bosky, grew so close to the window that they had made something of a shade to the room since morning, so that it was the coolest in the house. It was probably this sense of coolness that refreshed him so far as to place him within the power of sleep. He had thought it impossible when he entered the house that he should be able to find such a relief, exhausted as he had been. But now he had scarcely put his head on the pillow before he was asleep.

Several hours had passed before he opened his eyes again. He was conscious that a great change of some sort, that he could not at once define, had taken place. The room was in shadow where before it had been lighted by flecks of sunshine, but this was not the change which appealed to him with striking force; nor was it the sense of being refreshed, of which he was now aware. There was a curious silence in the world—the change had something to do with the silence. He felt as he had done in the parlour of Ruthallion Mill when he had been talking to the miller and the machinery had suddenly stopped for the breakfast hour. That was his half-awakened thought.

The next moment he was fully awake, and he knew what had happened: when he had fallen asleep the sound of the waves had been in his ears without cessation, and now the sea was silent.

He thought that he had never before been in such a silence. It seemed strange, mysterious, full of awful suggestions. It seemed to his vivid imagination that the world, which a short time before had been full of life, had suddenly swooned away. The hush was the hush of death. The silence was the silence of the tomb. "'Tis thus," he thought, "that a man awakens after death—in a place of awful silences."

And then he felt as if all the men in the world had been cut off in a moment, leaving him the only man alive.

It continued unbroken while he lay there. It became a nightmare silence—an awful palpable thing like a Sphinx—a blank dumbness—a benumbing of all Nature—a sealing-up of all the world as in the hard bondage of an everlasting Winter.

He sprang from his couch unable to endure the silence any longer. He went to the window and looked out, expecting to see the flat unruffled surface of the channel, where the numberless waves had lately been, sparkling with intolerable, brilliance, and every wave sending its voice into the air to join the myriad-voiced chorus that the sea made.

He looked out and started back; then he drew up the blind and stared out in amazement, for where the sea had been there was now no sea.

He threw open the window and looked out. Far away in the utter distance he saw what seemed like a band of glittering crimson on the horizon. Looking further round and to the west he saw that the sun was more than halfway down the slope of the heavens in that quarter and it was of the darkest crimson in colour—large, but no longer fiery.

Then there came a murmur to his ears—the murmur of a multitude of people; and above this sound came a hoarse, monotonous voice, crying:

"I heard one say to me: 'There shall be no sea—there shall be no more sea'; and the sun shall be turned into darkness and the moon into blood, before the great and terrible Day of the Lord. Repent—repent—repent!"

Far away he could see the figure of the man. He stood on the summit of the cliff beyond the path, and, facing the sinking sun, he was crimson from head to foot. Seen at such a distance and in that light he looked an imposing figure—a figure that appealed to the imagination, and not lacking in those elements which for ages have been associated with the appearance of a fearless prophet uplifting a lean right arm and crying "Thus saith the Lord." Wesley listened and heard his cry:

"There shall be no more sea! Repent—repent—repent!"

"There shall be no more sea! Repent—Repent—Repent!"

CHAPTER XIX

What think you now, sir?" Hartwell asked of Wesley when the latter had descended the stairs and entered the little parlour of the house.

"I am too greatly amazed to think," replied Wesley. "But since you put thinking into my head, I would ask you if you think it unnatural that a great ebb should follow an unusually high tide?"

It was plain that Hartwell was greatly perturbed.

"Unnatural? Why, has not everything that has happened for the past three days been unnatural?" he cried. "Sir, I am, I thank God, a level-headed man. I have seen some strange things in my life, both in the mines and when seafaring; I thought that naught could happen to startle me, but I confess that this last—I tell you, sir, that I feel now as if I were in the midst of a dream. My voice sounds strange to myself; it seems to come from someone apart from me—nay, rather from myself, but outside myself."

"'Tis the effect of the heat, dear friend," said Wesley. "You should have slept as I did."

"I did sleep, sir; what I have been asking myself is 'Am I yet awake?' I have had dreams before like to this one—dreams of watching the sea and other established things that convey to us all ideas of permanence and regularity, melting away before my very eyes—one dread vision showed me Greta Cliff crumbling away like a child's mound built on the sand—crumbling away into the sea, and then the sea began to ebb and soon was on the horizon. Now, I have been asking myself if I am in the midst of that same dream again. Can it be possible? Can it be possible?"

He clapped his hand to his forehead and hastened to the window, whence he looked out. Almost immediately he returned to Wesley, saying:

"I pray you to inform me, sir, if this is the truth or a dream—is it really the case that the sea has ebbed so that there is naught left of it?"

"You are awake, my brother," said Wesley, "and 'tis true that the sea hath ebbed strangely; but from the upper windows 'tis possible to see a broad band of it in the distance. I beseech of you to lie down on your bed and compose yourself. This day has tried you greatly."

The other stared at him for a few moments and then walked slowly away, muttering:

"A mystery—a mystery! Oh, the notion of Dick Pritchard being a true prophet! Was it of such stuff as this the old prophets were made? God forgive me if I erred in thinking him one of the vain fellows. Mr. Wesley's judgment was not at fault; he came hither to preach against him; but not a word did he utter of upbraiding or reproof."

Wesley saw that the man was quite overcome. Up to this moment he had shown himself to be possessed of a rational mind, and one that was not easily put off its balance. He had only a few hours before been discussing Pritchard in a sober and unemotional spirit; but this last mystery had been too much for him: the disappearance of the sea, which had lately climbed up to the doors of Porthawn, had unhinged him and thrown him off his balance. If the phenomenon had occurred at any other time—under any less trying conditions of weather—he might have been able to observe it with equanimity; but the day had been, as Wesley said, a trying one. The intense heat was of itself prostrating, and demoralising even to Wesley himself, and he had schooled himself to be unaffected by any conditions of weather.

Suddenly Hartwell turned toward his visitor, saying:

"And if the man was entrusted to predict the falling away of the sea, is there anyone that will say that the remainder of his prophecy will not be fulfilled?"

"I entreat of you, brother, to forbear asking yourself any further questions until you have had a few hours' sleep," said Wesley.

"What signifies a sleep now if before this time to-morrow the end of all things shall have come?" Hartwell cried almost fiercely. "Nay, sir, I shall wait with the confidence of a Christian; I shall not be found as were the foolish virgins—asleep and with unlighted lamps. There will be no slumber for me. I shall watch and pray."

"Let us pray together, my brother," said Wesley, laying his hand on the man's shoulder affectionately. He perceived that he was not in a mood to be reasoned with.

It was at this moment that the door was opened and there entered the room the miller and Jake 'Pullsford.

Wesley welcomed their coming; he had hopes that they would succeed in persuading his host to retire; but before they had been in the room for more than a few minutes Hartwell had well-nigh become himself again.

The newcomers were not greatly affected by anything that had happened. They were only regretful that the mist of the morning had prevented them from reaching the Red Tor in time for the preaching. They had started together, but had stopped upon the way to help a party of their friends who were in search of still another party, and when the strayed ones had been found they all had thought it prudent to remain at a farm where they had dined.

"On our way hither we met with one who had been to the preaching," said Jake. "He told us something of what we had missed."

"Were you disappointed to learn that no reference had been made to the very matter that brought me back to you?" asked Wesley.

Jake did not answer immediately. It was apparent that he had his own views on this matter, and that he had been expounding them to his companion on their walk from the farm to the coast.

"Mr. Wesley, 'tis plain to me that the skill at divination shown by that man comes from below, not from above," he said. "And do you suppose that our enemies will take back any of the foul things they have said about our allying ourselves with sorcery when they hear of the wonderful things that are now happening?"

"Brother," said Wesley, "if the principles of the Truth which we have been teaching are indeed true, they will survive such calumnies—nay, they will take the firmer hold upon all who have heard us by reason of such calumnies. The gold of the Truth has oft been tried by the fire of calumny and proved itself to be precious."

"You saw the man play-acting in his sackcloth?" said the carrier.

Wesley shook his head sadly.

"'Twas deplorable!" he said. "And yet I dare not even now speak against him—no, not a word."

"What, sir, you do not believe that he is a sorcerer and a soothsayer?" cried Jake.

"I have not satisfied myself that he is either," replied Wesley. "More than once since I saw how much evil was following on his predictions I have felt sure that he was an agent of our Arch-enemy, but later I have not felt quite so confident in my judgment. No, friend, I shall not judge him. He is in the hands of God."

"And I agree with Mr. Wesley," said the miller.

Jake Pullsford, with his hands clasped behind him and his head craned forward, was about to speak, when Hal Holmes entered the room. He was excited.

"Have you seen it?" he cried before he had greeted anyone. "Have you seen it—the vision of his trance at the Mill—the tide sliding away as it hath never done before within the memory of man?—the discovery of the bare hollow basin of the sea? Have you been within sight of the Dog's Teeth?"

"We—Mr. Hartwell and I—have not been out of doors for six hours; but we are going now," said Wesley. "We have seen some of the wonders that have happened; we would fain witness all."

"Oh, sir," said the blacksmith, "this one is the first that I have seen, and seeing it has made me think that we were too hasty in condemning poor Dick Pritchard. We need your guidance, sir. Do you hold that a man may have the gift of prophecy in this Dispensation, without being a sorcerer, and the agent of the Fiend?"

"Alas! 'tis not I that can be your guide in such a matter," said Wesley. "You must join with me in seeking for guidance from above. Let us go forth and see what is this new wonder."

"'Tis the vision of his trance—I saw it with these eyes as I passed along the high ground above the Dog's Teeth Reef—the reef was well-nigh bare and naked," said Hal. "Who is there of us that could tell what the bottom of the sea looked like? We knew what the simple slopes of the beach were—the spaces where the tide was wont to ebb and flow over are known to all; but who before since the world began saw those secret hidden deeps where the lobsters lurk and crabs half the size of a man's body—I saw them with these eyes a while agone—and the little runnels—a thousand of them, I believe, racing through channels in the slime as if they were afraid to be left behind when the sea was ebbing out of sight—and the sun turned all into the colour of blood! What does it all mean, Mr. Wesley—I do not mean the man's trance-dream, but the thing itself that hath come to pass?"

"We shall go forth and be witnesses of all," said Wesley.

He was not excited; but this could not be said of his companions; they betrayed their emotions in various ways. Mr. Hartwell and the miller were silent and apparently stolid; but the carrier and the smith talked.

Very few minutes sufficed to bring them to the summit of the cliff that commanded a full view seaward. At high tide the waves just reached the base of these cliffs, and the furthest ebb only left bare about a hundred feet of sand and shingle, with large smooth pebbles in ridges beyond the groins of the out-jutting rocks. But now it was a very different picture from that of the ordinary ebb that stretched away to the horizon under the eyes of our watchers.

The sandy breadth, with its many little ribs made by the waves, sloped into a line of sparse sea weed, tangled tufts of green and brown, and some long and wiry, and others flat with large and leathery bosses, like the studs of a shield. But beyond this space the rocks of the sea-bed began to show, There they were in serrated rows—rocks that had never before been seen by human eyes. Some lay in long sharp ridges, with here and there a peak of a miniature mountain, and beyond these lines of ridges there was a broad tableland, elevated in places and containing huge hollow basins brimming over with water, out of which every now and again a huge fish leaped, only to find itself struggling among the thick weeds. Further away still there was a great breadth of ooze, and then peak beyond peak of rocks, to which huge, grotesque weeds were clinging, having the semblance of snakes coiled round one another and dying in that close embrace.

Looking over these strange spaces was like having a bird's-eye view of an unexplored country of mountains and tablelands and valleys intersected by innumerable streams. The whole breadth of sea-bed was veined with little streams hurrying away after the lost sea, and all the air was filled with the prattling and chattering that went on through these channels.

And soon one became aware of a strange motion of struggling life among the forests of sea weed. At first it seemed no more than a quivering among the giant growths; but soon one saw the snake's head and the narrow shoulders of a big conger eel, from five to seven feet long, pushed through the jungle of ooze, to be followed by the wriggling body; there were congers by the hundred, and the hard-dying dog-fishes by the score, flapping and forcing their way from stream to stream. Stranded dying fish of all sorts made constant movements where they lay, and whole breadths of the sea-bed were alive with hurrying, scurrying crabs and lobsters and cray-fish. Some of these were of enormous size, patriarchs of the deep that had lurked for ages far out of reach of the fisherman's hook, and had mangled many a creel.

The weirdness of this unparalleled picture was immeasurably increased by its colouring, for over all there was spread what had the effect of a delicate crimson gauze. The whole of the sea-bed was crimson, for it was still dripping wet, and glistening with reflections of the red western sky. At the same time the great heat of the evening was sucking the moisture out of the spongy sea weeds, and there it remained in the form of a faint steam permeated with the crimson light.

And through all that broad space under the eyes of the watchers on the cliff there was no sign of a human being. They might have been the explorers of stout Cortez who stared at the Pacific from that peak in Darien. It was not until they had gone in silence for a quarter of a mile along the cliff path that they saw where the people of the village had assembled. The shore to the westward came into view and they saw that a crowd was there. The sound of the voices of the crowd came to their ears, and above it the hard, high monotone like that of a town crier uttering the words that Wesley had heard while yet in his room:

"There shall be no more sea. Repent—repent—repent."

Once more they stood and looked down over the part of the coast that had just been disclosed—the eastern horn of Greta Bay, but no familiar landmark was to be seen; on the contrary, it seemed to them that they were looking down upon a new and curious region. The line of cliffs was familiar to their eyes, but what was that curious raised spine—that long sharp ridge stretching outwards for more than a mile on the glistening shore?

And what was that strange object—that huge bulk lying with one end tilted into the air on one shoulder of that sharp ridge?

All at once Wesley had a curious feeling that he had seen all that before. The sight of that mighty bulk and the knowledge that it was the heavy ribbed framework of a large ship seemed familiar. But when or how had he seen it?

It was not until Hartwell spoke that he understood how this impression had come to him.

"You see it—there—there—just as he described it to us when he awoke from his trance?" said Hartwell.

And there indeed it was—the fabric of the East Indiaman that had been wrecked years before on the Dog's Teeth Reef, and there was the Dog's Teeth Reef laid bare for the first time within the memory of man!

It was the skeleton of a great ship. The outer timbers had almost wholly disappeared—after every gale for years before some portion of the wreckage had come ashore and had been picked up by the villagers; but the enormous framework to which the timbers of the hull had been bolted had withstood the action of the waves, for the ship had sunk into a cradle of rock that held her firmly year after year. There it lay like the skeleton of some tremendous monster of the awful depths of the sea—the Kraken—a survival of the creatures that lived before the Flood. The three stumps of masts which stood up eight or ten feet above the line of bulwarks gave a curious suggestion to a creature's deformed legs, up in the air while it lay stranded on its curved back.

And the crimson sunset shot through the huge ribs of this thing and spread their distorted shadows sprawling over the sands at the base of the reef and upon the faces of the people who stood looking up at this wonder.

"There it is—just as he saw it in his trance!" said Hal Holmes. "He saw it and related it to us afterward. What are we to say to all this, Mr. Wesley? All that he predicted so far has come to pass. Are we safe in saying that yonder sun will be setting over a blazing world to-morrow?"

"I do not dare to say anything," replied Wesley. "I have already offered my opinion to Mr. Hartwell, which is that there may be a kind of sympathy between the man and the earth, by whose aid he has been able to discover the whereabouts of a spring in the past and to predict these marvels of tides."

"That is a diviner's skill derived from the demons that we know inhabit the inside of the earth," cried Jake Pullsford. "He has ever had communication with these unclean things."

"That works so far as the tides are concerned," said the smith. "It stands to reason that the demons of the nether world must know all about the ebb and flow; but how did he foresee the laying bare of yonder secret?" He pointed to the body; of the wreck.

"Was it not the same demons that dragged the ship to destruction on the reef, and is't not within their province to know all that happens below the surface of the sea?" said the carrier.

"Doubtless," said the smith. "But I find it hard to think of so moderately foolish a fellow as Dick Pritchard being hand in glove with a fiend of any sort, and not profiting more by the traffic—as to his secular circumstances, I should say."

"And I find it hard to think of him as urging men to repent, if he be an ally of the Evil One," said Hartwell.

"This is not a case in which the wisdom of man can show itself to be other than foolishness," said Wesley. "But I am now moved to speak to the people who have come hither to see the wonder. Let us hasten onward to the highest ground. My heart is full."

He went on with his friends to a short spur of the cliff about twenty feet above the shingle where groups of men and women were straying; most of them had been down to the wreck and nearly all were engaged in discussing its marvellous appearance. Some of the elder men were recalling for the benefit of the younger the circumstances of the loss of the great East Indiaman, and the affluence that had come to a good many houses in the Port, when the cargo began to be washed ashore before the arrival of the Preventive men and the soldiery from Falmouth.

But while the larger proportion of the people were engaged in discussing, without any sense of awe, the two abnormal tides and the story of the wreck, there were numbers who were clearly terror-stricken at the marvels and at the prospect of the morrow. A few women were clinging together and moaning without cessation, a girl or two wept aloud, a few shrieked hysterically, and one began to laugh and gibber, pointing monkey hands in the direction of the wreck. But further on half a dozen young men and maidens were engaged in a boisterous and an almost shocking game preserved in Cornwall and some parts of Wales through the ages that had elapsed since it was practised by a by-gone race of semi-savages. They went through it now in the most abandoned and barbaric way, dancing like Bacchanalians in a ring, with shouts and wild laughter.

John Wesley, who knew what it was to be human, had no difficulty in perceiving that these wretched people were endeavouring in such excesses to conceal the terror they felt, and he was not surprised to find a number of intoxicated men clinging together and singing wildly in the broad moorland space that lay on the landward side of the cliffs.

"This is the work of Pritchard the water-finder, and will you say that 'tis not of the Devil?" cried Jake Pullsford.

"Poor wretches! Oh, my poor brothers and sisters!" cried Wesley. "Our aim should be to soothe them, not to denounce them. Never have they been subjected to such a strain as that which has been put upon them. I can understand their excesses. 'Let us eat and drink, for to-morrow we die'—that is the cry which comes from all hearts that have not been regenerated.'Tis the cry of the old Paganism which once ruled the world, before the sweet calm of Christianity brought men from earth to heaven. I will speak to them."

He had reached the high ground with his friends. There was a sudden spur on the range of low cliffs just where the people were most numerous. They had come from all quarters to witness the wonders of this lurid eve, and, as was the case at Wesley's preaching, everyone was asking of everyone else how so large an assembly could be brought together in a neighbourhood that was certainly not densely populated. On each side of him and on the beach below there were crowds, and on every face the crimson of the sinking sun flamed. He went out to the furthest point of the cliff-spur and stood there silent, with uplifted arms.

In a moment the whisper spread:

"Mr. Wesley has come—Mr. Wesley is preaching!"

There was the sound of many feet trampling down the pebbles of the beach. The people flowed toward him like a great wave slowly moving over that place now forsaken by the waves. The young men and maidens who had been engaged in that fierce wild dance among the wiry herbage flocked toward him, their faces shining from their exertions, and stood catching their breath. The old men who had been staring stolidly through the great ribs of the hulk, slouched through the ooze and stood sideways beneath him, their hands, like the gnarled joints of a thorn, scooped behind their ears lest they should lose a word. The women, with disordered hair, tears on their faces, the terror of anticipation in their eyes, waited on the ground, some kneeling, others seated in various postures.

Then there came a deep hush.

He stood there, a solitary figure, black against the crimson background of the western sky, his arms still upraised. It might have been a statue carved out of dark marble that stood on the spur of the cliff.

And then he began to speak.

His hands were still uplifted in the attitude of benediction; and the words that came from him were the words of the Benediction.

"The Peace of God which passeth all understanding."

The Peace of God—that was the message which he delivered to that agitated multitude, and it fell upon their ears, soothing all who heard and banishing their fears. He gave them the message of the Father to His children—a message of love, of tenderness—a promise of protection, of infinite pity, of a compassion that knew no limits—outliving the life of the world, knowing no change through all ages, the only thing that suffered no change—a compassion which, being eternal, would outlive Time itself—a compassion which brought with it every blessing that man could know—nay, more—more than man could think of; a compassion that brought with it the supreme blessing that could come to man—the Peace of God which passeth all understanding!

He never travelled outside this message of Divine Peace, although he spoke for a full hour.

And while he spoke the meaning of that message fell upon the multitude who listened. They felt that Peace of which he spoke falling gently upon them as cold dew at the close of a day of intolerable heat. They realised what it meant to them. The Peace descended upon them, and they were sensible of its presence. The dread that had been hanging over them all the day was swept away as the morning mist had been dispersed. The apprehension of the Judgment was lost in the consciousness of a Divine Love surrounding them. They seemed to have passed from an atmosphere of foetid vapours into that of a meadow in the Spring time. They drank deep draughts of its sweetness and were refreshed.

When he had begun to speak the sun was not far from setting in the depths of a crimson sky, and before he had spoken for half an hour the immense red disc, magnified by the vapours in the air, was touching the horizon. With its disappearance the colour spread higher up the sky and drifted round to the north, gradually changing to the darkest purple. Even then it was quite possible for the people to see one another's features distinctly in the twilight, but half an hour later the figure of the preacher was but faintly seen through the dimness that had fallen over the coast. The twilight had been almost tropical in its brevity, and the effect of the clear voice of many modulations coming out of the darkness was strange, and to the ears that heard it, mysterious. Just before it ceased there swept upon the faces of his listeners a cool breath of air. It came with a suddenness that was startling. During all the day there had not been a breath. The heat had seemed to be so solid, and now the movement of the air gave the impression of the passing of a mysterious Presence. It was as if the wings of a company of angels were winnowing the air, as they fled by, bringing with them the perfume of their Paradise for the refreshing of the people of the earth. Only for a few minutes that cool air was felt, but for that time it was as if the Peace of God had been made tangible.

When the preacher ended with the words with which he had begun, the silence was like a sigh.

The people were on their knees. There was no one that did not feel that God was very nigh to him.

And the preacher felt it most deeply of all. There was a silence of intense solemnity, before the voice was heard once more speaking to Heaven in prayer—in thanksgiving for the Peace that had come upon this world from above.

He knew how fully his prayer had been answered when he talked to the young men and maidens who had been among his hearers. The excitement of the evening had passed away from all of them. At the beginning of his preaching there had been the sound of weeping among them. At first it had been loud and passionate; but gradually it had subsided until at the setting of the sun the terror which had possessed them gave place to the peace of the twilight, and now there was not one of them that did not feel the soothing influence that comes only when the angel of the evening hovers with shadowy outspread wings over the world.

They all walked slowly to their homes; some belonged to Porthawn and others to the inland villages of the valley of the Lana, as far away as Ruthallion, and the light breeze that had been felt during the preaching became stronger and less intermittent now. It was cool and gracious beyond expression, and it brought with it to the ears of all who walked along the cliffs the soothing whisper of the distant sea. The joyous tidings came that the sea was returning, and it seemed that with that news came also the assurance that the cause for dread was over and past.

And all this time the preacher had made no allusion to the voice that had sounded along the shore in the early part of the evening predicting the overthrow of the world. All that he had done was to preach the coming of Peace.

"You may resume your journeying, Mr. Wesley, as soon as you please. May he not, friend Pullsford?" said Hartwell when he had returned to his house. "There is no need for us to keep Mr. Wesley among us when we know that he is anxious to resume his preaching further west. You never mentioned the man's name, sir, and yet you have done all—nay, far more than we thought it possible for you to accomplish."

"There is no need for me to tarry longer," replied Wesley. "But I pray of you, my dear friends, not to think that I do not recognise the need there was for me to return to you with all speed. I perceived the great danger that threatened us through Pritchard, and I was glad that you sent for me. I hope you agree with me in believing that that danger is no longer imminent."

"I scarce know how it happened," said Hartwell; "but yesterday I had a feeling that unless you preached a direct and distinct rebuke to Pritchard, the work which you began here last month would suffer disaster, and yet albeit you did no more than preach the Word as you might at any time, making no reference to the things that have happened around us, I feel at the present moment that your position is, by the Grace of God, more promising of good than it has ever been."

"Ay," said Jake Pullsford. "But I am not so sure that the vanity of that man should not have been crushed. There is no telling to what length he may not go after all that has happened. The people should ha' been warned against him, and his sorceries exposed.".

"Think you, Jake, that the best way to destroy the vanity of such as he would be by taking notice of what he said and magnifying it into a menace?" said Hartwell. "Believe me, my friend, that Mr. Wesley's way is the true one. Dick Pritchard's vanity got its hugest filip when he heard that Mr. Wesley had come back to preach against him. It will receive its greatest humiliation when he learns that Mr. Wesley made no remark that showed he knew aught of him and his prophecies."

"He will take full credit to himself for what has happened—of that you may be sure," said Jake, shaking his head. "Ay, and for what did not happen," he continued as an afterthought. "Be certain that he will claim to have saved the world as Jonah saved the Ninevites. He will cling to Jonah to the end."

"I am glad that I came hither when you called for me, my brethren," said Wesley. "Let us look at the matter with eyes that look only at the final issue. I would fain banish from my mind every thought save one, and that is spiritual blessing of the people. If they have been soothed by my coming—if even the humblest of them has been led to feel something of what is meant by the words 'the Peace of God,' I give thanks to God for having called me back. I have no more to say."

And that was indeed the last word that was said at that time respecting Pritchard and his utterances. Wesley and his friends felt that, however deeply the people had been impressed by the natural phenomena which had followed hard on his predictions of disaster to the world, he would not now be a source of danger to the work which had been begun in Cornwall. Wesley had, by his preaching, showed that he would give no countenance to the man. Those who thought that it would be consistent with his methods and his Methodism to take advantage of the terror with which the minds of the people had become imbued, in order to bring them into the classes, that had already been formed, were surprised to find him doing his utmost to banish their fears. He had preached the Gospel of Peace, not of Vengeance, the Gospel of Love, not of Anger.

Awakening shortly after midnight, Wesley heard the sound of the washing of the waters on the pebbles at the base of the cliffs. There was no noise of breaking waves, only the soft, even lisp and lap of the last ripples that were crushed upon the pebbles—grateful and soothing to his ears.

Suddenly there came to him another sound—the monotone of the watchman calling out of the distance:

"Repent—repent—repent! The Day of the Lord is at hand. Who shall abide the Day of His Wrath? Repent—repent—repent!"

CHAPTER XX

The sunlight was in his room when he awoke. He had a sense of refreshment. A weight seemed lifted off his heart. He remembered how he had awakened the previous morning in the same bed with a feeling of perplexity. He had found it impossible to make up his mind as to the course he should pursue in regard to Pritchard. He had been fearful of being led to rebuke a man who might have been made the means of leading even one sinner to repentance. He asked himself if he differed as much from that man as the average churchman did from himself in his methods. He knew how grievous he regarded the rebukes which he had received from excellent clergymen who looked on his field preaching with the sternest disapproval; and who then was he that he should presume to rebuke a man who had been led by his zeal beyond what he, Wesley, thought to be the bounds of propriety?

He had felt great perplexity on awakening on that Sunday morning; but he had been given help to see his way clearly on that morning of mist, and now he felt greatly at ease. He had nothing to reproach himself with.

He recalled all the events of the day before—all that his eyes had seen— all that his ears had heard; and now that he had no further need to think about Pritchard, it was surprising how much he had to recall that had little to do with that man. He himself felt somewhat surprised that above all that had been said to him during the day the words that he should dwell longest upon were a few words that had fallen from Mr. Hartwell. He had hinted to Mr. Hartwell that John Bennet had acted so grossly in regard to him, through a mad jealousy; and Mr. Hartwell, hearing this, had lifted up his hands in amazement, and said:

"Absurdity could go no further!"

When Hartwell said those words Wesley had not quite grasped their full import; his attention had been too fully occupied with the further extravagance which he had witnessed on the part of Pritchard. But now that his mind was at ease he recalled the words, and he had sufficient selfpossession to ask himself if his host considered that the absurdity was to be found in Bennet's fancying that he, Wesley, was his rival. If so, was the absurdity to be found in the fancy that such a young woman could think of him, Wesley, in the light of a lover; or that he should think of the young woman as a possible wife?

He could not deny that the thought of Nelly Polwhele as his constant companion had more than once come to him when he was oppressed with a sense of his loneliness; and he knew that when he had got Mr. Hartwell's letter calling him back to Porthawn he had felt that it might be that there was what some men called Fate, but what he preferred to call the Hand of God, in this matter. Was he being led back to have an opportunity of seeing her again, and of learning truly if the regard which he thought he felt for her was to become the love that sanctified the marriage of a man with a woman?

Well, he had returned to her, and he had seen (as he fancied) her face alight with the happiness of his return. For an hour he had thought of the gracious possibility of being able to witness such an expression upon her face any time that he came from a distant preaching. The thought was a delight to him. Home—coming home! He had no home; and surely, he felt, the longing for a home and a face to welcome him at the door was the most natural—the most commendable—that a man could have. And surely such a longing was not inconsistent with his devotion to the work which he believed it was laid upon him to do while his life lasted.

He had seen her and talked with her for a short time, and felt refreshed by being under the influence of her freshness. But then he had been forced to banish her from his mind in order to give all his attention to the grave matter which had brought him back to this place. He had walked by her side through the mist the next day, and never once had he allowed the thought of her to turn his eyes away from the purpose which had called him forth into the mist of the morning. He thought of her thoughtfulness in the matter of the mariner's compass with gratitude. That was all. His heart was full of his work; there was no room in it for anything else.

But now while he sat up in the early sunshine that streamed through his window he felt himself free to think of her; and the more he thought of her the more he wondered how he could ever have been led to believe what he had already embodied in a book respecting the advantages of celibacy for the clergy. A clergyman should not only have a knowledge of God; a knowledge of man was essential to success in his calling; and a knowledge of man meant a wide sympathy with men, and this he now felt could only be acquired by one who had a home of his own. The influence of the home and its associations could not but be the greatest to which a man was subject. The ties that bind a man to his home were those which bind him to his fellow-men. The *res angusta domi*, which some foolish persons regarded as detrimental to a man's best work, were, he was now convinced, the very incidents which enabled him to do good work, for they enabled him to sympathise with his fellows.

Theologians do not, any more than other people, feel grateful to those who have shown them to be in the wrong; but Wesley had nothing but the kindliest feelings for Nelly Polwhele for having unwittingly led him to see that the train of reasoning which he had pursued in his book was founded upon an assumption which was in itself the result of an immature and impersonal experience of any form of life except the Academic, and surely such a question as he had discussed should be looked at from every other standpoint than the Academic.

Most certainly he was now led to think of the question from very different standpoints. He allowed his thoughts to wander to the girl herself. He thought of her quite apart from all womankind. He had never met any young woman who seemed to possess all the charms which endear a woman to a man. She was bright as a young woman should be, she was thoughtful for the needs of all who were about her, she had shown herself ready to submit to the guidance of one who was older and more experienced than herself. He could not forget how she had promised him never again to enter the playhouse which had so fascinated her. Oh, she was the most gracious creature that lived—the sweetest, the tenderest, and surely she must prove the most devoted!

So his imagination carried him away; and then suddenly he found himself face to face with that phrase of Mr. Hartwell's *"Absurdity could go no further."*

And then, of course, he began to repeat all the questions which he had put to himself when he had started on his investigations into the matter. Once more he said:

"Where lies the source of all absurdities?"

And equally as a matter of course he was once again led in the direction that his thoughts had taken before until he found himself enquiring if the world held another so sweet and gracious and sympathetic.

It was not until he was led once more to his starting-point that he began to feel as he had never done before for those of his fellow-men who allowed themselves to be carried away by dwelling on the simplest of the questions which engrossed him.

"'Tis a repetition of yesterday morning," said he. "We set out pleasantly enough in the mist, and after an hour's profitless wandering we found ourselves at the point whence we had started—ay, and the young woman was waiting for us there in person."

Was that morning's wandering to be typical of his life? he wondered. Was he to be ever straying along a misty coast, and evermore to be finding himself at the point whence he had started, with Nelly Polwhele waiting for him there?

An absurdity, was it?

Well, perhaps—but, after all, should he not be doing well in asking Mr. Hartwell what had been in his mind when he had made use of that phrase?

Mr. Hartwell had undoubtedly something in his mind, and he was a level-headed man who had accustomed himself to look at matters without prejudice and to pronounce an opinion based on his common sense. It might be that he could see some grave reason why he, Wesley, should dismiss that young woman forever from his thoughts—forever from his heart.

But, of course, he reserved to himself the right to consider all that Mr. Hartwell might say on this matter, and—if he thought it right—to exercise his privilege of veto in regard to his conclusions. He was not prepared to accept the judgment of Mr. Hartwell without reserve.

Following this line of thought, he quickly saw that whatever Mr. Hartwell might have to say, and however his conclusions might be put aside, it would be necessary for him, Wesley, to acquaint all those men who were associated with him in his work with his intention of marrying a certain young woman. There were his associates in London, in Bristol, in Bath, and above all there was his brother Charles. Would they be disposed to think that such a union would be to the advantage or to the detriment of the work to which they were all devoted?

The moment he thought of his brother he knew what he might expect. Up to that moment it had really never occurred to him that any objection that might not reasonably be overruled, could be offered to his marrying Nelly Polwhele. But so soon as he asked himself what his brother would say when made aware of his intention, he perceived how it was conceivable that his other friends might agree with Mr. Hartwell. For himself, he had become impressed from the first with some of those qualities on the part of Nelly Polwhele which, he was convinced, made her worthy of being loved by the most fastidious of men. He had long ago forgotten that she was only the daughter of a fisherman, and that she owed her refinement of speech to the patronage of the Squire's daughters whose maid she had been.

But what would his brother say when informed that it was his desire to marry a young woman who had been a lady's maid? Would not his brother be right to assume that such a union would be detrimental to the progress of the work in which they were engaged? Had they not often talked together deploring how so many of their brethren in the Church had brought contempt upon their order through their loss of self-respect in marrying whomsoever their dissolute patrons had ordered them to marry? What respect could anyone have for his lordship's chaplain who was content to sit at the side table at meals and in an emergency discharge the duties of a butler, and comply without hesitation to his lordship's command to marry her ladyship's maid, or, indeed, any one of the servants whom it was found desirable to have married?

The thing was done every day; that was what made it so deplorable, he and his brother had agreed; and in consequence day by day the influence of the clergy was declining. Was he then prepared to jeopardise the work to which he had set his hand by such a union as he was contemplating?

He sprang to his feet from where he had been sitting by the window.

"Heaven forgive me for having so base a thought!" he cried. "Heaven forgive me for being so base as to class the one whom I love with such creatures as his patron orders his chaplain to marry! She is a good and innocent child, and if she will come to me I shall feel honoured. I shall prove to all the world that a woman, though lowly-born, may yet be a true helpmeet for such as I. She will aid me in my labours, not impede them. I know now that I love her. I know now that she will be a blessing to me. I love her, and I pray that I may ever love her truly and honestly."

It was characteristic of the man that the very thought of opposition should strengthen him. An hour earlier he had been unable to assure himself that his feeling for her was love, but now he felt assured on this point: he loved her, and he had never before loved a woman. She was the first fruit of his mission to Cornwall. She had professed the faith to which even he himself had failed to attain until he had been preaching for years. Bound to her by a tie that was the most sacred that could exist between a man and a woman, his most earnest hope was to hold her to him by another bond whose strands were interwoven with a sympathy that was human as well as divine. His mind was made up at last.

He was early at breakfast with his host, but he did not now think it necessary to ask Mr. Hartwell what he had meant by his reference to the absurdity of John Bennet's jealousy. The morning gave promise of a day of brilliant sunshine and warmth. There was nothing sinister in the aspect of the sun, such as had been noted on the previous day.

"Ah, sir," said Hartwell, "you came hither with a blessing to us all, and you will leave with a sense of having accomplished by the exercise of your own judgment far more than we looked for at such a time. The boats have put out to the fishing ground once more, and the dread that seemed overhanging our poor friends sank with the setting sun last evening."

"Not to me be the praise—not to me," said Wesley, bowing his head in all humility. After a few moments he raised his head quite suddenly, saying:

"You have referred to my judgment, dear friend; I wonder if you think that in many matters my judgment is worthy to be depended on?"

"Indeed, sir, I know of no man in the world whose judgment in all reasonable matters I would accept sooner than yours," replied Hartwell. "Why, Mr. Wesley, who save you would have foreseen a way of avoiding the trouble which threatened us by such means as you adopted? Were not we all looking for you to administer a rebuke to the man whose vanity carried him so far away from what we held to be discreet? Was there one of us who foresaw that the right way of treating him was to let him alone?"

"I dare not say that 'twas my own judgment that guided me," said Wesley. "But—I hope, friend Hartwell, that I shall never be led to take any step that will jeopardise your good opinion of my capacity to judge what course is the right one to pursue in certain circumstances."

"Believe me, Mr. Wesley, after the events of yesterday I shall not hesitate to say that you were in the right and I in the wrong, should I ever be disposed to differ from you on a matter of moment. But I cannot think such a difference possible to arrive," said Hartwell.

"Differences in judgment are always possible among good friends," said Wesley.

"I should like to have a long talk with you some day, Mr. Wesley, on the subject of the influence of such powers as are at the command of Pritchard," said Hartwell. "Are they the result of sorcery or are they a gift from above? I have been thinking a great deal about that trance of his which we witnessed. How was it possible for him to foresee the place and the form of that wreck, think you?"

"Howsoever his powers be derived," replied Wesley, "the lesson that we must learn from his case is that we cannot be too careful in choosing our associates. For myself, I have already said that I mistrusted him from the first, as I should any man practising with a divining rod."

"We should have done so, too, sir, only that we had become so accustomed to his water-finding, it seemed as natural to send for him when sinking a well as it was to send for the mason to build the wall round it when the water was found."

This was all that they said at that time touching the remarkable incidents of the week. Both of them seemed to regard the case of Pritchard as closed, although they were only in the morning of the day which the man had named in his prediction. Mr. Hartwell even assumed that his guest would be anxious to set out on his return to the west before noon, and he was gratified when Wesley asked for leave to stay on for a day or two yet.

Wesley spent an hour or two over his correspondence, and all the time the matter which he had at heart caused him to lay down his pen and lie back in his chair, thinking, not upon the subject of his letters, but upon the question of approaching Nelly Polwhele, and upon the question of the letter which he would have to write to his brother when he had seen the girl; for whether she accepted him or refused him, he felt that it was his duty to inform his brother as to what had occurred.

The result of his meditations was as might have been expected. When a man who is no longer young gives himself up to consider the advisability of offering marriage to a young woman with whom he has not been in communication for much more than a month, he usually procrastinates in regard to the deciding scene. Wesley felt that perhaps he had been too hasty in coming to the conclusion that a marriage with Nelly would bring happiness to them both. Only a few hours had elapsed since he had, as he thought, made up his mind that he loved her. Should he not refrain from acting on such an impulse? What would be the consequence if he were to ask the young woman to be his wife and find out after a time that he should not have been so sure of himself? Surely so serious a step as he was contemplating should be taken with the utmost deliberation. He should put himself to the test. Although he had been looking forward to seeing the girl this day, he would not see her until the next day—nay, he was not confident that he might not perceive that his duty lay in waiting for several days before approaching her with his offer.

That was why, when he left the house to take the air, he walked, not in the direction of the village, where he should run the best chance of meeting her, but toward the cliffs, which were usually deserted on week days, except by the Squire's grooms, who exercised the horses in their charge upon the fine dry sand that formed a large plateau between the pathway and the struggling trees on the outskirts of Court Park.

He went musing along the cliff way, thinking of the contrast between this day and the previous one—of the contrast between those sparkling waves that tossed over each other in lazy play, and the slime and ooze which had lain bare and horrid with their suggestions of destruction and disaster. It was a day such as one could scarcely have dreamt of following so sinister a sunset as he had watched from this place. It was a day that made him glad that he had not uttered a harsh word in rebuke of the man who had troubled him—indeed he felt most kindly disposed toward Pritchard; he was certainly ready to forgive him for having been the means of bringing him, Wesley, back to this neighbourhood.

He wondered if it had not been for Pritchard, would he have returned to Ruthallion and Porthawn. Was the affection for Nelly, of which he had become conscious during his journeying in the west, strong enough at that time to carry him back to Porthawn, or had it matured only since he had come back to her?

He wondered and mused, strolling along the path above the blue Cornish waters. Once as he stood for a while, his eyes looked longingly in the direction of the little port. He felt impatient for more than a few moments—impatient that he should be so strict a disciplinarian in regard to himself. It was with a sigh he turned away from where the roofs of the nearest houses could just be seen, and resumed his stroll with unfaltering feet. He had made his resolution and he would keep to it.

But he did not get further than that little dip in the cliffs where he had once slept and awakened to find Nelly Polwhele standing beside him. The spot had a pleasant memory for him. He remembered how he had been weary when he had lain down there, and how he had risen up refreshed.

Surely he must have loved her even then, he thought. What, was it possible that he had known her but a few days at that time? His recollection of her coming to him was as that of someone to whom he had been attached for years.

He smiled as he recalled the tale which he had once read of the magician Merlin, who had woven a bed of rushes for the wife of King Mark, on which she had but to lie and forthwith she saw whomsoever she wished to see. Well, here he was in the land of King Mark of Cornwall, and there was the place where he had made his bed....

He had been contemplating the comfortable hollow between the rocks, thinking his thoughts, and he did not raise his eyes for some time. When he did he saw Nelly Polwhele coming toward him, not along the cliffs, but across the breadth of moorland beyond which was the Court Park.

CHAPTER XXI

Tis by a happy chance we are brought together," Wesley said while he held her hand.

But Nelly Polwhele made haste to assure him that it was not by chance; she had been with her young ladies at the Court, she said, and from the high ground she had spied upon him on his walk, and had come to him through the sparse hedges of the park.

He smiled at the eagerness with which she disclaimed such an ally as chance. He had not had a wide experience of young women, but he had a shrewd conviction that the greater number of them would have hastened to acknowledge his suggestion rather than to repudiate it. She was innocent as a child.

"By whatsoever means we have been brought together, I for one must think it happy," said he. "Do you go to your friends yonder every day?"

"Oh, no, sir; but they have charged me to keep them apprised of your preaching since you came hither, and thus I went to them yesterday—that was after your morning preaching—and to-day to tell them of the evening. Oh, sir, surely there was never aught seen that would compare with the happenings of yester eve! Even while I was rehearsing all to my young ladies, I had a feeling that I was telling them what I had seen in a dream. I do think that I have had a dream more than once that was strangely like all that was before my eyes—a dream of drowning and seeing in a blood-red light the mysteries of the sea-bed."

"A strange thing, my child! I have never seen a stranger thing," said he. "It did not seem a wonder to me that the people were so agitated."

"They thought for sure that the end of the world had come," said she. "And indeed I began to feel that poor Dick Pritchard had truly been sent to warn us."

"And how was his warning taken by many?" he cried. "Worse than the Ninevites were some that I saw here. Of sackcloth there was none on their limbs—of repentance their hearts were empty. I hope, my child, that you did not see some of those whom I saw here—dancing—wild—pagan creatures of the woods! And their dance! Pagan of the worst—an orgy of the festival of the god Saturn—an abomination of Baal and Ashtoreth. And I asked myself, 'Is it possible that this is how a solemn warning of the coming of the Dreadful Day is taken by a Christian people? But you, I trust, did not see all that came before me?"

"I saw enough to tell me that Dick Pritchard's warning was not a true one," said she. "I was by the side of father below the wreck. He had seen the *Gloriana* founder, and if Dick Pritchard had prophesied that he should live to look upon her hull again after all the years that have passed, he would have laughed. And some of the men about us on the beach that had never been bare of water since the world began, talked like wild men. If the world was to come to an end before another set o' sun they meant to enjoy themselves—the Court—they whispered of breaking through the doors of the Court and feasting for once and for the last time. One of them—David Cairns is his name—cried that at the Day of Judgment all men were equal, and he would head any band of fellows that had the spirit to face the Squire and call for the key of the cellar. Father called him a rascal, and he replied. Some were taking his part and some the part of father, when the cry went up that Mr. Wesley was nigh. That was the end of the strife, sir."

"To tell me this last is to gladden my heart, my dear," he said, and again he clasped one of her hands in both his own. But he did not do so with the fervour of a lover. His heart was not dwelling upon the purpose which he had been considering since he rose; the girl's story had absorbed him. "And now I hope that the good folk will settle down once more into their quiet and useful lives," he added.

"They will not be able to do so for some time," she replied, shaking her head. "All who were present at the preaching have already returned to their work; the boats that were idle for nearly a week put out to the fishing early in the morning; but there are other places where Dick Pritchard's talk was heard, and the miners made it a good excuse for quitting their labour."

"Poor fellows, I shall go among them at once; I may be able to help them," said he.

"Do you think of going at once, sir?" she asked quickly.

"At once," he replied. "Is there any time to lose?"

"And you will not return to us?"

Her question came from her like a sigh—a sigh that is quickly followed by a sob.

He looked at her for some moments in silence. He had a thought that if he meant to tell her that he loved her, no better opportunity would be likely to present itself. This was for the first few moments, but his thought was succeeded by a feeling that it would be a cruelty to shock this innocent prattling child with his confession. She could not be otherwise than shocked were he to tell her that his desire was to get her promise to marry him. He would adhere to his resolution to wait. He would make another opportunity if one did not present itself.

"If it be God's will I shall return to you," he said. "Yes, in good time—in good time."

"I am glad," she said. "It was because I feared that you would go away at once and not return for a long time, that I made haste to reach you when I saw you from the park."

"Why should my going affect you, Nelly?" he asked. He wondered if the opportunity which he looked for, and yet was anxious to avoid, would persist in remaining within easy reach.

"I—I—the truth is, sir, that I wanted—I wished greatly—to ask your advice," she said.

"I hope you will not find that you have placed overmuch dependence on me," he said. "Let us walk along the cliffs and talk as we pursue our way. Not that I am anxious to leave this spot; it bears many happy memories to me. Was it not here that you came to me on the day of my first preaching, ministering to my needs?"

She flushed with pleasure.

"Ah, sir, all I did was as nothing compared with the good that has come to me through your words. I want your counsel now. I am sometimes very unhappy by reason of my doubts in a matter on which I should have none."

"Tell me your grief, dear child. Have you not lived long enough to know that when the cause of your unhappiness is told to another, it weighs less heavily upon you? What, did you not confide in me on Saturday? 'Tis surely not from that man Bennet that——"

"Oh, no; he has naught to do with my trouble. It comes not from anyone but my own self—from my own foolishness. You have a mind to hear the story of a young girl's foolishness who knew not her own mind—her own heart?"

"If you are quite sure that you wish to tell it to me. You may be assured that you will find in me a sympathetic listener. Is there any one of us that can say in truth that his heart or hers has not some time been guilty of foolishness?"

"The worst of it is that what seems foolishness to-day had the semblance of wisdom yesterday. And who can say that to-morrow we may not go back to our former judgment?"

"That is the knowledge that has come to you from experience."

"It has come to me as the conclusion of my story—such as it is."

"'Tis sad to think that our best teacher must ever be experience, my child. But if you have learned your lesson you should be accounted fortunate. There are many to whom experience comes only to be neglected as a teacher."

"I have had experience—a little—and all that it has taught to me is to doubt. A year ago I thought that I loved a man. To-day I do not know whether I love him or not—that is all my poor story, sir." She had not spoken fluently, but faltering—with many pauses—a little wistfully, and with her eyes on the ground.

He stopped suddenly in his walk. He, too, had his eyes upon the ground. He had not at once appreciated the meaning of her words, but after a pause it came upon him: he understood what her words meant to him.

She loved another man.

How could he ever have been so foolish as to take it for granted that such a girl as this was free? That was the first thought which came to him. Had he not heard how every youth for miles round was in love with Nelly Polwhele? Had he not seen how one man had almost lost his senses through love of her?

And yet he had been considering the question of asking her to marry him, assuming from the very first that she must be free! He had been considering the matter from his own standpoint, asking himself if it would not be well to be assured of his own love for her before telling her that he loved her; and he came to the conclusion that he should not use any undue haste in saying the words which, he hoped, would link their lives together. He had never entertained a suspicion that he might be too late in making his appeal to her. It was now a shock to him to learn, as he had just done, that he was too late.

It took him some time to recover himself.

"I ask your pardon," he said. "I pray you to tell to me again what you have just said."

"I am well-nigh ashamed to say it, sir," she murmured. "I am afraid that you may not think well of me. You may think that there is some truth in the reports that have gone abroad concerning me."

"Reports? I have heard no reports. I thought of you as I found you, and all that I thought was good. I think nothing of you now that is not good. Ah, child, you do not know what direction my thoughts of you have taken! Alas! alas!"

It was her turn to be startled. He saw the effect that his words had produced upon her, and he hastened to modify it. He felt that he had no right to say a word that might even in a distant way suggest to her the direction in which his thoughts—his hopes—had so recently led him.

"Have I spoken too vaguely?" he said. "Surely not. But I will be explicit, and assure you that from the day we walked through the valley side by side I have thought of you as a good daughter—an honest and innocent young woman, thoughtful for the well-being of others."

"Oh, sir, your good opinion is everything to me!" she cried. "But I feel that I have not earned it truly. Vanity has ever been my besetting sin—vanity and fickleness. That is what I have to confess to you now before asking you for your counsel."

"God forbid that I should give you any counsel except that which I am assured must be for your own well-being. Tell me all that is weighing on your heart, and, God helping me, I will try to help you."

"I will tell you all—all that I may tell, sir.'Tis not much to tell, but it means a great deal to me. In brief, Mr. Wesley, a year ago I was at Bristol and there I met a worthy man, who asked me to marry him. I felt then that I loved him so truly that 'twould be impossible for me ever to change, and so I gave him my promise. I had been ofttimes wooed before, but because my heart had never been touched the neighbours all affirmed that I had the hardest heart of any maiden in the Port. They may have been right; but, hard-hearted or not, I believed that I loved this man, and he sailed away satisfied that I would be true to him."

"He was a mariner?"

"He is a master-mariner, and his ship is a fine one. He sailed for the China Seas, and 'twas agreed that after his long voyage we were to be married. That was, I say, a year ago, and I was true to him until— —"

She faltered, she gave him a look that he could not understand, and then all at once she flung herself down on the short coarse herbage of the cliff, and began to weep with her hands over her face.

He strove to soothe her and comfort her, saying she had done naught that was wrong—giving her assurance that a way out of her trouble would surely he found if she told him all.

"What am I to do?" she cried, looking piteously up to him, with shining eyes. "What am I to do? I got a letter from him only on Friday last, telling me that he had had a prosperous voyage and had just brought his ship safe to Bristol, and that he meant to come to me without delay. Oh, sir, 'twas only when I had that letter I found that I no longer loved him as I did a year ago."

"Is there another man who has come between you, my child?" he asked gravely.

"Heaven help me! there is another," she faltered.

"And does he know that you are bound by a promise to someone else? If so, believe me he is a dishonourable man, and you must dismiss him from your thought," said he.

She shook her head.

"He is an honourable man; he has never said a word of love to me. He knows nothing of my love for him. He at least is innocent."

"If he be indeed a true man he would, I know, give you counsel which I now offer to you; even if he suspected—and I cannot but think that if he sees you and converses with you, no matter how seldom, he will suspect—the sad truth—he will leave your side and so give you an opportunity of forgetting him, and all may be well."

"Ah, sir, think you that 'tis so easy to forget?"

"Have you not just given me an instance of it, Nelly? But no; I will not think that you have forgotten the one to whom you gave your promise. I like rather to believe that that affection remains unchanged in your heart, although it be for a while obscured. You remember how we lost our way on the morning of yesterday? We saw not the shore; 'twas wreathed in mist; but the solid shore was here all the same, and in another hour a break dispersed the mist which up till then had been much more real to us than the shore; the mist once gone, we saw the substance where we had seen the shadow. Ah, dear child, how often is not the shadow of a love taken for the true—the abiding love itself. Now dry your tears and tell me when you expect your true lover to come to you."

"He may arrive at any time. He will come by the first vessel that leaves Bristol river. He must have left already. Oh, that sail out there may be carrying him hither—that sail— —"

She stopped suddenly, and made a shade of one hand over her eyes while she gazed seaward. After a few moments of gazing she sprang to her feet crying:

"The boats—you see them out there? What has happened that they are flying for the shore? They should not be returning until the night."

He looked out across the waters and saw the whole fleet of fishing smacks making for the shore with every sail spread.

"Perhaps the boats have been unusually successful and thus have no need to tarry on the fishing ground," he suggested.

She remained with her eyes upon them for a long time. A look of bewilderment was upon her face while she cried:

"Oh, everything is topsy-turvy in these days! Never have I known all the boats to make for the shore in such fashion, unless a great storm was to windward, and yet now——"

She caught him by the arm suddenly after she had remained peering out to the southern horizon with an arched hand over her eyes.

"Look there—there!" she said in a whisper, pointing seaward. "Tell me what you see there. I misdoubt my own eyes. Is there a line of white just under the sky?"

He followed the direction of her finger. For some moments he failed to see anything out of the common; the sea horizon was somewhat blurred—that was all. But suddenly there came a gleam as of the sun quivering upon a thin sword blade of white steel out there—it quivered as might a feather in the wind.

"'Tis a white wave," he said. "See, it has already widened. A great wave rolling shoreward."

"List, list," she whispered.

He put his hand behind his ear. There came through the air the hollow boom of distant thunder, or was it the breaking of a heavy sea upon a rocky coast? The sound of many waters came fitfully landward, and at the same moment a fierce gust of wind rushed over the water—they marked its footsteps—it was stamping with the hoofs of a war-horse on the surface of the deep as it charged down upon the coast.

Before the two persons on the cliff felt it on their faces, bending their bodies against its force, a wisp of mist had come over the sun. Far away there was a black cloud—small, but it looked to be dense as a cannon ball. She pointed it out, and these were her words:

"A cannon ball!—a cannon ball!"

The gust of wind had passed; they could hear the trees of the park complaining at first and then roaring, with the creaking of branches as it clove its way through them. Flocks of sea birds filled the air—all were flying inland. Their fitful cries came in all notes, from the plaintive whistle of the curlew and the hoarse shriek of the gull to the bass boom of a bittern.

Then the cannon ball cloud seemed to break into pieces in a flame of blue fire, more dazzling than any lightning that ever flashed from heaven to earth, and at the same instant the sun was blotted out, though no cloud had been seen approaching it; the pall seemed to have dropped over the disc, not to have crept up to it.

"A storm is on us," he said. "Whither can we fly for shelter?"

"The stones of Red Tor," she replied; "that is the nearest place. There is plenty of shelter among the stones."

"Come," he cried, "there is no moment to be lost. Never have I known a storm fall so quickly."

She was tarrying on the cliff brow watching the progress of the fishing boats.

"They will be in safety before disaster can overtake them," she said.

Then she turned to hasten inland with him; but a sound that seemed to wedge its way, so to speak, through the long low boom, with scarcely a quiver in it, of the distant thunder, made her look round.

She cried out, her finger pointing to a white splash under the very blackness of the cloud that now covered half the hollow of the sky dome with lead.

"Never have I seen the like save only once, while the great gale was upon us returning from Georgia," said he. "'Tis a waterspout."

It was a small spiral that came whirling along the surface of the water whence it had sprung, and it made a loud hissing sound, with the swish of broken water in it. It varied in height from three feet to twenty, until it had become a thick pillar of molten glass, with branching capitals that broke into flakes of sea-foam spinning into the drift. Its path through the sea was like the scythe-sweep of a hurricane on the shore. Its wake was churned up like white curd, and great waves fled from beneath its feet.

Wesley and his companion stood in astonishment, watching that wonder. Its course was not directly for the cliff where they were standing; but they saw that if it reached the shore it would do so a hundred yards or thereabouts to the westward.

They were not wrong. It reached the shore not farther away from them. It struck the sand where the sun had dried it, and in a moment it had scooped out a hollow eight or ten feet deep; then it whirled on to the shingle. They heard the noise as of the relapse of a great wave among the pebbles, sweeping them down beneath the scoop of its talons; only now it seemed as if the prow of a frigate had dashed into the ridge of pebbles and was pounding its way through them. It was a moving pillar of stones that struck furiously against the stones of the cliff—an avalanche in the air that thundered against the brow, breaking away a ton of rock, and turning it into an avalanche that slid down to the enormous gap made in the shingle. At the same instant there was the roar of a cataract as the whirling flood of the waterspout broke high in the air and dropped upon the land. It was as if a lake had fallen from the skies in a solid mass, carrying everything before it.

It was the girl who had grasped Wesley by the arm, forcing him to rush with her to the higher ground. Together they ran; but before they reached it they were wading and slipping and surging through a torrent that overflowed the cliff, and poured in the wave of a waterfall over the brink and thundered upon the rocks beneath.

They only paused to take breath when they reached the highest ledge of the irregular ground beyond the cliff pathway. There was a tangle of lightning in the air—it fell from a cloud that had black flowing fringes, like a horse's tail trailing behind it, and it was approaching the shore. They fled for the rocks of the Bed Tor.

If he had been alone he never would have reached the place. The air was black with rain, and he and his companion seemed to be rushing through a cloud that had the density of velvet. It was a blind flight; but this girl of the coast needed not the lightning torch that flared on every side of them to guide her. She held his arm, and he suffered himself to be led by her. She even knew where the sheltering rocks were to be found; they had not to search for them. At the back of the slight eminence that had formed his pulpit, half a dozen basalt boulders of unequal size lay tumbled together. Two of them were on end and three others lay over them, the remaining one lying diagonally across the arched entrance to what had the appearance of the ruin of a doorway four feet high. The high coarse herbage of the place, with here and there a bramble branch, was thick at this place, and if the girl and the companions of her childhood had not been accustomed to play their games here, calling the hollow between the stones their cave sometimes, their palace when it suited them, it would have escaped notice.

She bent her head and crept under the stones of the roof, and he followed her. They had a depth of scarcely three feet behind them, for the bank of the mound against which the stones lay sloped naturally outward, and the height was not more than four feet; but it was a shelter, although they had to kneel upon its hard floor. It was a shelter, and they had need of one just then. The cloud had burst over them just as they reached their hospitable cleft in the rocks, and the seventh plague of Egypt had fallen upon the rude amphitheatre of the Red Tor—it was hail mingled with fire; and when a pause came, as it did with a suddenness that was more appalling than the violence of the storm, the ninth plague was upon them. The darkness might have been felt. They could see nothing outside. They knew that only ten yards away there was another pile of rocks with a few stunted trees springing from their crevices; but they could not even see this landmark. Farther away, on a small plateau, was the celebrated rocking-stone of Red Tor; but it seemed to have been blotted out. They could hear the sound of the wind shrieking over the land, making many strange whistlings and moanings through the hollows among the stones—they could hear the sound of thousands of runnels down the banks, but they could see nothing.

In that awful black pause Wesley began to repeat the words of the eighteenth Psalm:

"The Lord is my rock, and my fortress, and my deliverer; my God, my strength, in whom I will trust; my buckler, and my high tower....

"In my distress I called upon the Lord, and cried unto my God: he heard my voice out of his temple, and my cry before him, even into his ears.

"Then the earth shook and trembled; the foundations also of the hills moved and were shaken, because he was wroth.

"There went up a smoke out of his nostrils, and fire out of his mouth devoured: coals were kindled by it.

"He bowed the heavens also, and came down: and darkness was under his feet.

"And he rode upon a cherub, and did fly: yea, he did fly upon the wings of the wind.

"He made darkness his secret place; his pavilion round about him were dark waters and thick clouds of the skies.

"At the brightness that was before him his thick clouds passed, hail stones and coals of fire.

"The Lord also thundered in the heavens, and the Highest gave his voice; hail stones and coals of fire.

"Yea, he sent out his arrows, and scattered them; and he shot out lightnings, and discomfited them.

"Then the channels of waters were seen, and the foundations of the world were discovered at thy rebuke, O Lord, at the blast of the breath of thy nostrils....

"For thou wilt light my candle: the Lord my God will enlighten my darkness."

Before he had come to the last stanza the battle of the elements had followed the brief truce.

The first flash was blinding, but before they had instinctively put their hands up to their eyes they had seen every twig of the skeleton trees outlined against the background of fire—they had seen the black bulk of the rocking-stone, and for the first time they noticed that it had the semblance of a huge hungry beast crouching for a leap. The thunder that followed seemed to set the world shaking with the sway of the rocking-stone when someone had put it in motion.

"Is it true?—is it, indeed, true?" cried the girl between the peals of thunder. He felt her hands tighten upon his arm.

"The Rock of Ages is true," he said; but the second peal swallowed up his words.

He heard her voice when the next flash made a cleft in the cloud:

"Is it true—the prophecy—has it come?"

Then he knew what was in her mind.

"Do you fear it?" he cried, and he turned his face toward her. Another flaring sword made its stroke from the heavens, and by its blaze he saw that she was smiling while she shook her head.

He knew that she had no fear. Across his own mind there had flashed the same thought that had come to her, taking the form of the question which she had put to him: "Is the prophecy about to be realised?"

He felt perfectly tranquil in the midst of the storm; and the reflection that the tranquillity of the girl was due to his influence was sweet to him. The roar of the thunder had become almost continuous. They seemed to be the centre of a circle of livid flame. The intervals of darkness were less numerous than those during which the whole sky became illuminated. The floods came rather more fitfully. For a few minutes at a time it seemed as if an ocean had been displaced, as if an ocean had been suspended above them, and then suddenly dropped with the crash of a waterfall. Immediately afterward there would be a complete cessation of rain and the crash of waters. The thunder sounded very lonely.

More than once there were intervals of sudden clearness in the air. For minutes at a time they could see, even after the blinding flash of a javelin of lightning, every object outside their sheltering place; then suddenly all would be blotted out. At such moments it seemed as if the blackness above them was solid—a vast mountain of unhewn marble falling down upon them. They had the impression of feeling the awful weight of its mass beginning to crush them. They became breathless—gasping.

Once a flash fell close to them, and there was a noise of splintering wood and the hiss of water into which a red-hot bar has been dipped. A second afterward a blazing brand was flung in front of them, and the smoke hung dense in the heavy air. By the light that was cast around they saw that one of the trees growing on the little mound close to them had been struck and hurled where it lay.

It blazed high for a few minutes, and then the girl cried out. She had got upon her feet, though forced to keep her head bent. He thought that she was pointing out to him the thing that had happened; but in a moment he perceived that her eyes were fixed upon some object beyond the mound that had been struck. It was, however, only when the next flash came that he saw out there the figure of a man—he recognised him: it was Pritchard.

He stood bareheaded with his sackcloth garment clinging to him— the lightning was reflected from it as if it had been made of steel, for the water was streaming down its folds—on the summit of the rocks that were piled together on the slope of the bank not twenty yards away. He was gesticulating, but his bare arms were above his head.

So much Wesley saw in the single glimpse that was allowed to him. After the flash the darkness swallowed him up once more; but even before the next flash came he was visible, though faintly, by the light of the blazing tree, for the trunk had not fallen directly between where he was standing and the shelter. The red light flickered over his body, and showed his attitude— his hands were now clasped over his head, and he was facing the quarter whence the storm was coming. Then there fell another torrent of rain and hail, and he was hidden by that watery sheet for some minutes. Suddenly, as before, the rain ceased, and there was another interval of clearness, that showed him standing with his arms extended. And when the thunder peal rolled away his voice was heard calling out passionately, though his words were indistinct; they were smothered in the noise of the thousand torrents of the Tor.

In a moment Wesley had pushed himself through the opening of his shelter and hurried to his side. He caught him by the arm.

"Come!" he cried. "Have you not read, 'Thou shalt not tempt the Lord thy God'? Man! is this a time to seek destruction?"

The man turned upon him.

"It has come—it has come—the great and terrible Day, and I am its prophet!" he shouted. "You did not believe me. I was mocked more than any prophet; but it has come. All has been fulfilled, except calling to the rocks and the mountains. No voice has called to them but mine. I have called to the rocks to cover me and the hills to hide, but none else. But you will join me—you will add your voice to mine that the Scriptures may be fulfilled, John Wesley. Call upon them as I do. Fall upon us, O rocks—cover us, O hills!"

He stretched out his arms once more and bowed his head on every side, shouting out his words, amid the blaze of the lightning and the rattle of the thunder.

"Wretch!" cried Wesley, but then he checked himself. He had now no doubt that the man had become a maniac. "My poor friend—brother—let me be your guide at this time. Let us talk over the matter together. There is a place of safety at hand."

"What, you, John Wesley, talk of safety; know you not in this dread hour that the Scripture must be fulfilled?" shouted the man. "What will your judgment be who would make the Holy Writ to be a vain thing? I tell you, sir, that it will be a lie if you do not join with me in calling upon the rocks to fall upon us? This is the place that was prophesied of—these are the very rocks—yonder are the very hills. They will not move—they must be stubborn until another voice be joined with mine. O rocks, fall—fall—fall!"

Wesley grasped one of the frantic arms that were outstretched. He could not temporise with the wretch again.

"You shall not dare!" he cried. "I may not stand by and hear such a mockery."

The man wrenched his arm free.

"The mockery is yours, sir," he shouted. "You will not save the truth of the Scriptures when it is left for you to do so. Think of your own condemnation, man—think that there are only two of us here, and if we remain silent we are guilty of blasphemy, for we are preventing the fulfilment of this prophecy."

A discharge of lightning that had the semblance of a pair of fiery fetters went from hill to hill, and when Wesley recovered the use of his eyes he saw that the man was pointing to the slight eminence on which the rocking-stone was poised.

"It has been shown to me—thank God that it has been shown to me before 'tis too late," he cried. "If you, John Wesley, refuse to aid me, power shall be given me alone to fulfil the Scriptures. The rocks shall obey me. I am the chosen vessel."

A torrent of rain swept between them, with the sound of a huge wave striking upon the flat face of a cliff. Wesley spread out his arms. One of them was grasped by the girl, who had crept to his side, and he felt himself guided back to the shelter.

He lay back upon the sloping rock thoroughly exhausted, and closed his eyes.

A minute had passed before he opened them again, hearing the girl cry out.

Another of the comparatively clear intervals had come, and it was sufficient to show the great rocking-stone in motion and the figure that was swaying it. To and fro it went on its heels' keel, the man making frantic efforts to increase the depth to which it rose and fell. To and fro, to and fro it swayed, and every fall was deeper than the last, until at last it was swinging so that the side almost touched the rock beyond. The man thrust his shoulder beneath the shoulder of the moving mass of stone, pushing it back every time it bowed toward him. Never before had it swung like this. At last it staggered on to the edge of the cup on which it was poised—staggered, but recovered itself and slipped into its place again. It swung back and jerked out of the cup as before. One more swing, with the man flinging his whole weight upon it; for a second it trembled on the edge of the hollow fulcrum, and then—it failed to return. It toppled slowly over upon the granite rock. For a moment its descent was retarded by the man, who was crushed like a walnut beneath it, then with a crash of broken crags it fell over the brink of the height to the ground, fifteen feet beneath.

Wesley left the girl with her hands pressed against her eyes and hurried to the fallen mass. A man's hand projected from beneath it—nothing more. But for this it would have been impossible to say that a body was beneath it. The mighty stone did not even lie flat on the ground; it had made a hollow for itself in the soft earth. It had buried itself to the depth of a foot, and beneath its base Pritchard lay buried.

CHAPTER XXII

Not until the afternoon had the storm moderated sufficiently to allow of Wesley and his companion returning to Porthawn. For a full hour after the fall of the rocking-stone they remained together in the shelter. They were both overcome by the horror of what they had witnessed. Happily the charred crown of branches which remained on the tree that had been struck down, after the rain had extinguished the blaze, was enough to hide the fallen stone, and that ghastly white thing that lay thrust out from beneath it like a splash of lichen frayed from the crag. But for another hour the tempest continued, only with brief intervals, when a dense and smoky greyness took the place of the blackness. It seemed as if the storm could not escape from the boundary of the natural amphitheatre in the centre of which was the mound which Wesley had used as his pulpit; and to that man whose imagination was never a moment inactive, the whole scene suggested a picture which he had once seen of the struggle of a thousand demons of the Pit, around a sanctified place, for the souls of those who were safe within the enclosure. There were the swirling black clouds every one of which let loose a fiery flying bolt, while the winds yelled horribly as any fiends that might be struggling with obscene tooth and claw, to crush the souls that were within the sacred circle. The picture had, he knew, been an allegory; he wondered if it were not possible that certain scenes in Nature might be equally allegorical. He hoped that he was not offending when he thought of this citadel of his faith—this pulpit from which he had first preached in Cornwall—being assailed by the emissaries of the Arch-enemy, and jet remaining unmoved as a tower built to withstand every assault of the foe.

The whole scene assumed in his imagination a series of fierce assaults, in all of which the enemy was worsted and sent flying over the plain; he could hear the shrieks of the disappointed fiends—the long wail of the wounded that followed every impulse; and then, after a brief interval, there came the renewed assault—the circling tumult seeking for a vulnerable point of entrance. But there it stood, that pulpit from whose height he had preached the Gospel to the thousands who had come to hear him, and had gone forth to join the forces that are evermore at conflict with the powers of evil in the world, There stood his pulpit unmoved in the midst of the tumult. He accepted the symbolism, and he was lifted up by the hope that his work sent forth from this place would live untouched by the many conflicts of time.

He was able to speak encouraging words to his companion every time the thunder passed away; and he was more than ever conscious of the happiness of having her near to him at this time. He knew that he had loved her truly; for his love had been true enough and strong enough to compel him to give her the advice that precluded his ever being able to tell her of his own feeling for her. The joy of her gracious companionship was not for him; but he would do all that in him lay to assure her happiness.

He knew that he was able to soothe her now that she had received a shock that would have been too much for most women. The horror of the mode of the man's death, quite apart from the terror of the tempest, was enough to prostrate any ordinary man or woman. It was very sweet to him to feel her cling to his arm when they crawled back to their shelter. He laid his hand tenderly upon the hand that clasped him, and he refrained from saying a word to her at that moment. When the storm had moderated in some measure he spoke to her; and he was too wise to make any attempt to turn her thoughts from the tragedy which, he knew, could not possibly fade from her mind even with the lapse of years.

"He predicted truly so far as he himself was concerned," he said gravely. "The end came for him as he said. Poor wretch! He may have possessed all his life a curious sense beyond that allowed to others—an instinct—it may not have been finer than the instinct of a bird. I have read that one of the desert birds will fly an hundred miles to where a camel has fallen by the way. The camel itself has, we are told, an instinct that guides it to water. But I do not say that he was not an agent of evil. There is evidence to prove that sorcery can give the power to predict what seems to be the truth, but it is only a juggling of the actual truth. The manner of that poor wretch's death makes one feel suspicious. He predicted the end of the world; well, the world came to an end, so far as he was concerned. You perceive the jugglery? But his was a weak mind. He may have been lured on to his own destruction. However this may be, his end was a terrible one. I grieve that it was left for us to witness it."

She shook her head.

"I shall never forget to-day," she said. "I had a feeling more than once when the lightning was brighter than common, and the world seemed to shake under the rattle of the thunderclap, that the next moment would be the last."

"There was no terror on your face—I saw it once under the fiercest flash," said he.

"At first—ah, I scarce know how I felt," said she. "But when I heard your words saying, 'Rock of Ages,' my fear seemed to vanish."

"The lines ring with the true confidence that only the true Rock of Ages can inspire," said he.

And thus he gradually led her thoughts away from the ghastly thing that she had seen, though he had begun talking to her about it. At this time the storm, which had been hurtling around the brim of the huge basin of the valley, had succeeded in its Titanic efforts to free itself from whatever influence it was held it fettered within the circle; and though the rain continued, there was only an occasional roll of thunder. The roar that now filled the valley was that of the sea. It came to them after the storm like the voice of an old friend shouting to them to be of good cheer.

And all that the preacher said to her was founded upon the text that the sea shouted for them to hear. For a time at least the horror that she had looked upon passed out of her mind; and when he pointed out to her that the rain had almost ceased, she suffered herself to be led away from their place of shelter by the further side of the central mound, without straining her eyes to see where the rocking-stone lay; she had not even a chance of noting the strangeness brought about by the disappearance of a landmark that she had seen since she was a child. But as they walked rapidly toward the little port, a cold fear took hold of her.

"Can a single cottage remain after such a storm—can anyone be left alive?" she cried, and he saw that the tears were on her face.

"Do not doubt it," he said. "To doubt it were to doubt the goodness of God. Some men are coming toward us. I have faith that they bring us good news."

Within a few minutes they saw that it was Mr. Hartwell and two of his men who had come in search of Wesley. Before they met, Nelly had asked how the port had fared—the boats, what of the boats?

"All's well," was the response, and her hands clasped themselves in joy and gratitude.

Never had such a tempest been thrown on the coast, Hartwell said, but absolutely no damage had been done to building, boat, or human being. Some trees had been struck by the lighting in the outskirts of the park, and doubtless others had suffered further inland; but the fishing boats having had signs of the approach of the storm, had at once made for the shore, and happily were brought to the leeward of the little wharf before the first burst had come.

When he had told his tale he enquired if either of them had seen anything of Pritchard.

"He appeared suddenly where we saw him yesterday," he continued, "and his cry was that we should join him in calling upon the rocks to fall on us. He would not be persuaded to take shelter, and he was seen to wander into what seemed to be the very heart of the storm."

Wesley shook his head, and told his story.

The man whose prophecy of the end of the world had spread within certain limits a terror that was recalled by many firesides, and formed a landmark in the annals of two generations, was the only one who perished in the great thunderstorm, which undoubtedly took place within a day or two of the date assigned by him to see the destruction of the world.

John Wesley had no choice left him in the matter. His host insisted on his going into a bed that had been made as warm as his copper pan of charcoal could make it, after partaking of a spiced posset compounded in accordance with a recipe that was guaranteed to prevent the catching of a cold, no matter how definitely circumstances conspired in favour of a cold.

His garments had become sodden with rain from the waterspout at the outset of the storm, and he had been forced to sit for several hours in the same clothes. He could not hope to escape a cold unless by the help of this famous posset, the housekeeper affirmed; and she was amazed to find him absolutely docile in this matter. She had been voluble in her entreaties; but she came to the conclusion that she might have spared herself half her trouble; she had taken it for granted that she was talking to an ordinary man, who would scoff at the virtues of her posset, and then make all his friends miserable by his complaints when he awoke with a cold on him. Mr. Wesley was the only sensible man she had ever met, she declared to her master, with the sinister expression of a hope that his example of docility would not be neglected by others.

He went to bed, and after listening for some hours to the roaring of the sea, he fell asleep. The evening had scarcely come, but he had never felt wearier in all his life.

He slept for eight hours, and when he awoke he knew that he had done well to yield, without the need for persuasion, to the advice of the housekeeper. He felt refreshed in every way; and after lying awake for an hour, he arose, dressed himself, and left the house. This impulse to take a midnight walk was by no means unusual with him. He had frequently found himself the better for an hour or two spent in the darkness, especially beside the sea. Midnight was just past. If he were to remain in the air for some time, he might, he thought, be able to sleep until breakfast-time.

The night was cool, without being cold, and there was a sweet freshness in the air which had certainly been wanting when he had walked along the cliffs in the afternoon. The thunderstorm did not seem at that time to have cleared the atmosphere. He was rather surprised to find that there was such a high sea rolling at this time, and he came to the conclusion that there had been a gale while he was asleep. Clouds were still hiding the sky, but they held no rain.

He shunned the cliff track, going in the opposite direction, which led him past the village, and on to the steep sandy bay with its occasional little peninsulas of high rocks, the surfaces of which were not covered even by Spring tides. Very quiet the little port seemed at this hour. Not a light was in any window—not a sound came from any of the cottages. He stood for a long time on the little wharf looking at the silent row of cottages. That one which had the rose-bush trained over the porch was the home of the Polwheles, he knew, and he remained with his eyes fixed upon it. It seemed as if this had been the object of his walk—to stand thus in front of that house, as any youthful lover might stand beneath the lattice that he loved.

He had his thoughts to think, and he found that this was the time to think them. They were all about the girl who slept beyond that window. He wondered if he had ever loved her before this moment. If he had really loved her, how was it that he had never before been led to this place to watch the house where she lay asleep? Was it possible that he had fancied he knew her before he had passed those hours with her when the storm was raging around them? He felt that without this experience he could not possibly have known what manner of girl she was.

And now that he had come to know her the knowledge came to him with the thought that she was not for him.

He had set out in the morning feeling that perhaps he had been too hasty in coming to the conclusion that because, when far away from her he had been thinking a great deal of his own loneliness and the joy that her companionship would bring to him, he loved her. That was why he had wished to put himself to the test, and he had fancied that he was doing so when he had walked in the opposite direction to that in which the village lay so that he might avoid the chance of meeting her.

But in spite of his elaborate precautions—he actually thought that it had shown ingenuity on his part—he had met her, and he had learned without putting the question to her that she was not for him. He recalled what his feeling had been at that moment. He had fancied that he knew all that her words meant to him; but he had deceived himself; it was only now that he knew exactly the measure of what they meant to him. It seemed to him that he had known nothing of the girl before he had passed those dark hours by her side.

At that time it was as if all the world had been blotted out, only he and she being left alone.

This feeling he now knew was what was meant by loving—this feeling that there was nothing left in the world—that nothing mattered so long as he and she were together—that death itself would be welcome if only it did not sunder them.

And he had gained that knowledge only to know that they were to be sundered.

It was a bitter thought, and for a time, as he stood there with his eyes fixed upon the cottage, he felt as if so far as he was concerned the world had come to an end. The happiness which he had seen before him as plainly as if it had been a painted picture—a picture of the fireside in the home that he hoped for—had been blotted out from before his eyes, and in its stead there was a blank. It did not matter how that blank might be filled in, it would never contain the picture that had been torn away from before him when she had of her own free will told him the story of her love.

He felt the worst that any man can feel, for the worst comes only when a man cries out to himself:

"Too late—too late!"

He was tortured by that perpetual question of "Why? Why? Why?"

Why had he not come to Cornwall the previous year? Why had he not seen her before she had gone to Bristol and given her promise to the other man?

But this was only in the floodtide of his bitterness; after a space it subsided. More reasonable thoughts came to him. Who was he that he should rail against what had been ordered by that Heaven in whose ordering of things he had often expressed his perfect faith? What would he say of any man who should have such rebellious thoughts? Could this be the true love—this that made him rebel against the decree of an all-wise Providence? If it was true it would cause him to think not of his own happiness, but of hers.

Had he been thinking all the time of his own happiness? he asked himself. Had she been denied to him on this account? He feared that it was so. He recalled how he had been thinking of her, and he had many pangs of self-reproach when he remembered how in all the pictures of the future that his imagination had drawn he was the central figure. He felt that his aim had been an ignoble one. Selfishness had been the foundation of his love, and therefore he deserved the punishment that had fallen upon him.

'He continued his walk and went past the cottage on which his eyes had lingered. For a mile he strolled, lost in thought along the sandy bay, disturbing the sea birds that were wading about the shallow pools in search of shell fish. The tide was on the ebb and he walked down the little ridges of wet beach until he found himself at the edge of that broad grey sea that sent its whispering ripples to his feet. He had always liked to stand thus in winter as well as summer. Within an hour of dawn the sea seemed very patient. It was waiting for what was to come—for the uprising of the sun to turn its grey into gold.

He never failed to learn the lesson of the sea in all its moods; and now he felt strengthened by looking out to the eastern sky, though it was still devoid of light. He would have patience. He would wait and have faith. Light was coming to the world, and happy was the one to whom was given the mission of proclaiming that dawn—the coming of the Light of the World.

Even when he resumed his stroll after he had looked across the dun waters he became conscious of a change in the eastern sky. The clouds that still clung to that quarter were taking on to themselves the pallor of a pearl, and the sky edge of the sea was lined with the tender glaze that appears on the inner surface of a white shell, and its influence was felt upon the objects of the coast. The ridges of the peninsular rocks glimmered, and the outline of the whole coast became faintly seen. It was coming—the dawn for which the world was waiting was nigh. The doubts born of the night were ready to fly away as that great heron which rose in front of him fled with winnowing wings across the surface of the sea.

CHAPTER XXIII

The first faint breath of the dawn—that sigh of light of which the air was scarcely conscious—made him aware as he walked along the sands of the fact that the beach was strewn with wreckage. He found himself examining a broken spar upon which he had struck his foot. Further on he stumbled over a hen-coop, and then again a fragment that looked like the cover of a hatchway.

He had heard nothing about a vessel's having come ashore during the tempest of the morning; but there was nothing remarkable in the sudden appearing of wreckage on this wild Cornish coast. Almost every tide washed up something that had once been part of a gallant ship. Wreckage came without anyone hearing of the wreck from which it had come. He examined the broken spar, and his fancy showed him the scene at the foundering of such a ship as the *Gloriana*, whose carcase had been so marvellously uncovered on the Sunday evening. He had had enough experience of seafaring to be able to picture the details of the wreckage of such a ship.

He left the beach and went on to the ascent of the higher part of the shore, thinking that it might be that when the dawn strengthened it might reveal the shape of some craft that had run ashore on the outer reef at this dangerous part of the coast; and even before he reached the elevated ground the dawn light had spread its faint gauze over the sea, and the shapes of the rocks were plain. He looked out carefully, scanning the whole coast, but he failed to see any wreck between the horns of the bay.

But when he had continued his slow walk for a few hundred yards he fancied that he saw some objects that looked dark against the pale sands. At first he thought that he was looking at a rock that had some resemblance to the form of a man; but a movement of a portion of the object showed that it was indeed a man who was standing there.

Wesley had no mind for a companion on this stroll of his, so he went a short way inland in order to save himself from being seen, and he did not return to the sandy edge of the high ground until he judged that he had gone beyond the spot where he had seen the man. Turning about, he found that he had done what he intended: he saw the dark figure walking from where he had been, in the direction of the sea.

But by this time the light had so increased that he was able to see that the man was walking away from the body of another that was lying on the beach.

He had scarcely noticed this before the man stopped, looked back, and slowly returned to the body. But the moment he reached it Wesley was amazed to see him throw up his arms as if in surprise and then fling himself down on the body with his hands upon its throat.

Wesley knew nothing except that the man's attitude was that of one who was trying to strangle another. But this was surely enough. He shouted out and rushed toward the place with a menace.

The man was startled; his head went back with a jerk, but his hands did not leave the other's throat. Wesley had to drag him back by the collar, and even then he did not relax his hold until the body had been lifted up into a sitting position. The moment the man's fingers were loosed the head fell back upon the sand.

Wesley threw himself between the two, and the instant that he turned upon the assailant he recognised John Bennet.

"Wretch!" he cried, "what is it that you would do? What is it that you have done—murderer?"

Bennet stared at him as if stupefied. Then he burst into a laugh, but stopped himself suddenly.

"Mr. Wesley, is it?" he cried. "Oh, sir, is't you indeed that pulls my hands off his throat? There is something for the Devil to laugh at in that."

"Man, if you be a man and not a fiend, would you strangle one whom the sea has already drowned?" cried Wesley.

"I have the right," shouted Bennet, "for he would be dead by now if I had not succoured him."

"If it be true that you saved him from an imminent death, at that time, wherefore should you strive to murder him now?" said Wesley.

"I did not see his face then—it was dark when I stumbled on him. Only when I turned about when the dawn broke I saw who he was. Go your ways, Mr. Wesley. The man is mine by every law of fair play. Stand not between us, sir, or you shall suffer for it."

"Monster, think you that I shall obey you while a breath remains in my body? I shall withstand you to the death, John Bennet; you shall have two murders laid at your door instead of one."

The man laughed as before. Then he said:

"That is the point where the devils begin to laugh—ho! ho! John Wesley!"

"I have heard one of them," said Wesley.

"Oh, you fool, to stay my hand! Know you not that the man lying there is none other than he whom Nelly Polwhele has promised to marry?"

"And is not that a sufficient reason why you should do your best to save him—not take his life away?"

For more than a minute the man was too astonished to speak. At last he said:

"Is it that you are mad, John Wesley? Heard you not what I said?"

"Every word," replied Wesley.

"You cannot have taken in my words," the other whispered. "Think, sir, that is the foolish thing that stands between you and her—you love her—I have seen that."

Go your ways, Mr. Wesley. The man is mine by every law of fair play."

"And I stand between you and him—that is enough for the present moment," said Wesley quickly, facing the man, whom he noticed sidling round ready to leap upon the body lying on the beach.

Bennet saw that his cunning was overmatched. "Fool! I cry again," he said in a low tone. "Would not I slay a score such as you and he for her sake? A man's soul can only be lost once, and I am ready to go to perdition for her—I have counted the cost. The best of the bargain is with me! Out of my way, sir—out of my way!"

He took a few steps back, preparing to rush at the other. Wesley kept his eyes upon him and stood with his feet firmly planted to stand against his violence. But before the man could make his rush there was sudden flash of light in his face, dazzling him and Wesley as well. The light shifted.

Wesley turned to see whence it came. There was the sound of a hard boot on the pebbles and a man's voice said:

"Avast there! Don't move a hand. I have a pistol covering ye, and a cutlash is in my belt."

"You have come in good time, whoever you be," said Wesley. "But you will have no need to use your weapons, sir."

"Ay, ay, but if there's a move between ye, my gentlemen, I'll make spindrift o' your brains. Ye hear?" was the response.

The man, who had flashed his lantern upon them—the dawn was still very faint—came beside them and showed that he had not made an empty boast. Wesley perceived that he was one of the Preventive men, fully armed.

He kept the blaze of his lantern on Bennet's face and then turned it on Wesley, whom he appeared to recognise.

"In Heaven's name, sir, what's this?" he cried.

"Take no thought for us," said Wesley. "Here lies a poor wretch washed ashore. Give me your help to bring back life to him. No moment must be lost—the loss of a minute may mean the loss of his life."

He was already kneeling beside the prostrate figure. The Preventive man followed his example. They both exclaimed in one voice:

"He is alive!"

"God be thanked," said Wesley solemnly. "I feared——"

"You have treated him with skill, sir," said the man. "You did not give him a dram?"

"I have only been here a few minutes; the saving; of him from drowning is not due to me," said Wesley.

The man had his ration of rum in his knapsack, and was administering it, Bennet standing by without a word.

"We must get help to carry him to the nearest house," said the Preventive man.

"I shall hasten to the village," said Wesley. But he suddenly checked himself. He knew that Ben-net's cunning would be equal to such a device as to get rid of the revenue officer for the few minutes necessary to crush the life out of the man on the sand. "No, on second thought yonder man— his name is Bennet—will do this duty. John Bennet, you will hasten to the nearest house—any house save Polwhele's—and return with at least two of the fishermen. They will come hither with two oars and a small sail— enough sailcloth to make into a hammock for the bearing of the man with ease. You will do my bidding."

"I will do your bidding," said Bennet after a pause, and forthwith he hurried away.

"What is all this, sir?" asked the man in a low tone when he had gone. "I heard your voice and his—he is half a madman—they had the sound of a quarrel."

"You arrived in good time, friend," said Wesley. "You say this man was treated with skill in his emergency; if so, it must be placed to the credit of John Bennet. I can say so much, but no more."

"I'll ask no more from you, sir," said the other, slowly and suspiciously. "But if I heard of Ben-net's murdering a man I would believe it sooner than any tale of his succouring one. He is a bit loose in the hatches, as the saying is; I doubt if he will bear your message, sir."

"I shall make this sure by going myself," said

Wesley. "I am of no help here; you have dealt with the half drowned before now."

"A score of times—and another score to the back of the first," said the man. "I tell you this one is well on the mend. But a warm blanket will be more to him than an anker of Jamaica rum. You do well to follow Bennet. Would the loan of a pistol be of any confidence to you in the job?"

"There will be no heed for such now, even if I knew how to use one," said Wesley.

He perceived that the man had his suspicions. He hurried away when he had reached the track above the shingle.

It was quite light before he reached the nearest cottage, which stood about a hundred yards east of the Port Street, and belonged to a fisherman and boatwright named Garvice. The men and his sons had their tar-pot on the brazier and had already begun work on a dinghy which lay keel uppermost before them.

They looked with surprise at him when he asked if they had been long at work.

"On'y a matter o' quartern hour," replied the old man.

"Then you must have seen John Bennet and got his message?" said Wesley.

"Seen John Bennet? Ay, ay—still mad. Message? No message i' the world. What message 'ud a hare-brainer like to 'un bear to folk wi' the five senses o' Golmighty complete?" the old man enquired.

"Do you tell me that Bennet said naught to you about a half-drowned man needing your help?" asked Wesley.

"No word. Even if so rigid a madman ha' carried that tale think ye we'd be here the now?"

"'Tis as well that I came, though I thought it cruel to distrust him," said Wesley.

He then told the man what was needed, and before he had spoken a dozen words the old man had thrown down his tar-brush and was signalling his sons to run down one of the boats to the water.

"Paddle round in half the time takes t' walk," he said. "No back breakin', no bone shakin 's my morter. Down she goes."

Wesley was glad to accept a seat in the stern sheets of the small boat which was run down to the water, not twenty yards from the building shed; and when he returned with the three boatmen to that part of the coast from which he had walked, he found the man to whose aid he had come sitting up and able to say a word or two to the revenue man, who was kneeling beside him, having just taken his empty rum bottle from his mouth.

Old Garvice looked as if he felt that he had been brought from his work under false pretences. He plodded slowly across the intervening piece of beach a long way behind Mr. Wesley, and the Preventive man had reported the progress to recovery made by the other before the Garvice family had come up. The Garvices had had more than a nodding acquaintance with the revenue authorities before this morning.

"John Bennet is a bigger rascal than I thought, and that's going far," said the Preventive man when Wesley told him that no message had been given at the Port. "If I come face to face with him, them that's nigh will see some blood-letting. Why, e'en Ned Garvice, that I've been trying to lay a trap for this twelve year, lets bygones be bygones when there's a foundered man to succour."

"Where is 'un?" enquired the old man with pointed satire, looking round with a blank face.

The bedraggled man sitting on the beach was able to smile.

"Wish I'd had the head to bid you ask Neddy Garvice to carry hither a bottle of his French brandy—ay, the lot that you run ashore when the cutter fouled on the bank," said the Preventive man.

"Oh, that lot? Had I got a billet from you, Freddy Wise, I'd ha' put a stoup from the kegs o' the *Gorgon* into my pocket," said the old man wickedly. Mr. Wesley did not know that the *Gorgon* was a large ship that had come ashore the previous year, and had been stripped bare by the wreckers. "Oh, ay; the *Gorgon* for brandy and the *Burglarmaster* for schnapps, says I, and I sticks to that object o' creed, Freddy, whatsoe'er you says." The *Bourghermeister* was the name of another wreck whose stores the revenue men had been too slow to save some years before.

But while these pleasantries were being exchanged between the men Wesley was looking at the one in whose interests he was most concerned. He was lying with his head supported by a crag on which Fred Wise had spread his boat cloak. His face was frightfully pallid, and his forehead was like wax, only across his temple there was a long ugly gash, around which the blood had coagulated. His eyes were closed except at intervals when he started, and they opened suddenly and began to stare rather wildly. His arms hung down and his hands were lying limp on the beach palms up, suggesting the helplessness of a dead man. He was clearly a large and strongly built fellow, who could sail a ship and manage a crew, using his head as well as his hands.

The others were looking at him critically; he was so far recovered that they did not seem to think there was any imperative need for haste in the matter of carrying him to a bed; although they criticised him as if he were dead.

"Worser lads ha' gone down and heard of for nevermore," said the old fisherman. "Did he know that Squire Trevelyan buries free of all duty all such as the sea washes up 'tween tides? That's the Vantage to be drowned on these shores; but the Squire keeps that knowledge like a solemn secret; fears there'd be a rush—they'd be jammin' one t'other amongst crags as for who'd come foremost to his own funeral."

"Tis no secret o' gravity, Ned Garvice, that you give orders to your boys to carry you down in the cool o' the evening when you feel your hour's at hand, and lay ye out trim and tidy for the flood-tide, so that ye get a free funeral, and Parson Rodney's 'Earth t' earth' thrown into the bargain," said Wise.

"I've learned my sons to honour their father, and it puts 'un back a long way in their 'struction to be face to face wi' 'un as has a hardened scoff for his grey hairs," said the fisherman. "Go your ways, lads, and gather limpits so ye hear not evil words that shake your faith in your ancient father. But what I can't see is how he got them finger-marks on his neck."

He pointed to the man on the beach.

"They ha' the aspect o' finger marks, now ha' they not, sir?" said Wise meaningly, turning to Wesley.

"My thought, friends, amounts to this: I have heard that in cases of rescue from drowning quickness is most needful for the complete restoration of the sufferer," said Wesley. "Now, sirs, I ask you is this the moment for light gossip, when yonder poor fellow lies as if he had not an hour's life in his body?"

"There's summat i' that, too," said old Garvice, as if a matter which he had been discussing had suddenly been presented to him in an entirely new light.

"Oh, sir," said the Preventive man, "when a corpse has revived so far 'tis thought best that he should have a short rest; it kind o' way knits the body and soul together all the closer. The man is in no danger now, I firmly believe; but, as you say, there's no need for wasting any more time. Give us a heave under his other armpit, my lad. Heave handsomely; there's naught but a thin halfhour 'twixt him and eternity—mind that, and you won't jerk. Who's for his heels?"

The elder of Garvice's sons—a big lad of twenty—obeyed the instructions of the revenue man, and Wesley and the old fisherman went to the feet.

"'Vast hauling! Set me up on end," said the man over whom they were bending. He spoke in a low voice and weak; he did not seem to have sufficient breath to make himself heard.

"Hear that?" said the fisherman with a sagacious wink. "There's the lightsome and blithe quarter-deck voice o' your master-mariner when warping into dock and his missus a-waitin' for 'un rosy as silk on the pier-head.'Tis then that if so be that a man's genteel, it will out."

"'Vast jaw, my hearty!" murmured the man wearily.

"That's the tone that fills the air wi' th' smell o' salt beef for me whene'er I hears 'un—ay, sirs, salt beef more lifelike and lively than this high ship-master who I trow hath ofttimes watched a ration toddle round the cuddy table like to a guileless infant."

"Heave all, with a will!" cried Wise, and the four men raised the other as tenderly as a bulk so considerable could be taken off the ground, and bore him with some staggering and heavy breathing, down to where the youngest of the Garvice family was keeping the dinghy afloat over the rapidly shallowing sand.

An hour later, when the day was still young, Wesley was kneeling by his bedside giving thanks to Heaven for having allowed him to participate in the privilege of saving a fellow-creature from death.

CHAPTER XXIV

He slept for an hour or two, but awoke feeling strangely unrefreshed. But he joined Hartwell at breakfast and heard the news that the latter had acquired during his usual half-hour's stroll through the village.

After shaking his guest warmly by the hand, Hartwell cried:

"What, Mr. Wesley, was it that you did not believe you had adventure enough for one Summer's day, that you must needs fare forth in search of others before sunrise?"

Wesley laughed.

"I ventured nothing, my good friend," he said. "I came upon the shipwrecked man by the blessing of God, in good time. I have been wondering since I rose if he had suffered shipwreck. Did you learn so much at the village—and pray hath he fully recovered himself?"

"I dare not say fully, but he has recovered himself enough to be able to tell his story," replied Hartwell.

"And he was wrecked?"

"Only swamped at sea. He is a ship-master, Snowdon, by name, but 'twas not his own craft that went down, but only a miserable coasting ketch that ventured from Bristol port to Poole with a cargo of pottery—something eminently sinkable. Strange to say, Captain Snowdon set out from Bristol, wanting to go no further than our own port; for why? you ask. Why, sir, for a true lover's reason, which may be reckoned by some folk as no reason at all—namely a hope to get speedily by the side of his mistress, this lady being none other than our friend, the pretty and virtuous young woman known as Nelly Polwhele."

"Ah! Nelly Polwhele?"

"None other, sir. It seems that Nelly met this good master-mariner a year ago at Bristol, and following the usage of all our swains, he falls in love with her. And she, contrary to her usage of the stay-at-home swains who piped to her, replies with love for love. But a long voyage loomed before him, so after getting her promise, he sails for the China Seas and the coast of the Great Mogul. Returning with a full heart and, I doubt not, a full pocket as well, he is too impatient to wait for the sailing of a middle-sized packet for Falmouth or Plymouth, he must needs take a passage in the first thing shaped like a boat that meant to come round the Lizard, and this was a ketch of some ten ton, that opened every seam before the seas that the hurricane of yesterday raised up in the Channel, and so got swamped when trying to run ashore on some soft ground. Nelly's shipmaster, Mr. Snowdon, must have been struggling in the water for something like four hours, and was washed up, well-nigh at the very door of the young woman's cottage, and so—well, you know more of the remainder of the story than doth any living man—not even excepting the Captain himself."

"And the young woman—have you heard how she received her lover?" asked Wesley.

"Ah, that is the point at which Rumour becomes, for a marvel, discreetly silent," replied Hartwell. "I suppose it is taken for granted that the theme has been dealt with too frequently by the poets to have need to be further illustrated by a fisherman's daughter. Take my word for it, sir, the young woman, despite her abundance of womanly traits, is a good and kind and true girl at heart. She hath not been spoiled by the education which she received as companion to the Squire's young ladies."

"That was my judgment, too," said Wesley. "I pray that the man will be a good husband to her. His worldly position as the master of an East Indiaman is an excellent one."

"He will make her a very suitable husband," said Hartwell. "I must confess that I have had my fears for her. She is possessed of such good looks—a dangerous possession for such a young woman, sir. These, coupled with her intimate association with the Squire's daughters, might have led her into danger. A less sensible girl would certainly be likely to set her cap at someone a good deal above her in station—a dangerous thing—very dangerous!"

"No doubt, sir. And now you are disposed to think that her happiness is, humanly speaking, assured?"

"I think that she is a very fortunate young woman, and that the man is even more fortunate still. Old Polwhele, in his whimsical way, however, protests that he wishes the man whose intent it is to rob him of his daughter, had got drowned. He grumbled about the part you played in the matter—he was very whimsical. 'What, sir,' he grumbled to me just now, 'is Mr. Wesley not content with looking after our souls—is he turning his attention to our bodies as well? Old Polwhele has a nimble wit."

"It was not I, but John bennet, who was fortunate enough to restore the man: he treated him altogether skilfully, the revenue patrol-man told me."

Hartwell threw up his hands in surprise. Then he frowned. He was plainly puzzled for some time. At last he said:

"Mr. Wesley, if Bennet saved that man's life he must have stumbled on him while it was yet dark—too dark to let him see the man's face."

"But how should he know who the man was, even if he had seen his face?"

"He was acquainted with Mr. Snowdon at Bristol, and his grievance was that if Snowdon had not appeared, the girl would have accepted his own suit. Oh, yes; it must have been too dark for him to see the man's face, or it would have gone hardly with the poor fellow."

There was a considerable pause before Wesley said:

"You are right, it was too dark to allow him to recognise the man's features. Has he been seen at the village during the morning?"

"If he has I heard nothing of it," replied Hartwell, "it might be as well to say a word of warning to Mr. Snowdon respecting him; he is a madman, and dangerous. You do not forget the mad thing he said about you on Sunday, sir?"

"I have not forgotten it," said Wesley in a low voice. "I have not forgotten it. I think that I shall set out upon my journey this afternoon."

The pause that he made between his sentences was so slight as to suggest that they were actually connected—that there was some connection between the thing that Bennet had said and his own speedy departure.

His host, who was in good spirits after his walk in the early sunshine, gave a laugh and asked him in no spirit of gravity if he felt that it was necessary for him to fly lest Captain Snowdon should develop the same spirit of jealousy that had made Bennet fit for Bedlam.

Wesley shook his head and smiled.

"Need I ask your pardon for a pointless jest, sir?" cried Hartwell. "Nay, dear sir and brother, I hope you will find good reason for remaining with us for a few days still. You have had a trying time since you came, Mr. Wesley; and I do not think that you are fit to set out on so rude a journey."

"I confess that I feel somewhat exhausted," said Wesley, "but I have hope that an hour or two in the saddle will restore me."

Hartwell did his best to persuade him to reconcile himself to the idea of staying in the neighbourhood for at least another day, but without success.

"I must go. I feel that I must go, grateful though I be to you for your offer of hospitality," said Wesley.

"Then I will not say a further word. If it be a matter of feeling with you, I do not feel justified in asking you to change your intention," said Hartwell. "I shall give orders as to your horse without delay."

But the horse was not needed that day, nor was it likely to be needed for some time to come, for within the hour after breakfast Mr. Wesley was overcome by a shivering fit and compelled to take to his bed. It became plain that he had caught a chill—the wonder was that it had not manifested itself sooner, considering that he had sat for so long the day before in his saturated garments, and the very trying morning that he had had. Mr. Hartwell, who had some knowledge of medicine, and a considerable experience of the simpler maladies to which his miners were subject, found that he was more than a little feverish, and expressed the opinion that he would not be able to travel for a full week. Wesley, who, himself, knew enough about the treatment of disease to allow of his writing a book on the subject, agreed with him, that it was not necessary to send for a physician, who might possibly differ from both of them in his diagnosis.

For three days he remained in bed, and in spite of the fact that he would have nothing to say to the Peruvian bark which his host so strongly recommended, his feverish tendency gradually abated, and by careful nursing he was able to sit up in his room by the end of a week.

In the meantime he had many visitors, though he refrained from seeing any of them. His host told him that Miller Pendelley, Jake Pullsford, and Hal Holmes had driven more than once from Ruthallion when they heard of his illness; but of course the earliest and most constant of the enquirers after his health were Nelly Polwhele and her lover. Mr. Hartwell told him how greatly distressed they were, and perhaps it was natural, he added, that the girl should be the one who laid the greatest emphasis upon the fact that they were the cause of Mr. Wesley's suffering. She was undoubtedly a sweet and unselfish girl, Hartwell said; and he feared that Captain Snowdon thought that she was making too great a fuss in referring to the risks which he, Wesley, had run to bring her happiness. Snowdon, being a man, had not her imagination; and besides his life had been made up of running risks for the benefit of other people, and he was scarcely to be blamed if he took a less emotional view of, at least, the incident of Wesley's finding him exhausted on the shore in the early dawn.

"I spoke with him to-day," said Hartwell when his guest was able to hear these things, "and while he certainly showed himself greatly concerned at your sickness, he grumbled, half humorously, when he touched upon the way he was being neglected by the young woman. 'I am being hardly treated, sir,' he said. 'What is a simple master-mariner at best alongsides a parson with a persuasive voice? But when the parson adds on to his other qualities the dash and derring-do of a hero it seems to me that a plain man had best get into his boat, if so be that he have one, and sail away—it boots not whither, so long as he goes. Oh, ay, sir, I allow that your Mr. Wesley hath made short work of me.' Those were his words; and though they were followed by an earnest enquiry after your health, I could see that he would as lief that he owed his life to a more ordinary man."

"If I had not been overtaken by this sickness he would have had no cause for complaint," said Wesley. After a pause he touched with caution upon a matter over which he had been thinking for some time.

"Mr. Snowdon heard nothing about a rival other than myself in the young woman's regard?" he said.

"Oh, not he," replied Hartwell quickly. "Snowdon is not the fellow to listen to all that the gossips may say about Madam Nelly's liking for admiration—he knows well that so pretty a thing will be slandered, even when she shows herself to be wisely provident by seeking to have two strings to her bow. But, indeed, whatever her weakness may have been in the past, she hath been a changed girl since you first came hither. Captain Snowdon has no rival but yourself, sir, and I am certain that the honest fellow would not for the world that the young woman abated aught of her gratitude to you. He has too large a heart to harbour any thought so unworthy of a true man."

"God forbid that anything should come between them and happiness," said Wesley.

"'Tis all unlikely," said his host. "He must see that her love for him must be in proportion to her gratitude to you for having done all that you have done for him. If she did not love him dearly she would have no need to be half so grateful to you."

Wesley said nothing more on this point. He had not forgotten what Nelly had confided to him and the counsel which he had given her just before the hurricane had cut short their conversation on the cliffs. She had told him her story, confessing that the man to whom she had given her promise was less dear to her now that she was in daily expectation of meeting him after the lapse of a year than he had been when they had parted; and he had defined, in no doubtful language, the direction in which her duty lay.

For the rest of the time that they were together neither he nor she had made any reference to this matter; but he had not ceased to think upon it. After what Mr. Hartwell had said he felt reassured. He had brought himself to feel that he could only be happy if the girl's happiness were assured; and he believed that this could only be accomplished by her keeping the promise which she had given to a man who was worthy of her. However she might have fancied that her love had waned or turned in another direction during the year they had been parted, he was convinced that it would return, as true and as fresh as before, with the return of Captain Snowdon.

All that Hartwell had said bore him out in this view which he was disposed to take of the way of this maid with the man. Hartwell was a man of judgment and observation, and if there had been any division between the two people in whom they were interested, he would undoubtedly have noticed it. He had described the grievance of which Snowdon had complained in a humorous way; and Wesley knew that if the man felt that he had a grievance of the most grievous sort that can fall upon a man, he would not have referred to it in such a spirit.

And then the day came when Wesley was able to talk, without being hushed by his hospitable friend, of mounting his horse and resuming his journey in the west. He had many engagements, and was getting daily more anxious to fulfil them before the summer should be over.

"If it rested with me, sir," said Hartwell, "I would keep you here for another month and feel that I was the most favoured of men; but in this matter I dare not be selfish. I know what, with God's blessing, you seek to accomplish, and I feel that to stay you from your journey would be an offence."

"You have been more than good to me, my brother," said Wesley. "And now in parting from, you, I do not feel as did the Apostle Paul when leaving those friends of his who sorrowed knowing that they should see his face no more. I know that your sorrow is sincere, because I know how sincere is my own, but if God is good to us we shall all meet again after a season."

"That is what we look forward to; you have sown the good seed among us and you must return to see what your harvest will be," said Hartwell.

They agreed that his horse was to be in readiness the next morning. This was at their noon dinner, and they had scarcely risen from the table when the maidservant entered with the enquiry if Mr. Wesley would allow Captain Snowdon to have a word with him in private.

"I was expecting this visitor," said Hartwell. "It would be cruel for you to go away without receiving the man, albeit I think that you would rather not hear him at this time. Let me reassure you: he will not be extravagant in his acknowledgment of the debt which he owes to you; he is a sailor, and scant of speech."

"Why should I not see him?" said Wesley. "I am not afraid to face him! even a demonstration of his gratitude. Pray let him be admitted."

Very different indeed was the stalwart man who was shown into the room from the poor half-drowned wretch whom Wesley had helped to carry from the shore to the boat. Captain Snowdon stood over six feet—a light-haired, blue-eyed man who suggested a resuscitated Viking of the milder order, brown faced and with a certain indefinable expression of shrewd kindliness which might occasionally take the form of humour and make itself felt by a jovial slap on the back that would make most men stagger.

He was shy, and he had plainly been walking fast.

These were the two things that Wesley noticed when Hartwell was shaking hands with the man, and the latter had wiped his forehead with a handkerchief as splendid as the western cloud of a sunset in the Tropics—a handkerchief that seemed a floating section of the Empire of the Great Mogul—dazzling in red and yellow and green—a wonder of the silk loom.

"You and Mr. Wesley have already met, Mr. Snowdon," said Hartwell with a smile, and forthwith quitted the room.

Captain Snowdon looked after him rather wistfully. He seemed to be under the impression that Mr. Hartwell had deserted him. Then he glanced with something of surprise in the direction of Wesley, and was apparently surprised to see his hand stretched out in greeting. He took the hand very gingerly and with nothing of a seaman's bluffness or vigour.

"Seeing you at this time, Captain Snowdon, makes me have a pretty conceit of myself," said Wesley. "Yes, sir, I feel inclined to boast that I was one of the four who bore you from the high beach to the boat—I would boast of the fact only that I know I should never be believed. You do not seem to have suffered by your mishap."

"Thank you, sir, I am a man that turns the corner very soon in matters of that sort, and then I race ahead," replied the master-mariner.

"You have become accustomed to such accidents, sir," said Wesley.

"Ay, sir, the salt sea and me have ever been friends, and more than once we have had a friendly tussle together, but we bear no malice therefor, neither of us—bless your heart, none whatever," said Snowdon. "Why, the sea is my partner in trade—the sea and the wind, we work together, but you, Mr. Wesley, I grieve to see you thus, sir, knowing that 'twas on my account. What if you'd been finished off this time—wouldn't the blame fall on me? Shouldn't I be looked on as your murderer?"

"I cannot see on what principle you should, sir," said Wesley. "In the first place the chill from which I have now, by the blessing of Heaven, fully recovered, was not due to my having been one of the four men who carried you down the beach, though I should have no trouble in getting anyone to believe that I suffered from exhaustion. No, Mr. Snowdon, I had contracted the complaint before I was fortunate enough to come upon you in my early morning's walk."

"Anyway, sir, you earned my gratitude; though indeed, I feel as shy as a school miss to mention such a word in your presence. If I know aught of you, Mr. Wesley, and I think that I can take the measure of a man whether he be a man or a parson, if I know aught of you, sir, I repeat, you would be as uneasy to hear me talk of gratitude as I should be to make an offer to talk of the same."

"You are right in that respect, Mr. Snowdon. Between us—men that understand each other—there need be no protestation of feeling."

"Give me your hand, sir; you have just said what I should like to say. I feel that you know what I feel—you know that if there was any way for me to prove my gratitude— —="

"Ah, you have said the word again, and I understood that it was to be kept out of our conversation. But I am glad that you said so much, for it enables me to say that you have the means of showing your gratitude to Heaven for your preservation, and I know that you will not neglect such means. You will be a good husband to Nelly Polwhele—that is the way by which you will show how you appreciate the blessing of life!"

Captain Snowdon's face became serious—almost gloomy—as gloomy as the face of such a man can become. He made no reply for a few moments. He crossed the room and looked out of the window. Once more he pulled out his handkerchief and mopped his brow with that bit of the gorgeous. Orient.

Then he turned to Wesley, saying:

"Mr. Wesley, sir, I have come to you at this; time to talk about Nelly Polwhele, if I may make so bold."

"I can hear a great deal said about Nelly Polwhele so long as it is all that is good," said Wesley.

"I am not the man to say aught else," said Snowdon. "Only—well, sir, the truth is I don't quite know what to make of Nelly."

"Make her your happy wife, Captain Snowdon," said Wesley.

"That's what I look forward to, sir; but she is not of the same way of thinking, worse luck!"

"You cannot mean that she—she—what, sir, did not she give you her promise a year ago?"

"That she did, sir; but that's a year ago. Oh, Mr. Wesley, I believe that all of her sex are more or less of a puzzle to a simple man, and in matters of love all men are more or less simple, but Nelly is more of a puzzle than them all put together."

"How so? I have ever found her straightforward and natural—all that a young woman should be.".

"Ay, sir; but you have not been in love with her."

Wesley looked at him for a moment or two without a word. Then he said:

"Pray proceed, sir."

"The truth is, Mr. Wesley, the girl no longer loves me as she did, and all this time my love for her has been growing," said Snowdon. "Why, sir, she as good as confessed it to me no later than yesterday, when I taxed her with being changed. 'I must have another year,' she said. 'I cannot marry you now.'Twould be cruel to forsake my father and mother,' says she. 'You no longer love me, or you would not talk like that,' says I, and she hung her head. It was a clear minute before she said, 'That is not the truth, dear. How could I help loving you when I have given you my promise. All I ask is that you should not want me to marry you until I am sure of myself— another year,' says she. Now, Mr. Wesley, you are a parson, but you know enough of the affairs of mankind to know what all of this means—I know what it means, sir; it means that another man has come between us. You can easily understand, Mr. Wesley, that a well-favoured young woman, that has been educated above her station, should have her fancies, and maybe set her affections on someone that has spoken a word or two of flattery in her ear."

"I can scarce believe that of her, Mr. Snowdon. But she was at the Bath a few months ago, and perhaps—Mr. Snowdon, do you think that any words of mine—any advice to her—would have effect?"

The sailor's eyes gleamed; he struck his left palm with his right fist.

"Why, sir, that's the very thing that I came hither to beg of you," he cried. "I know in what esteem she holds you, Mr. Wesley; and I said to myself yesterday when I sat on the crags trying to worry out the day's work so that I might arrive at the true position of the craft that I'm a-trying to bring into haven—says I, "'Tis trying to caulk without oakum to hope to prevail against a young woman that has a fancy that she doesn't know her own mind. But in this case if there's anyone living that she will listen to 'tis Mr. Wesley.' Those was my words."

"I cannot promise that I shall prevail with her; but I have confidence that she will at least hearken to me," said Wesley.

"No fear about that, sir," cried the other, almost joyfully. He took a step or two toward the door, having picked up his hat, which he stood twirling for a few moments. Then he slowly turned and faced Wesley once again.

"Mr. Wesley," he said in a low voice. "Mind this, sir: I would not have you do anything in this matter unless you feel that 'twould be for the good of the girl. 'Tis of the girl we have to think in the first place—the girl and her happiness. We must keep that before us, mustn't we, sir? So I ask of you as a man of judgment and wisdom and piety to abstain from saying a word to her in my favour unless you are convinced that I am the man to make her happy. Look at me, sir. I tell you that I will not have the girl cajoled into marrying a man simply because she has given him her promise. What! should she have a life of wretchedness simply because a year ago she did not know her own mind?"

"Captain Snowdon, give me leave to tell you that you are a very noble fellow," said Wesley. "The way you have acted makes me more certain than ever that Nelly Polwhele is the most fortunate young woman in Cornwall, no matter what she may think of the matter. Since I have heard you, sir, what before was a strong intention has become a duty. Hasten to Nelly and send her hither."

The man went to the door quickly, but when there he hesitated.

"To be sure 'twould be better if you was to speak to her without her knowing that I had been with you; but we cannot help that; we are not trying to trick the girl into keeping her promise," said he.

"The knowledge that you have been with me would make no difference to her," said Wesley. "She knows that I would not advise her against my judgment, to please even the man who, I know, loves her truly as man could love woman."

Captain Snowdon's broad back filled up the doorway in an instant.

CHAPTER XXV

John Wesley sat alone in the room, thinking his thoughts. They were not unhappy, though tinged with a certain mournfulness at times. The mournful tinge was due to the reflection that once more he must reconcile himself to live alone in the world. For a brief space he had had a hope that it might be given to him to share the homely joys of his fellow-men. He now saw that it was not to be; and he bowed his head to the decree of the Will which he knew could not err.

Alone? How could such a reflection have come to him? How could he who sought to walk through the world with the Divine companionship of the One to whom he trusted to guide his steps aright feel lonely or alone?

This was the thought that upheld him now. He could feel the hand that he knew was ever stretched out to him. He touched it now as he had touched it before, and he heard the voice that said:

"I have called ye friends."

He was happy—as happy as the true man should be who knows that the woman whom he loves is going to be made happy. He now perceived that everything had been ordered for the best, this best being the ultimate happiness of the woman whom he loved. He now saw that although he might strive to bring happiness to her, he might never succeed in doing so. Even if she had loved him her quick intelligence could not fail to whisper to her what the people around them would be saying out loud—that John Wesley had married the daughter of a humble fisherman of Cornwall, and that that was no match for him to make. She would hear it said that John Wesley, who was ever anxious for the dignity of the Church to be maintained, had shown himself to be on the level with my lord's greasy, sottish chaplain, who had showed himself ready to marry my lady's maid when commanded to do so by his master, when circumstances had made such an act desirable.

Would such a young woman as Nelly Polwhele be happy when now and again she should hear these whispers and the consciousness was forced upon her that John Wesley was believed to have made a fool of himself?

But even to assume what her thoughts would be was to assume that she had loved him, and this she had never done. He was convinced that she had never ceased to love the man to whom she had given her promise. To be sure, she had told him when they had been together on the cliffs that someone else had come into her life. But that he believed to be only a passing fancy of hers. It was impossible that such a young woman, having given her promise to so fine a fellow as Captain Snowdon, should allow his place in her heart to be taken by anyone else.

He wondered if the Squire had a son as well as daughters. Nelly had talked to him often enough about the young ladies, but not a word had she breathed about a young gentleman. If there was a son, would it be beyond the limits of experience that this village girl should be captivated by his manners—was it beyond the limits of experience that the young man might have been fascinated by the beauty of the girl and so have talked to her as such young men so often did, in a strain of flattery that flattered the poor things so that they were led to hope that an offer of marriage was approaching?

He resolved to make enquiry on this point from Nelly herself should she still maintain that her affection had changed. But meantime——

His lucubrations were interrupted by the sudden return of Captain Snowdon. He was plainly in a condition of great excitement. His coat was loose and his neckerchief was flying.

"We are too late, Mr. Wesley," he cried. "We are too late. The girl has given both of us the slip. I called at the cottage to fetch her hither. I did not find her at home. This is what was put into my hand."

He thrust out a piece of paper with writing upon it.

"I cannot stay—I dare not stay any longer where I am forced to see you every day, and am thus reminded of my promise which I know I cannot now keep. Please try not to follow me; 'twould be of no use. I must be apart from you before I make up my mind. I am very unhappy, and I know that I am most unhappy because I have to give pain to one who is the best of men.

"Nelly."

"You have read it?" cried Snowdon. "I had no notion that her whimsies would carry her so far. Oh, she is but a girl after all—I tell you that she is no more than a girl."

"She is a girl, and I think that she is the best that lives, to be a blessing to a good man's life," said Wesley, returning the letter to his trembling hand.

"The best? The best? She has made a fool of the man who would have died to save her from the least hurt, and you call her the best!" he cried, walking to and fro excitedly, crumpling up the letter with every stride.

"She is the best," said Wesley. "Sir, cannot you see that those lines were written by a woman who is anxious to be true to herself? Cannot you see that her sole fear is that she may do an injustice to the man who loves her?"

"You see things, sir, that none other can see; I am but a plain man, Mr. Wesley, and I can see naught in this letter save the desire of a fickle young woman to rid herself of a lover of whom she has grown weary. Well, she has succeeded — she has succeeded! She exhorts me not to follow her. She need not have been at the trouble to do so: I have no intention of following her, even if I knew whither she has gone. Have you any guess as to the direction she has taken? Not that I care — I tell you, sir, I have no desire to follow her. Who do you suspect is her lover?"

"Mr. Snowdon," said Wesley, "her lover stands before me in this room. The poor child has had her doubts, as any true girl must have when she thinks how serious a step is marriage, and the best way that you can dissipate such doubts is to show to her that you have none.'Tis left for you to prove yourself a true man in this matter, Captain Snowdon, and I know that, being a true man, you will act as a true man should act."

"I know not what you would suggest, sir, but I can promise you that if you hint that I should seek to follow her, you make a mistake," said Snowdon.

"She may go whithersoever she pleases. I have no mind to be made a fool of a second time by her. I have some self-respect still remaining, let me tell you, Mr. Wesley."

"You may be sure that no advice to sacrifice it will come from me, sir," said Wesley. "Oh, Mr. Snowdon, did not you come to me an hour ago to ask me to be your friend in this matter? Did you not ask me to give my advice to the young woman of whom we have been speaking? Was not that because you believed that my advice would be right?"

"I know that it would have been right, Mr. Wesley; but now — —"

"If you could trust to me to give her good advice, why cannot you prove that this was your hope, by hearkening to the advice which I am ready to give to you?"

The big man, who was standing in the middle of the room, had made several passionate attempts to speak, but none of them could be called successful. When Wesley had put his last question, he tried to frame a reply. He put out an arm with an uplifted forefinger and his lips began to move.

Not a word would come. He looked at Wesley straight in the face for a long time, and then he suddenly turned away, dropped into the nearest chair, and bent his head forward until his chin was on his hand, and he was gazing at the floor.

Wesley let him be. He knew something of men and their feelings, as well as their failings.

There was a long silence before the man arose and came to him, saying in a low voice:

"Mr. Wesley, I will trust to your judgment. I will do whatsoever you bid me."

Wesley grasped him by the hand.

"I had no doubt of you, my friend," he said. "I felt that any man whom Nelly Polwhele loved — —"

"Ay, loved — loved!" interjected Snowdon.

"Loves — loves — in love there is no past tense," said Wesley. "She loved you, and she loves you still — she will love you forever. You will come with me, and I know that mine will be the great happiness of bringing you together. What greater happiness could come to such as I than this which, by the grace of Heaven, shall be mine?"

"She gave you her confidence? You know whither she has fled?"

Wesley shook his head.

"She told me nothing; remember that I have not seen her since you returned to her," he said. "But I think that I can say whither she has gone.'Tis but six or seven miles from here. Have you heard of Ruthallion Mill?"

The mariner struck the palm of his left hand with his right fist. The blow had weight enough in it to make the casements quiver.

"Wherefore could I not have thought of the Mill?" he cried.' "I was fool enough to let a thought of Squire Trevelyan's Court come into my mind."

"I have no doubt that we shall find her at the Mill," said Wesley. "The miller has been a second father to her, and, besides, he has a daughter. 'Tis to friends such as these that she would go for succour and sympathy in her hour of trouble." Captain Snowdon mused for a moment.

"How do I know that they will be on my side, Mr. Wesley?" he asked. "They may reckon that she has been ill-used — that she has a right to change her mind and to choose whomsoever she will."

"Mr. Snowdon," said Wesley, "it doth not need that one should be possessed of a judgment beyond that of ordinary people to decide the right and the wrong of this affair in which we all take a huge interest. Come, sir, let us prepare for the best and not for the worst. What, are you a master-mariner and yet have not learned that the best way to stamp out a mutiny is by a display of promptitude. Let us lose no time over the discussion of what the result of our action may be—let us act at once."

He went to the door..

"Nay, sir; but you are a sick man—how will you make this journey?" said Snowdon.

"I am no longer a sick man," said Wesley. "I would not give a second thought to the setting out upon a journey to the Mill on foot. But there will be no need for this. Mr. Hartwell will lend us his light cart; it will hold three."

"Three? But we are but two, sir."

"Ay, Mr. Snowdon—only two for the journey to the Mill; but we shall need an extra seat for our return."

A few words to Mr. Hartwell and his easy running waggon was at the door. The drive through the valley of the Lana on this lovely afternoon had an exhilarating effect upon Captain Snowdon, for Wesley took care that their conversation should be-on topics far removed from their mission at this time. He wished to be made acquainted with his companion's views respecting many matters of the Orient. Was it possible that the Jesuits had sent missionaries to the Indies and even to China? Had Captain Snowdon had any opportunity of noting-the result of their labours? Had Captain Snowdon learned if the Jesuits discountenanced any of the odious native customs such as the burning of widows—the throwing of infants into the sacred river of Ganges? Or did the missioners content themselves with simple preaching?

The journey to the Mill was all too short to allow of Captain Snowdon's answering more than a few of the questions put to him by the discreet Mr. Wesley, and it was not until they were turning down the little lane that the ship-master came to an abrupt end of his replies, and put the nervous question to his companion:

"Shall we find her here, or have we come on a wild-goose chase?"

In a few minutes they were in her presence—almost in her presence; they caught sight of her flying through the inner door when they entered the Mill room.

The miller, in his shirtsleeves and wearing his working apron, gave a loud laugh and shouted "Stop thief!" but his daughter and her mother were looking grave and tearful. They moved to the door by which Nelly had made her escape, but checked themselves and returned to greet Wesley and Snowdon. They hoped that the sun had not been overwarm during the drive through the valley, and that Mr. Wesley had fully recovered from his sickness.

The miller came to the point with his usual directness.

"You have come to carry the girl home with you, I doubt not?" he said; and forthwith his wife and daughter made for the door.

Captain Snowdon looked ill at ease. He glanced toward the outer door.

"How oft have I not told her that a judgment would fall upon her for the heartburnings that she brought about—all through her kindness o' heart?" continued the miller. "Poor daughter! But they all go through the same course, Captain, of that you may be assured, albeit I doubt not that you think that so dread a case as yours has never been known i' the world before. When the marriage day draws nigh, the sweetest and the surest of them all has a misgiving. Don't be too ready to blame them, sir. The wonder is that when she sees so many errors hurried into under the name of marriage, any maid can bring herself to take upon her the bondage." Captain Snowdon nodded sideways and looked shyly down.

"Nature is stronger than experience, miller," said Wesley. "I am bold enough to think that you could give Mr. Snowdon a pinch of your experience in your garden, after you have told Nelly that I seek a word with her here. I am pretty certain that I shall have completed my task before your experiences as a married man are exhausted."

"Right, sir," said the miller. "Captain, I show you the door in no inhospitable spirit. I'll join you in the turning of a pinion."

Captain Snowdon seemed pleased to have a chance of retiring, returning to the open air; he hurried out by one door, while the miller went through the other and shouted for Nelly. His wife's remonstrance with him for his unfeeling boisterousness reached Wesley, who was now alone in the room.

He was not kept long waiting. Nelly entered, the miller leading her by the hand, and then walking slowly to the outer door..

"My dear, you know why I have come hither," said Wesley, taking her hand in both of his own. "You asked for my counsel once, and I gave it to you. I could only give it to you at that time in a general way. I had not seen the man to whom you had given your promise; but having seen him, and knowing what manner of man he is—and I am something of a judge of a man's character—I feel that I would be lacking in my duty to you, dear child, if I were to refrain from coming to you to plead for—for your own happiness."

"Have I forfeited all your esteem by my behaviour, sir?" she cried, still holding his hand and looking at him with piteous eyes. "Do you think of me as a light-minded girl, because I confessed to you—all that I did confess?"

"I have never ceased to think of you with affection," he said.

"Ah! the affection of a man who is esteemed by all the world, for a poor girl who touched the hem of his life, and then passed away never to be seen by him again."

She spoke in a curious tone of reproach. He looked at her, asking himself what she meant.

"Child, child, you little know how I have thought of you," he said slowly. "Do you believe that the path of my life has been so gilded with sunshine that I take no count of such hours as we passed together when we walked through the valley, side by side—when we sat together on the cliffs?"

She gave a little cry of joy and caught up his hand and kissed it.

He was startled. He turned his eyes upon her. She was rosy red. Her head was bowed.

In that instant he read her secret.

There was a long silence. Only occasionally a little sob came from her.

"Child," he said in a low voice. "Child, you have been very dear to me."

She looked up with streaming eyes.

"Say those words again—again," she cried in faltering tones.

"They are true words, my dear," he said. "The life which it has been decreed that I shall lead must be one of loneliness—what most men and all women call loneliness. Such joys of life as love and marriage and a home can never be for me. I have given myself over body and soul to the work of my Master, and I look on myself as separate forever from all the tenderness of life. They are not for me."

"Why should they not be for you? You have need of them, Mr. Wesley?"

"Why should they not be for me, do you ask?" he cried. "They are not for me, because I have been set to do a work that cannot be done without a complete sacrifice of self. Because I have found by the bitterest experience, that so far as I myself am concerned—I dare not speak for another—these things war against the Spirit. If I thought it possible that a woman should be led to love me I would never see her again."

"Oh, do not say that—do not say that!" she said piteously.

"I do say it," he cried. "Never—never—never would I do so great an injustice to a woman as to marry her. I tell you that I would think of it as a curse and not a blessing. I know that I have been appointed to do a great work, and I am ready, with God's help, to trample beneath my feet everything of life that would turn my thoughts from that work. The words are sounding in my ear day and night—day and night, 'If any man come to Me and hate not his father and mother and wife and children and brethren and sisters—yea, and his own life also, he cannot be my Disciple.'"

He stood away from her, speaking fervently. His face, pale by reason of his illness, had become paler still: but his resolution had not faltered, his voice had not broken.

She had kept her eyes fixed upon him. The expression upon her face was one of awe.

She shuddered when he took a step toward her and held out a thin white hand to her. She touched it slowly with her own.

"Nelly," he said, "there is a joy in self-sacrifice beyond any that the world can give. I look on you as one of my children—one of that Household of Faith who have told me that they had learned the Truth from my lips. My child, if you were called on to make any great sacrifice for the Truth, would you not make it? Although I may seem an austere man to you, I do not live so far apart from those who are dear to me as to be incapable of sympathising with them in all matters of their daily life. I think you knew that or you would not have confessed to me that you fancied your love had suffered a change."

She rose from her chair, and passed a hand wearily across her face.

"A fancy—it was a fancy—a dream—oh, the most foolish dream that ever a maiden had," she said. "Has it ever been known that a maiden fancied she loved the shadow of a dream when all the time her heart was given to a true man?"

"Dear child, have you awakened?" he asked.

"My dreaming time is past," she replied.

"I may bid Captain Snowdon to enter?" he said.

"Not yet—not yet—I must be alone; I will see him in another hour."

He kissed her on the forehead, and went with unfaltering feet into the sunshine.